Visco

David Fell

Habitat Press

Habitat Press

Prologue

Joanna Castle was about seven years old when she was first asked what she wanted to be when she grew up. She didn't know. She had a vague idea that she wanted to be a superhero, but all the superheroes seemed to be boys. She didn't want to be Batman or Superman or James Bond.

The adults seemed concerned that she didn't have an answer – everyone else seemed to know that they wanted to be a ballerina or an astronaut or a vet – so they kept on asking her. By now she knew about Wonderwoman and Supergirl and Storm, but there was still a problem. She couldn't quite put her finger on it.

One day, this time having been asked by her grandmother, and with Jo having reached the grand old age of eleven, she managed her first satisfying response:

"I want to save people from the baddies, granny! Like in the books. But I don't want to be like... like Jack Reacher, saving everybody by beating everyone else up or shooting them! I want to do it with love, and care. Not guns. Not violence. Could I save people like that granny, do you think? Without all the drama? Could I save the world like that?"

Her grandmother didn't know. And, in the end, Jo became a fire-fighter.

Except, it turned out not to be the end.

Part One: Last Year

Late Summer

It was late summer and another hot day. Out in London's green-belt the heat was a little less spirit-sapping than in the city itself, but the car's electronic display suggested that the temperature hadn't really changed. Jo Castle was glad of the vehicle's air-conditioning. So was her father John.

"Climate change, eh?" he said. John knew far more about it than she did. Or, at least, he had once upon a time known far more than she did. She glanced over, checking.

"Well, they predicted more extremes, didn't they?" Jo said. The heatwave was into its sixth week. Cities far to the south had long since adapted to the heat, but London seemed peculiarly resistant to this kind of change. Millions of people still lived in homes without proper cooling systems; thousands of people still set about their normal outdoor activities without suitable protection; several hundred people – as the media over the past couple of weeks had screamingly reported – had already died from exposure, exhaustion and dehydration.

Jo's father had been watching the road ahead but turned now to gaze from the side window. An anonymous housing estate slid by, its public spaces empty at this time of day save for a smattering of thin and struggling trees and, in their inadequate shade, a handful of unsettling youths. Desiccated litter and elaborate recycling bins competed for space near the poorly maintained doors and stairwells. A futile municipal sign declared that both ball games and dogs were forbidden from the hard bleached surfaces that once grew grass.

John Castle was dressed, as ever, in smart trousers, flawlessly polished brown shoes, a freshly ironed shirt, tie and a well-tailored jacket. He looked like a university professor, probably the engineering department; and this was indeed exactly what he was. His glasses were perched precisely on the end of his nose; but, as Jo had noticed without remark when she picked him up, his tie was oddly askew.

"Not far now, I think," she said. This was their second day of reconnaissance. The first, last week, had not gone well. Jo had done the background research between shifts: they had done the short-listing together. John had consulted with at least two of his other children, but to little effect. Jo carried a modicum of resentment at the burden she was yet again bearing, but her dominant sensation was of merely continuing to be the helpful middle daughter. She expected it of herself; she could hardly blame her brothers and sisters for expecting it too.

Her father had coped well in the first few years after his wife had left him. Some of that, Jo felt, had been a sort of macho belligerence acting as its own proof; but some, at least, seemed a genuine adaptability in the face of what had, undoubtedly, been a devastating loss. His focus had always been his work and he had relied heavily on the landscape of support provided by his wife and, to a lesser extent, his middle daughter. As a parent he had engaged with his children like the professor he was: intellectual problems, challenging homework and conversational speculation were all greeted with genuine interest; emotional complications, relationships, spiritual questions – these were deflected or avoided completely. He was an engineer at heart, and in hand and in thought too.

The first signs had come when some of that engineering acumen began miscalculating. Jo had not seen them. They happened in seminars, in the drafting of a paper, during repartee at a formal university dinner. By the time Jo noticed on a perfectly ordinary visit to say hello, John already knew. He saw the fleeting furrow on her brow as he lost his way during a rudimentary explanation of the repairs he had conducted on the reconditioned foot massager that she had bought him for Christmas. With characteristic immediacy and precision he explained the diagnosis. Early onset. Likely to be rapid. Limited scope for amelioration. Zero scope for avoidance.

"Ah, look, there it is," she said. A gravel aperture, flanked by firs and a tasteful sign, beckoned them towards the converted nineteenth century building hiding behind a couple of further bends, a car park and another copse, this time of silver birch. "Looks nice," Jo added. She hated these empty platitudes. She knew he hated them too. She could not think of anything else to say.

"We're a bit early," she continued. "Do you want to look at the brochure again?" She twisted to rummage among the assortment of papers on the rear seat. Everything was on-line these days, of course, and she and her father had already looked at 'The Pines' web-site. She could easily have called up the same site on her notebook but she had discovered that it upset him. Anything electronic had a high risk of setting him off, either confusing him directly or reminding him of his confusion and of what was already beginning so quickly to disappear.

Once his anxiety began - she had also discovered - it could take a long time to bring him back.

"Nice bedrooms," she pointed out. "And the garden's lovely." She fought hard against the sudden choke in her throat, forcing her shoulders rigid and turning her misting eyes away from his. The gardens. He loved gardens, and gardening. During last week's reconnaissance he had become completely engrossed with the watering system in the glasshouse at 'Oak Heights'. Mid-sentence he simply wandered off. The deputy manager – far more experienced in these matters, of course, than Jo – barely broke stride, continuing her affectless description of how much the residents enjoyed this particular part of the wonderful facilities and how well they had all adapted since the pandemic. Jo, for her part, absorbed none of what the woman was saying and in fact barely noticed the disappearance of her father: she was instead transfixed by the residents.

Jo had, it was true, attended incidents at institutions like 'Oak Heights' over the years: she recalled a minor kitchen fire, and a couple of occasions where one or other piece of equipment had collapsed, trapping residents and staff alike amid an octopus of cord, canvas and twisted metal piping. She had, on such occasions, assessed these environments in terms of logistics and hazard, entry points and exit routes, turning circles and awkward stairwells. Now, her entire perspective was altered.

Oddly, the things she saw were not by and large alarming. The building, for example, was well-laid out, clean, bright and well-furnished. The staff, too, came across as friendly, professional and concerned, and there was no sign of Nurse Ratched. It was impossible to summon anxiety on the basis of the food, or the décor, or the mediocre artworks in the corridors.

Discomfort came instead from the occasional glimpse of contraptions designed for lifting or supporting or manoeuvring the delicate yet unwieldy bodies of those that lived here, or when seeing a trolley of drugs pass by, or – as happened on a couple of occasions – when witnessing some of the support staff cleaning and changing a heavily soiled bed.

But such discomfort was as nothing compared to the gut-tightening response evoked by the residents themselves. They were just people, Jo knew that. She kept reminding herself. Just people. Once upon a time, and not that long ago, these people had been doing jobs, going on holiday, looking forward to Christmas, looking forward to seeing their children and their grandchildren. Once upon a time, and not that long ago, these people had been living at home, making their dinner, making a cup of tea, heading to the shops to buy a loaf of bread. Now – now, something shattering had happened. Something inside their minds had broken. Something had gone awfully, horribly wrong and we, the rest of us, did not want to have to look. So we hid them from sight.

Whether we did it as a collective, obliging our governments to fund and care for these people, or whether we did it as individual families, the upshot was the same: we, we the conscious, we the mobile, we the young and the functioning and the terrified, we liquidate assets and write cheques and pay money to have someone else hide our decrepit elders, hide our shame, hide the very future that awaits so many of us. Please, no, anything; I do not want to have to look.

But Jo stood in the glasshouse, as the deputy manager droned on and John wandered off, looking. She saw an elderly lady in a dressing gown seated in a wicker chair in a perfectly beautiful, sunny spot, her head lolling sideways, her mouth open, her eyes focused on something invisible and far, far away. Behind her, another elderly lady, dressed in her day clothes, walking in a small circle, muttering rhythmically, gesturing in a tight repeated fashion, first the left hand pointing, then the right hand, a strange curtailing wave. Pace, gesture, mutter; pace, gesture, mutter; pace, gesture, mutter. Out of mind, out of sight.

Jo, sitting now in the car-park of 'The Pines' felt, again, that she might be about to faint. She had nearly fallen in the glasshouse of 'Oak Heights', saving herself only by propping herself on the metal trellis that happened to be available. "For fuck's sake!" she had shouted silently at herself. "Pull yourself together!" She had, she reminded herself, seen far worse things. Far worse. Building collapses where people had been crushed to death. Traffic accidents where people had been sliced into pieces. Motorway pile-ups where children had been burned so badly she had wondered whether it might have been better not to save them.

Fiercely she told herself: these people – these ordinary people – are not in pain. They are well looked after. There are people here who care for them. They are safe. They are warm, they eat, they sleep soundly.

And she realised – she realised the distance created by the word 'they'. That is how it works. 'They' are the others, the other, the Not Us. How could we put ourselves here? How could we abandon 'us'? We cannot. We abandon 'them'. We abandon 'they'. And that is completely fine, day after day after day after day, until one day – it is not them. It is not them, it's you. It is your father. Her father. One day, soon, her father was going to be in this place, or a place just like it; and he would be staring, uncomprehending, and sitting, immobile and slack-jawed. And she gripped the trellis, and she stared from the car window, and she fought back the tears and the disbelief.

"Hey." His voice came from far away. She felt his hand on her knee. "Do you think it would be all right if I took my jacket off? Do you think they'll mind? I'd like to take my jacket off. It's very warm. Isn't it warm? I think it's very warm. Climate change, eh?"

Early Summer

It was early summer. To the city's east, beyond the regenerated dockyards, the air was edgy. Somewhere nearby the money had run out, so while the warehouses at one end had become new urban living, those at the other were still full of vagabonds and mystery. Jo Castle's step-brother Mike Smith had been invited to a party by his friend Tom. The party was in one of these mysterious buildings.

"Man, stop looking so fucking scared!" said Tom. He had been living in London for all of twelve months so he now believed himself completely au fait with the city's geography, culture and patterns of criminality.

Mike was not convinced. Dusk was falling. It had been a warm day, again, and both the young men were wearing just t-shirts and jeans. Earlier, Mike had made some remark about the heat and then climate change, but Tom had responded with undisguised derision. Tom's 'all that eco-crap' shtick had been funny back when they'd met in sixth form, but Mike was finding it increasingly wearing. He was not entirely sure why they were still friends. He wasn't entirely sure, either, why he had accepted Tom's invitation.

"It won't really get going until 11," said Tom. For a moment Mike wondered if Tom had now accepted the reality of climate change and was proposing a new tipping point, some feedback indicator beyond which the reality of global calamity would finally become apparent to the powers-that-be, but then he realised that Tom was talking about the party. "I thought we should just check it out early. You know, so we know where it is and everything." Mike nodded, aware that Tom was probably as nervous as he was. Mike decided to say nothing and just go with the flow.

The flow took them to a bar that Tom claimed was as cool as it got these days, though something seemed amiss to Mike, as though the clientele had all heard that it was a cool bar and, rather than making cool or being cool, were waiting for the coolness to arrive. Neither Mike nor Tom constituted that coolness and Mike soon found himself eavesdropping on a conversation behind them in which a young man, just a few years older than him, was telling his mates about his new job.

"So listen," the young man persisted, pushing through some obvious mockery and disbelief from his companions, "the guy owns yachts, big ones, six of them, they don't really go anywhere, there's one in Nassau and one off Long Beach and one in Monaco, that sort of thing."

"A software billionaire, you said?"

"That's right, yeah, one of the ones you haven't heard of but like one of the fifty wealthiest guys on the planet..."

"And he's asked you to help him?"

"Fuck off," the young man responded, still attempting to outgun the guffaws, "the outfit I'm working for, my new job, they do 'lifestyle management' for high net worth individuals..."

"You mean they help oligarchs spend their money?" More guffaws.

"So the job I get is to check up on the yachts, just look over the maintenance contracts and shit, make sure that all his needs are being met..."

"You help him meet his needs!"

"...and it turns out that, you know, he doesn't like to decide in advance which yacht he'll be on next, sort of thing, he just sort of rocks up, unannounced."

"Well, they're his yachts, I suppose."

"Like visiting your shed or something..."

"Yeah, you wouldn't want to have to notify anyone you were visiting your fucking shed!"

"So anyway," the young speaker continued, "he wants all of his yachts to be ready for him, twenty four hours a day, three sixty five days a year, just in case he decides to rock up." For the first time since he listened in, Mike realised, the entire group had gone quiet. "And that means full staff team, fully loaded kitchen, helicopter pad scrubbed and ready, all the time. All the time. And get this – I had to sort the flowers." The group's silence rippled as the image of flowers breezed incongruously across the meadows of their imagination. "He likes the decks to be decked. Fresh flowers. Every fucking day. On every one of these six massive yachts, all over the world, every day, all yesterday's flowers are taken away, all the hanging baskets and vases and table displays and shit, taken away and replaced with today's fresh flowers." The breeze stilled completely. "Thirty thousand dollars per month, per yacht. Just for the fucking flowers."

"Did you hear that?" asked Mike, an hour or so and a couple of beers later, as he and Tom sought one more venue before hitting the party.

"Hear what?" Tom wondered.

"The thing about the flowers, the billionaire's flowers, on his yachts."

"Yeah man, wicked!" said Tom, gleefully. "Imagine having that much money!"

"You what?" Mike spluttered. "That sounded *good* to you?"

"Too fucking right," said Tom, pulling back his shoulders and lengthening his stride. "Oh, don't tell me, you thought it was appalling or disgusting or outrageous..."

"That's because it is appalling and disgusting and outrageous..."

"...just because some guy who worked really hard and who is probably really smart came up with some idea that made millions of people's lives better and who now has shed loads of money and he spends it on stuff he likes and you, some wanked-up leftie liberal, you think it's unfair or unjust or whatever and you don't think for a second about all the people employed to keep his boats clean and to grow the fucking flowers and who look after his helicopter, I suppose you'd far rather all that money was shared out in some hippy dippy bollocks way among all the poor and deserving and sad little bastards who never did anyone any harm..."

It became clear that Tom's rant would continue unbroken for some minutes to come, and Mike tuned out. There was, Mike privately conceded, an argument that the money being spent by this obscenely wealthy individual would indeed be creating jobs and providing livelihoods for other people, who would in turn be spending their earnings on a whole variety of other things, and the whole thing went round and round creating more jobs and more money, and that was, when you thought about it, pretty amazing. But it was surely and simply obscene – Mike could feel his emphasis on the word in his head – that people, even here in London, one of the wealthiest cities on the planet, were hungry and homeless, while that man spent millions each year on flowers. On flowers that he wouldn't even see, or smell.

"I..." Mike hazarded, sensing a pause in Tom's exposition.

"Here, this looks good," said Tom, before even a second syllable had escaped Mike's throat, and suddenly the moment was gone and the second bar of their evening yawned and swallowed them whole.

It turned out to be similarly devoid of the ineffable presence that everyone inside seemed to be seeking and it was not long before the two young men decided it was time to find the warehouse.

"Spliff?" Tom proffered, as they walked purposefully east, away from the money and back towards the edge. It was not far past eleven. Mike had a couple of tokes, of both the first and the immediately successive second joint, but things had changed since their shared sixth-form smokes, Mike was not sure what, and he found himself hanging and holding back.

Mike was glad he had; he doubted he would have coped otherwise. The interior of the warehouse delivered an overwhelming assault on the senses. A labyrinthine affair of exposed brick and twisted girders, asymmetric stairwells and incongruous corridors, unexpected arches and ceilings at the wrong height, the building seemed to be pumping like the exposed organ of a traumatised beast. Low-lit bodies filled one room after another; stroboscopic light writhed to the left and right; music, at astonishing volume, morphed from one sound system to the next as the boys drifted through the space.

Tom consulted his phone, mouthed something inaudible, laughed, and talked some more. Mike nodded, vaguely, and followed. They forced their way up a crowded staircase, left, along a corridor and left again into a darker, stiller space. There were perhaps a dozen, maybe twenty people, a handful strewn on the floor, a handful more propping up the walls. Towards the rear, by the blacked-out window, the man with the supplies. Tom leaned close and then back to Mike.

"Says he's got some good Ket, some MDMA, some coke and a couple of nice synthetics. What do you fancy?"

Mike could feel himself beginning to squirm, his spine tightening and his arms twisting. He tried desperately to suppress it. His face grimaced, eyebrows flickering up in a sign that could as easily have been understood as a desire to escape as indifference to which narcotic was preferable. It was manifestly unacceptable to run away. He had known that this scene would come to pass, but could fathom neither why he had allowed himself to be here nor why he so wanted to be here.

"I reckon the synthetics," said Tom. "Fuck knows what they're called, but he says they take you up not down, and I don't fancy that..." Tom was gesturing towards the horizontal figures around the room, some seemingly comatose, some merely paralyzed, eyes wide and sightless.

"OK," Mike nodded, still mystified at himself. He didn't want to do this; and, yet, here he was, still here. He watched the transaction, the empty nods of conclusion between the parties, and suddenly he was again trailing Tom as they wove along another crowded corridor. A few moments later they were sitting crossed-legged against a cold brick wall in a dimly-lit and sparsely filled storage area. Tom had found a smooth tile somewhere along the way, which he wiped carefully with the front of his t-shirt before beginning to chop at the lumpy crystalline powder with a card.

"Woo hoo!" he exclaimed, his chopping movements carefully controlled, rapid ups, downs and swipes in a concentrated space to avoid spillage. "Roll the note?"

Robotic, seemingly even further away from himself, Mike took the tenner Tom was holding towards him – the purchase of drugs being the last refuge for cash – and began rolling the tube. Four narrow lines lay on the tile. "Go for it," said Tom. Mike leant forward and down, the tube to his nostril. He breathed slowly in, out, then deeply and smoothly in as the tube slid along the first line. He switched nostril, did it again and handed the rolled note to Tom.

The party was amazing. Here and there people passed out, or vomited heavily, or both. Blurred faces and bodies swept by, grinning inanely. People were having sex in this room, and that one, and that one over there. Every time the terrifying emptiness swam into the guts, or the neck, or even the mind, another cold brick wall, another methodical chopping ritual, another line of something white. Noise, more noise. Laughter. Something was on fire, nothing huge, but the flames were lovely. More white powder. An incredibly beautiful girl. Inaudible conversations, gibberish, dancing. Another incredibly beautiful girl, different from the previous, or maybe the same. Wave of fear; another line. Victory! Superhuman powers, lordliness over the earth, dominion. Eye contact and charm, electricity and touch, another beautiful girl. Ideas of pure insight. Infinite happiness and unending exhilaration. Another line. Scintilla of doubt, of anxiety, of clay – another line.

Was there booze? Someone else's drugs? Whose line is it anyway? Wow, this music is amazing! And that girl – did you see her? Fuck, I don't know. Woo hoo, another fire! I love the fires. This is awesome! Another line? Some guy with a chainsaw, great arcs of sputtered light as he chopped something metallic in half, in time with the music, sparks to the rhythm, beauty and the bass. Jesus, we're nearly out, we'd better find the man...

Dawn arrived, somehow. Great lakes of bottles, some whole, many broken, filled the rooms. Bodies soaked in sweat, piss and alcohol lay in misshapen piles. Bleak faces and empty eyes tracked the occasional mover. The man had long gone. The fear was coming up with the sun. Mike was very cold. He hadn't seen Tom for – for a while. Hours? Days? Minutes? His legs ached, his back ached, his neck ached. His teeth hurt. His jaw muscles were tight like snare drums. His pockets were empty. His soul was empty.

He pushed through the bottles and the bodies and the bleakness to find a balcony, overlooking the river. Or was it a dock? He couldn't tell; it didn't matter. It was horribly cold. Through the thin, damp t-shirt the low sun gently brushed his chest. It was not yet high enough to ease the chills, but the clear blue sky foretold a warmth the very prospect of which helped. Mike folded his bare arms and leant on the railing, and immediately sprang back – the metal was freezing. He crossed his arms more tightly. He gazed slowly across the water, the riverside buildings, the cranes, old and new. He noticed the moorhens, then the gulls. He watched a well-apportioned rodent trot calmly along the brickwork at the edge of the warehouse.

He could not tell whether or not he was still high. He could see things, and hear things, but they did not make sense. Was this, really, what it was all about? He and several hundred other people had consumed unknowable quantities of narcotics and participated in a prolonged bout of corybantic seething. Innumerable young bodies had been profoundly sick. Great swathes of the past hours had already disappeared irrevocably from the minds supported by those bodies; and, almost without exception, all would claim to have had a fantastic time.

They were all, all of them, as fleeting and disposable as the flowers on a yacht. And just as pointless.

Mike wondered where Tom might be. Sad, worried, cold and bewildered, he headed back into the silent warehouse to begin the search.

Christmas

It was Christmas. Jo and Mike were leaning on the balcony surrounding the central atrium of London's largest shopping centre.

"No. I don't get it," said Mike. He had travelled down that morning. "Why are we here?" he asked.

"I thought it would be interesting," Jo explained. "I came here a couple of months ago, there was a collision in one of the service bays, we had to cut a guy out. It wasn't too bad, he'll probably be back on his feet by now, but we were obviously on the underside of the shopping centre, it was amazing, all the ducts and cables and delivery vans and concrete." She paused, gazing at the scene below them. "It was the complete opposite of... this," she added, with a muted sweep of her hand. "I've never been here before. I wanted to see what it looked like."

Mike swung his gaze from his step-sister's face and looked, to see what it was like. He saw shops, people and bags. He saw windows teeming with sparkly things. He saw doorframes bulging with plastic holly, trinkets and price tags. He saw great piles of jumpers and board games, towers of biscuits and scarves, acres of cologne and socks, watches and ear-rings, decorative vases and sportswear and multi-coloured stationery. He saw innumerable people moving – it seemed to him – like some sort of thick gas, flowing between the shops, stickily building up near concession stands selling doughnuts, slowly accreting more of the bulging bags as it glooped along.

"Well," he said, "I'm glad we didn't come here to shop."

Jo chuckled. Mike continued, in a plaintive tone: "I always thought Christmas was supposed to be a happy time." He allowed his gaze to sweep slowly across the crowds and back to his step-sister's face: "I don't see too many happy-looking people," he said.

Jo looked at him, a gawky nineteen year-old inside the bright baggy clothes then trendy among those purporting to disdain youthful fashion. She had known him since he was eleven, when their parents first met. She could feel his discomfort, like an itchy shirt.

"Well, maybe they'll enjoy themselves later," she said. "They're all thinking about their families and their friends. They're thinking about next week. They're thinking about how wonderful it will be when little Jonny opens his presents and his face lights up."

Mike harrumphed. "Maybe," he acknowledged. "But it looks... desperate. Don't you think? It makes me feel... It makes me feel that the only way people can cope with their awful jobs and their empty lives is to buy a whole load of shiny stuff, a whole load of stuff that no one really needs and nobody's impressed by. It'll all be in the bin or under the stairs by the middle of January. It just seems mad. Desperate."

Jo watched the animation change his body. The slouch that bent him against the flawlessly polished balcony railing slowly stiffened, lifting him upright and, suddenly, tall. Still growing, Jo thought; inside and out.

"That seems a bit harsh," she said, gently. "I think most of these people are trying hard, they've been working all year, and this is their party. They know how ridiculous it all is. They know they're buying too much stuff. Yes, they're being manipulated by all the hype, sure;

but they're not being..." She looked for the right word. She found herself watching a woman, perhaps her own age, temporarily at a halt outside a shop selling garish ties and cufflinks, consulting her phone while standing in a small puddle of bags at her ankles. The woman appeared prosperous – well dressed, poised – but also slightly dishevelled. Her elegant clothing was no longer as well manicured as it had been when she left home this morning. A few tresses of hair had escaped. "Control," Jo chose. "They're not being controlled."

It was Mike's turn to look at Jo. Beneath a nondescript anorak she was dressed, as always, as if she was not that interested in how she looked. She was of average height and her mid-length dark hair was pulled back into a simple pony-tail. The loose shapelessness of her clothing made it impossible to see her firefighter's physique. She had been twenty five when they met. He trusted her completely.

"Look over there," Mike pointed. A large man, somewhere in the second half of his thirties and dressed in careful elastic and fold-hiding cotton, was struggling with his lumbering gait alongside his even larger wife. There were three children, two on foot and one still in a buggy. The handles and tray of the buggy were draped with bags emblazoned with the logos of various second- and third-tier brands, trophies of the expedition-to-date. The youngest child appeared to be drinking from a bottle; the two other children and both adults were eating pastries. Flakes sprayed from the man's face as he barked inaudibly at one or other or all of the children. "What am I supposed to think?" said Mike. "Those kids don't have a chance, do they? No amount of cheap plastic toys or whatever is going to save them. They're facing a future of... of obesity and heart disease." He paused, briefly. "I'm sure the parents really do love them, and they probably think they're doing the right thing and are probably trying their best..." His face was contorted with distress; Jo thought he might actually cry out.

"And it's hardly their fault, is it?" Mike resumed, his gaze drifting across the massy, gassy crowd beneath them. "Once upon a time we're all just beautiful little children in the school nativity play, hoping to be a ballerina or an astronaut or whatever..."

He trailed off, frustration overtaking his ability to form sentences. His body twisted, tension working through his uncertain muscles, before he slowly resumed his slump against the balcony. Jo edged a little closer and rested a hand on his shoulder.

"I had to rescue a family like that last week," she told him, allowing her hand to fall slowly from his shoulder and down along his arm. "We got a call about 8, 8.15 in the evening. They'd put up their Christmas tree and it turned out that the lights were dodgy. Well, the plug. And the tree itself, plastic, you know, it hadn't passed the regulations, some dodgy import they'd picked up from the market. The plug overheated and set fire to the tree while the family were having dinner, by the time they noticed what was happening the whole living room was on fire. No smoke detector. They rushed into the street, mum dad and a couple of kids, they were still just standing there when we arrived with the blue light."

He was still staring down into the Christmas crowd. She continued to look at the side of his face.

"So, no-one hurt, and we put the fire out easily enough. But they'd put most of the presents under the tree, so they were all gone. And the house won't be fit for Christmas." She paused again. "I don't know what they'll do; stay with relatives I suppose. But I got to look at their house, you know, and you're right – it's not their fault. A couple of my colleagues were pretty fierce, criticising them for having a sub-standard fitting on the lights, and for the tree – not to the family's faces, of course, but afterwards, on the ride back to the station. I got a bit upset. You should have seen their house. The sofa, the kitchen table, all the knick knacks in the hallway and on the dresser. It was obvious they had no money, or hardly any, but they wanted a nice house, just like everyone else, and they'd bought the best they could, but it was rock-bottom stuff, you know, stuff at the absolute margin, stuff that wasn't going to last five minutes. Stuff that... oh, I don't know. Stuff that they thought they had to have in order to be normal."

Mike watched the shoppers ebbing and flowing below as he listened. Here and there someone was wearing a festive hat, or a pretend beard, or was dressed as an elf. It was not clear whether these people were enthusiastic civilians, promotional agents acting on behalf of some in-house retailer or the shopping centre's security staff operating under a corporate edict of compulsory jollity.

As Jo stopped speaking the centre's piped music, subliminally bland until that point, changed key and pace. Mike supposed that some well-honed algorithm, carefully monitoring the CCTV feeds, had decided that now was the time to inject some additional verve. The punters were clearly flagging. It was important not to let them stop spending.

"Normal," said Mike, out loud. Jo relaxed a little, and laughed. "Well, you know what I mean," she said.

He turned to look at her. "When did you decide to become a firefighter?" he asked.

"Well," she began – and stopped.

"No, don't worry, I'm still going to uni," he said, grinning with the satisfaction of having accurately read her face. "I'm just wondering, I suppose, when you really knew that you wanted to... I don't know, help people like that."

She smiled back. It was a good question. She was a classic middle child, born into an academic family and surrounded by siblings – two older, two younger – all of whom excelled at school, passed exams and followed their parents' footsteps into illustrious careers. She had been 'helping' since she was five years old: helping in the kitchen, helping in the study, helping in the garden. She had been helpful at primary school and helpful at secondary school and when she had been deciding what to study at university – there having been no real possibility of not going – she had been drawn to 'environmental science' because that, too, seemed helpful. Help her family, help her friends, help the planet. It seemed – inevitable.

"I'm not sure," she said. She had worked for an environmental charity for a few years after graduating but came quickly to a feeling – and it was certainly a feeling rather than a view – that the help she was giving was too abstract, too far removed from people's real needs. She had applied to join the fire service around the same time she first met Mike. "Well you know when I started with the fire service, and I can't remember wanting to be a firefighter when I was a kid, but I think I always enjoyed helping people, it was just something I did. It wasn't something I decided; it was something I was. Something I am."

He nodded and returned his gaze to the increasingly boisterous Christmas throng. A group of young men, around his age, were joshing to the far left of his field of vision, moving more quickly than the crowd, bumping into people, laughing and talking too loudly and sending ripples of disapproval through the surrounding fluid. Several of them were sporting tinsel; a few had plastic reindeer antlers. Funny how easy it is, Mike thought, to transform teenagers from 'Threat' into 'Treat' with no more than some lollipops or flowers or inflatable antlers. The lads slowed down – a dollop of higher density in the generalised gas – only when they came close to a group of similarly spirited and decorated young women, moving at much lower speed and diagonally across their path. Postures and tone changed almost instantly. As the dance began, Mike noticed how painfully thin the teenage girls were. Jo saw it too.

"I'd like to help, I think." He spoke almost wistfully. "You know, try and do something positive or useful." Jo respected the long pause that followed. The awful Christmas music jangled on, and on. "A lot of the time I'm just confused," he continued. "Sometimes I feel totally certain about something, and then the next day I've completely changed my mind." He resumed his pause. "And other times it just feels pointless, and then other times I get so angry, and I don't know if I'm angry at them, or myself, or the system, or the media or the government or whatever. And if I try, I don't know, to say – no, I don't try, I don't even try, I just imagine trying – when I imagine trying to say 'Hey, can I help?' I simply feel like a ridiculous bundle of furiousness and I give up and run back inside my head." He paused again. "Furiousness. Is that even a word?" he pondered.

Jo laughed again. "I don't know," she said. "But if it wasn't, it is now."

Both of them resumed their cross-armed lean against the railing. The music, tinsel, twinkling lights and, above all, the shopping continued.

Autumn

I t was autumn. The cool city wind veered insolently between warm and cold. The lunchtime pedestrians in this rather chic part of London tried to keep up with the wind's vacillations, with scarves and hoods for some, bold bare arms and necks for others. Jo toyed with a breadstick as she watched a sudden crowd of leaves chase an older woman and her dog.

"Hey!"

The cry of greeting from her best friend Miranda Farnaby filled the small Italian restaurant, hauling Jo from her reverie and several other diners from their lunch. Jo stood so as to be engulfed by Miranda's usual hug, set to be even more enveloping than normal: Miranda had predicted a cold wind and appeared to be wearing about eight layers of clothing.

"Hello hello hello!" Miranda trilled, her excitement at once infectious, overwhelming and mysterious. They had been friends since primary school. "How's things?!" Various layers were being peeled off as she spoke, and a waiter was attempting bravely to catch or hold the various items flung gaily his way. "Come on come on! News news! How's single life? How's your dad? How was your holiday? Come on come on!"

Any residual melancholy was swiftly blown away. Jo grinned broadly as her dear friend, now settled in her chair and apparently concerned with rearranging all the items crowding the surface of the modestly-sized table between them, moved seamlessly onwards from her opening volley of questions into an apparently hilarious anecdote about her journey. It made little sense, not so much because the story itself was incomprehensible but because each episode within the story was conveyed with, or interrupted by, a chortle or guffaw or a burst of disbelieving air, to the point where it was almost like listening to a story in a foreign language. You got the gist from all the noises and hand-waving, but the details – well, the details were probably irrelevant anyway.

Jo simply sat there and drank it in. She and Miranda had grown up on the outskirts of the university where Jo's parents had taught, a windswept place of big skies and a slow-moving river. Over more than twenty years now their friendship had mimicked that start. There had been times where they had barely seen one another for a few years; times when they had been almost inseparable; times when they had squabbled, laughed, cried and fought. There had been holidays, rows about men, career crises and a couple of drunken snogs. Right now, they seemed to be in a place of relative calm: the past year or two had included a handful of nights out, a handful of nights in, a few discussions about babies and the occasional lunch.

"So, what are we having?" Miranda asked. "Nothing too big? I'm looking at the specials. The fish looks nice. What do you think? I think the fish. The fish is good here, isn't it?"

By the time the fish arrived the situation had stabilised and something more closely resembling a conversation was becoming feasible.

"So I was at this amazing conference a couple of weeks ago," Miranda continued. "Really interesting. All about the idea that people actually *like* creating waste, throwing stuff away. Makes them feel good, knowing that they've got more than they really need. Apparently the reason that people recycle is not that they think recycling is a 'good thing to do', or that the government's told them to do it. No, it's because people love throwing stuff away! Having a box for their plastic and a box for their tins and somewhere for the glass or whatever makes them feel like they're throwing away *more* stuff. If they just chuck it in one bin it feels like less. Having lots of bins is the same as having lots of cars or lots of televisions or lots of shoes. Turns out that all this recycling is the same as any other bit of modern life. It's actually increasing the amount of rubbish we make!"

She paused for long enough to take a mouthful of fish, but not long enough for Jo to contribute. "And it's men, mainly, apparently. They ran a lovely experiment somewhere, can't remember where, it doesn't matter anyway, this experiment, they were able to show that men actually compete with other men in their neighbourhood over the size of their recycling bags! Basically, if a man found himself living next door to a guy who produced lots of rubbish, over the next few weeks he increased the amount of rubbish he produced, which then affected the guy next door to him, and then the next door guy and so on down the street."

Another mouthful. "Unbelievable," she managed through a mainly full mouth. "Or not, I suppose. Ha ha!"

Miranda was a sociologist working in London's third most prestigious university, a mix of teaching and research. Ever since she had started her PhD, maybe even before then, the stories that Jo found most interesting were those where the big academic or theoretical stuff collided with the day-to-day stuff. Every lunch or dinner or drink was a sprawling mix of impenetrable gossip, full of completely unfamiliar names and back stories; uproarious reminiscences of teenage indiscretion, or twenty-something misdemeanour, mixed with endlessly mutating plans of future travels and adventure; and, like veins of silver, rambling tales that somehow sewed together the lives that Jo saw at work with the grand theories of Miranda's day job.

"What about food?" Jo asked, capitalising on what appeared to be a genuine pause in Miranda's monologue.

"Food? "

"Food. Food waste. All the leftovers. All the stuff that people buy and then leave in their fridge and then just throw away. All those lettuces. And chickens. Didn't I read somewhere that we only end up eating about ten per cent of all the food that's grown?"

Miranda paused again, more wholeheartedly this time. She had, during Jo's question, placed her cutlery so as to indicate that she had finished eating. She glanced down and experienced a pang of discomfort: she had by no means cleared her plate. Food was *so* complicated. That piece of fish. Why had she not finished it?

Miranda knew perfectly well how much edible food was thrown away every day. She actually lectured students on the pointless waste of effort and energy that went into producing all this food – the ploughing and planting of so many fields, the raising and husbanding of so many animals – that simply ended up in a bin. She had written articles about how the food industry and the government were in hock to one another, and how the dieting industry was supported by the same companies that sold the food that made people too fat in the first place. And she knew that the money spent helping people to lead 'healthy lives' was simply dwarfed by the billions spent every year persuading more people to eat more stuff containing more fat, sugar and salt than they really needed.

She knew all these things – but she knew, too, her own battles with food, her own desires, her own guilt, her own shame. Those two or three mouthfuls of fish on her plate sat there like a reminder, and a reprimand.

"We got called to a food bank the other day," said Jo, aware of the pause but not fully of Miranda's discomfort. "A delivery van had knocked over a load of pallets. Have you ever been to a food bank? Unbelievable. The pallets had fallen on top of some of the people, the customers, a couple of mums and a kid, she was only about eight." Jo's gaze became distant and drifted away from Miranda's face, back to the window and the city breezing by outside. "I met someone interesting though, really nice woman, Abena her name was. She worked there."

Miranda remained quiet. She invariably found it hard not to burst into someone else's story, but she was still somewhat caught by the fish, and there was something in Jo's face that was reeling her in.

"One of the mums was trapped under the pallets, they were all full with tins and bags of flour, that sort of thing, so it was crushing her legs, and the little girl had a nasty broken arm, she was crying quite badly, and some of the other people who'd come to get food were pretty distressed, you know, upset at what they'd seen. And these people, well, I'd made assumptions I suppose, but it was really weird. Some of them looked actually properly poor. But some of them – there were maybe twenty people still there by the time we arrived, I suppose – some of them looked quite normal, you know, normal clothes, normal shoes." She swivelled to look directly at Miranda. "But you could see it in their eyes. Something difficult. A mix of..." she hunted for the words, "... a mix of fear, and defeat. And shame, and exhaustion. And hunger. Obviously."

Jo looked back out of the window. "Hunger. In this day and age. In this city." A pair of high-end sports cars drove across their field of view and, in the opposite direction, a woman in her fifties carried her dog in an extravagantly branded handbag. Jo glimpsed the dog's heavily jewelled collar.

"So the woman I met, Abena," Jo continued, "she was our age, maybe a bit older, late thirties, early forties maybe. Tall. Kept smiling all the time. Well, not just smiling. It wasn't just her face; somehow her whole body glowed with positive energy. It was like standing next to some sort of cosmic radiator. She was talking with the injured girl, and talking with the mums, and talking with her colleagues, and talking with me and the rest of the crew, all the time. It was amazing. She was calm and jolly and in charge and…"

"Sounds like your mum," Miranda guessed.

"Ha! Maybe. Yes, maybe, if my mum had come from Ghana. Abena told me that she'd started as a volunteer but that she'd been so good at dealing with the paperwork that they'd offered her a job. Quite ironic, really. She was absolutely amazing with the people, but it was the paperwork that got her the job."

Miranda grunted with a mix of understanding and encouragement.

"I keep thinking about her…" Jo began, trailing off. Her tone had shifted and Miranda noticed one or two of their fellow diners turn to look at them: they were paying a decent amount for this lunch and they did not want to be disturbed. Loud was one thing; highlighting social injustice was quite another. "I don't know," Jo reflected. "I suppose I'm… envious of her?"

"Envious? You? Of what?" Miranda burst out. "You're the proper hero around here. Everybody loves firefighters. And you're a *girl* firefighter! You get to save people, every day! You're one of the good guys, up there with doctors and nurses – what have you got to be envious of?!"

"Yes, I know, I know. But there's something… incomplete about it. Yes, I get to save people from fires and car crashes now and again, or save a woman's legs like I did last week, and yes it's a fantastic feeling, but at the end of a scene we just climb back into the engine and drive back to base and we never see them again. I have no idea where that little girl is now, or how those two women are doing. And I know nothing at all about all the other people that were there, and how they're coping, and what they're going through..."

"Whoa, whoa! You can't do everything! It's not your job to save the world. And even if it was, you couldn't do it on your own."

"But that's what Abena *was* doing!" Jo almost shouted, startling Miranda and ensuring that most of the other diners in the restaurant were now irritated. "Every day she gets up at the crack of dawn or whatever, makes sure that there's plenty of all the right kinds of food, knows the names of literally hundreds of people, people she sees every day or every week, people whose lives she's a part of. They know who she is. She cares for them, and they care about her." She paused again. "And you know - Abena told me this - you know that some of these people won't switch their heating on when winter starts because they're scared they won't be able to pay the bills. She knows these people! They're not some story in the paper, those ones you read in January about some couple who've been found frozen to death in their front room in front of some two-bar heater that they'd been too scared even to switch on. She *knows* these people, knows their names." Jo took a mouthful of water. "And I'm sure they're grateful that me and the other guys turned up in a big shiny engine and lifted some big heavy stuff out of the way, but they have no idea who I am and – and I don't think they really care who I am."

Miranda waited until Jo's gaze swung once again to meet her own: "I bet Abena knows who you are."

Miranda's words made Jo laugh, and the laugh made her realise she was almost weeping. Flustered, she made a short series of grunts and sniffs, found a tissue, rubbed her nose and settled back into her chair.

"And so do I," Miranda continued. "And it seems to me that you're even more stressed than usual." It had been a longstanding joke between them that Jo was always stressed, indeed needed to be stressed otherwise she would be bored. "Mere lunch is clearly insufficient. Some serious drinking is, I think, required."

The prospect of serious drinking encouraged the stress to effervesce further into smiles and laughter. A plan was hatched, and their fellow diners relaxed again. Across the restaurant's various plates a few kilogrammes of leftover food lay ready for disposal, ready to join the further dozens of kilos that had already been generated in the kitchens that day. Later, the restaurant's bins would be emptied and the dozens of kilos would join the thousands of other kilos from hundreds of other London eateries and terrifying tonnes of food waste would trundle in the backs of lorries towards disposal facilities that were based along roads at the rear of the housing estates where Abena's customers lived.

As Jo and Miranda hugged goodbye outside the restaurant the breeze gusted fleetingly warm. "So, two weeks Thursday, yes?" confirmed Miranda. "Can't wait," said Jo. As she turned to go she narrowly missed treading on a small dog. Its owner grunted her disapproval with undisguised venom.

Winter

There was a cold snap at the very beginning of winter. Normally Jo would be wearing no more than additional layers – thick jumper, warm coat and a woolly hat on top of the usual nondescript shirt or t-shirt. Tonight, on the occasion of her first outing with Robert since they split up, things were different. She had sought advice from Miranda.

"What does the invite say?" asked Miranda from the screen.

"Well, it says 'Dinner suit'" –

"Not dress suit?"

"No, dinner suit, definitely dinner suit. And it says 7.30 for dinner. And it's at the 'Worshipful Company of Tanners and Drovers', one of those ancient City clubs, you know, just around the corner from St Paul's."

"And Robert invited you?"

"Well, yes, it was something we set up months and months ago, ages, before we split up, you know, and then he rang me a couple of weeks ago and asked if I'd still like to come." A pause.

"And?..." Miranda queried.

"And he said something about how he was hoping we could catch up. You know."

It had been serious with Robert Dunbar. Just over three years. Jo thought it might have gone all the way. And then it didn't.

"He's a bastard," said Miranda. "What is he after? Why are you going? Why did you say yes?"

"No, no, he's not a bastard..." Jo trailed off. Back in the summer she would have said he was a bastard, but that – she now thought – was because she had been so upset. It was not as if she had caught him shagging someone else, or that she had gone all weird on him, or even that they had started having terrible rows and it had all become unbearably painful. The reality was that he had carried on being as he had always been, and she had carried on being as she had always been, and somehow they had not really managed to grow something new, something 'us'. He had been the one to call it, for sure; but that, too, was just him being him.

"He's a bit of dick, sure," Jo resumed, "but he's basically a good guy and if this... this whatever-it-is is a way of staying in touch and maybe even building something new and grown-up for the future then, well, I'm up for that."

"Really?"

"Really."

"Well then, Ms Grown Up and Sophisticated, we'd better have you looking meltingly fucking sexy. Show me that first dress again."

It took perhaps an hour, this dress that dress, this scarf that scarf, this necklace that necklace. Jo had the kind of body – Miranda told her, as she had so many times before – that made anything look good. Perhaps that was why she took so little interest. She followed Miranda's instructions. By the time they were done she did, she admitted, look terrific. Lots of arm. Lots of neck. "And make sure you wear your hair high!" Miranda admonished.

It was all invisible now, buried beneath the winter coat and a thick scarf, both worn so as to cover her head as well as her neck. She had arranged to meet Robert a few minutes before the formalities were due to begin and was now just moments from the chosen wine bar.

It was a winter wonderland of sorts. Here in London's financial district, even before the arrival of the Christmas decorations that were surely just days away, the lights seemed ubiquitous: they trimmed every junction, every apex, every crane; they carousel horizontally, vertically, diagonally; they filled every towering glass edifice and spilled into the sky. The buildings themselves spiralled impossibly from street level into the heavens by means of metals and plastics that reflected and refracted the lights into yet more bewildering fragments. To look up was to become disoriented, dizzy. Down here at street level, the remaining older buildings – and they were surprisingly numerous – cowered, gloomy, their ancient windows only mutely registering the numberless sparkles above.

Even on the short walk from the station to the wine bar Jo passed three construction sites. Buildings only a few years old had already become redundant, overtaken by the relentless increase in value of the few square metres of flat land upon which they stood. Torn down, their entrails and skeletal parts despatched for recycling, they were being replaced by even taller, more distant, more synthetic entities, themselves destined for disarmingly brief lifetimes.

It did not make sense to Jo but she presumed, as she ducked into the wine bar – was the entrance artificially low to create a deliberate sense of nostalgia, or was it actually ancient? – that Robert would have some sort of explanation and she resolved to press him on the matter. It was potentially an empty question – she was not sure whether she was really interested in the answer – but it served to calm the nerves. It had been – how long? Five months? Six? She still was not sure how she felt. She knew that, for a while at least, it had been intense and fabulous. She knew that, for a while at least, it had seemed as though the whole marriage and babies thing had hovered just ahead, some sort of mirage or oasis that loomed over the next dune, perhaps beyond the next holiday or meeting of the families. And she knew, too, that, fundamentally, he was too wild, too changeable, too *liquid* for a lifetime – or even a few years – of the kind of regularity and evenness that life in that oasis entailed.

Maybe she, too, could not do it. All that focus on just one, or two or even three people?

Her frown dissipated quickly as she scanned the small, crowded bar, found Robert Dunbar's broad handsome smiling face and began the short navigation to the spot where he stood. It was not awkward. She returned his seemingly genuine smile, they embraced comfortably, he offered to take her coat, she mumbled a 'no thank you' since they would not be here long, he pointed to the two glasses of red wine at his elbow and hoped he hadn't been too presumptuous. No, she said, he hadn't, and took a sip.

"Thanks for coming," he said. "I really appreciate it."

They discussed her journey, the temperature outside, whether or not this was a nice wine bar, his journey and how far it was to the Worshipful Company of Tanners and Drovers.

"I'm sorry," he said, laughing in response to her arched emphasis of the phrase 'Worshipful Company of Tanners and Drovers'. "I know it's a bit ridiculous. This whole industry is just the most bizarre mix of centuries – dining clubs from the thirteenth century, handshakes from the eighteenth century, businesses from the twentieth century, financial models from the twenty first century..."

"And buildings from the twenty third century?" Jo cut across.

"Exactly!" he agreed. "Apart from this one..." They had to duck as they left. It was a hundred metres or so before they turned along a preposterously narrow alley and stopped before a large wooden door that looked to have been made by wizards. "Thirteenth century?" she whispered. His muffled guffaw was choked back as the door swung back, held open by a gentleman of indeterminate but considerable age. His uniform – a blurred assembly of scarlet, white, silver, black and buttons – prompted a fleeting glance of understanding between the two arrivals. They entered, were ushered silently to a cloakroom and were within minutes nestled among a hundred or so others in the pre-dinner vestibule.

"The 'pre-dinner vestibule'?" whispered Jo, her tone ratcheted a little further towards disdain. She had never visited one of the City's livery companies before and the environment was hard to believe. Wood panelling on all four walls had the colour of deep honey, as though it had been polished every day for five hundred years. It probably had been polished every day for five hundred years. The only parts of the panelling that were invisible were those covered by ancient oil paintings, exclusively of white male heads, presumably the sundry and various tanners and drovers that had at some point in the past been responsible for ensuring the ongoing success of the eponymous worshipful company. Above, a carved and painted wooden ceiling offered yet further evidence of the extreme longevity, considerable status and deep wealth of both the worshipful company and all those that had had the terrible good fortune to be in its embrace at some point or other over the preceding half millennium or so.

"Bloody hell," Jo managed. A livery company was essentially a glorified trade union, but this was a different universe from the fire service union facilities she was used to.

"You look great," Robert replied. "Come and meet some of my colleagues."

His new colleagues were very different from the old colleagues. When she first met him he was with the same environmental charity where she had worked before joining the fire service. She had gone along to one of those 'let's all meet up again' drinks. He was good-looking and different, clever but at an odd angle to the rest of them. They had hit it off almost immediately.

The charity had grown since her time and now it had sufficient assets to support a small team of financial specialists. He was one of them. He did money. Money for a good cause, to be sure, but money all the same. While the rest of them engaged with supporters, or developed campaigns, or managed projects in areas of the world affected by drought or deluge, he and a couple of others sat at their computers tracking markets, assessing risks, adjusting portfolios. He was too restless, of course. He stayed a couple of years and headed off back into the mainstream. Or so it seemed to Jo. It had not been too long after that that they had split up.

The new colleagues were witty and charming, all skilled at the art of holding a champagne flute and chatting with a complete stranger. The wit and charm continued as they filed through to the dining room, a setting even more grand and intimidating than the last. Solid silver and venerable cutlery sank ever-so-slightly into the white linen of the table cloths at each of the dozen or so circular dining tables; perfectly starched flunkies stood at each table, ready to pour the wine chosen carefully from the cellar to accompany the soup. All were here gathered to congratulate the worshipful company's new president, a man who had also founded the investment institution for which Robert – he explained – now worked.

"No, I don't get it," Jo said. She had actually understood it the first time and, indeed, the second, when one of Robert's colleagues had explained it to her as if she was a bear of very little brain. She had been drinking fairly steadily for a couple of hours now and thought it would be funny to indulge in some gentle mocking. She seemed to be getting on perfectly well with Robert – he had not given any sign that he intended making a drunken pass at her, and there was no sign either that this was some sort of set up - so Jo was feeling quite relaxed.

Robert explained again. On behalf of their clients ("Wealthy individuals," Jo confirmed) they bought and sold financial objects ("Things that don't exist in any physical sense," she chirped) normally shortly before they existed ("So, imaginary," she suggested) using money that had itself been created expressly for the purpose of buying the imaginary objects and which would disappear again as soon as the object that had been bought or sold was either sold or bought again. So long as – Robert emphasised – the value of the imaginary object flickered up or down during the few milliseconds in which they were owned, or even not owned, then the amount of temporary money would always go up, just a little, which meant that, if you had enough of it to start with, by the time it turned back into not-money then there would be some Actual Money left over. If there was enough Actual Money, then their clients would have more money and he, Robert, and his colleagues, over there, and over there, and their shareholders – there, and there – would also have more money. So everyone wins, he concluded.

It was hard to disagree. What a miracle it is! Jo thought. Without any reference to physical objects, material considerations or even such humdrum factors as 'value', an entire sub-culture of the financial community seemed to be living a virtual life predicated on:-

"Alchemy," Jo suggested. "It's basically alchemy, isn't it?"

"Well…" Robert looked at Jo, and around the room, and then back at the woman he'd loved. He knew she was tipsy; he knew she was playing, teasing; he knew that her passion could sometimes get the better of her and that it had been something of a risk to bring her here, to such an obvious manifestation of wealth and privilege. He agreed with her: it was a form of alchemy. And that made him some sort of wizard. He liked being a wizard, even if it was shallow, perhaps even fraudulent.

He had not brought her here to impress her: he knew well enough that she was not the kind of person it was wise to try to impress. How had she put it? 'If a man goes to a party with the intention of making an impression, that's generally the impression he creates.' It was partly why he'd fallen for her in the first place – she wasn't that impressed. There he was, all tall and handsome and clever and destined for the sunny uplands of success – and she just did not seem that bothered.

Perhaps – he found himself reflecting – he had actually needed more affirmation than she had ever been able to give him? They had found out the hard way, he supposed, that something was not right; but he had missed her since they split up and, though he was still not entirely sure of his motivations for getting back in touch, he really did hope that they could find some way of staying connected.

"No," she was saying, trampling through his momentary introspection: "Alchemy's too good a word for it. Alchemy has no victims. Well, maybe the lead. But it's hardly a sentient being." She paused, briefly, and only for a swig of wine. "No victims. Take the lead, cast the spell, lo! the gold, or whatever." Another swig. "You – this – this is not… benign." She almost hissed the word. For the first time in the whole evening Robert grimaced. Yes, there had been a risk, but, given how well everything seemed to have been going, he thought the moment of maximum peril had passed. "Someone, somewhere," she continued, "in fact, many someones, in lots of somewhere, there are people, right now, who have less, who have less than they otherwise would have done. This isn't simply 'wealth management' or looking after the pensions of loads of ordinary people or whatever. That's just bollocks, isn't it? Just bollocks…" She fizzled off. A gong sounded and a herald announced the name of the first after-dinner speaker. Robert, relieved, glanced at Jo. She smiled, a slightly untidy mix of apology, righteousness, victory and acceptance. She promised, with that smile, to behave, and she did.

The speeches were bland, the jokes insipid, the laughter and applause polite. Nothing remotely surprising occurred and soon it was time for carriages. "Time for carriages?!" Jo spluttered, but Robert had seen it coming and managed to smother her remark by helping her into her coat. "I'll get you a cab," he offered.

The freezing air sharpened the senses and Jo found her focus returned quickly. She was still drunk, she knew, because her knees were funny, but the bit of her brain controlling her mouth seemed once again stable.

"I wasn't too…" she asked.

"No, no," he said, warmly. "Quite mild really." He laughed, a memory clearly popping somewhere inside his head.

She slid her hand through the crook of his arm, not so close or tight as to be misinterpreted but just enough to signal the peace. "It was nice," she said. "You were nice."

"Maybe," he replied. "But you're right, of course." It was gone midnight and he watched their breath forming icy clouds as, around them, the infinite light show persisted, a great fractal approximation of the incomprehensible electronic frothing upon which the whole place span. "It's all a giant self-sustaining illusion, hanging on for one last hurrah. I can't believe it hasn't crashed again already."

"How do you do it?" she asked, and immediately regretted it. They had been warm and convivial all evening, she had not once pressed him on anything personal – and now, with surely just minutes, perhaps even less before they went their separate ways, she had put her great clumsy foot in it. It had been one of the last discussions they had had before they split: she had said to him "How you live your life is the politics you have," and he had had no reply. She had made him feel ashamed; and now she felt something similar, having put him there again.

But she had not. He saw it coming, caught it, and gently put it down. For a second she almost loved him again. The cab came to a halt. Robert had a word with the driver, putting the journey on account.

They hugged lightly, kissed cheeks and looked briefly and intently at one another.

"Thanks," they said, simultaneously. She was still laughing as the cab pulled away.

Spring

It was spring, not yet full bloom, that marvellous week or so beyond the equinox when the sap is at maximum acceleration. Even here in the big city, where the tarmac and brick have hegemony, the flora and fauna are determinedly oblivious to their subjugation. The street trees are a mix of impossible blossom and iridescent greens; the urban birds are chattering and pecking, ramped up on hunger and lust, audible even above the traffic.

Jo was walking to the tube station. Normally on a day like this she would be on her bicycle. Cycling was the only way to travel in the city, she felt. She loved the sense of freedom, the way it made the city visible, the steady flow of air on her face and blood in her veins. Miranda thought she was mad, of course: it's far too dangerous out there! In practice, Jo had long since discovered, the traffic was invariably moving so slowly that it was actually safer to cycle in the city than anywhere else.

Today, though, she was on a mission to buy presents. Birthdays for her mother, Miranda and Mike were all coming up. Normally her gifts were handmade - or at least hand-adjusted – but every few years she would wonder whether she was missing out on something, perhaps the possibility that the perfect gift was, in fact, available in a shop somewhere and that, really, it wasn't that big a deal to go on a bit of an expedition and buy a couple of nice things for the people she cared about. This was one of those years.

She preferred to do this kind of thing as efficiently as possible, so she was aiming to get all three gifts on a single outing. She was not completely sure what she would end up buying and did not want to risk transporting items either bulky or expensive on the bike. So, the tube it was.

She was travelling off-peak and mid-week, so the risks of sweaty congestion, either underground or in the shops, were reduced. It was one of her favourite features of her job. She had done a long weekend shift, was not due back on for another couple of days and so could pootle at her own pace, sort out a little life laundry and go shopping when things were quiet. She was planning a proper bike ride the next day, perhaps into the hills to the south of the city, or maybe the lakes out west. Either would be beautiful at this time of year. She was looking forward to it.

She was not even particularly anxious about the day ahead, un-accustomed though she was to the demands of modern shopping. Perhaps it was the weather. The short walk to the station took her along two streets of domestic gardens and diagonally through a small municipal park. She had no option but to absorb the full wonder of the spring – how could she, or anyone, fail to be lifted? She watched a pair of squirrels playing some sort of game, running circles around the trunk of a mature tree in the park; she saw a small brightly-coloured bird ferrying food into a bush, presumably to its nest; she saw a black-bird interrupt a preening pigeon, an unfathomable territorial dispute, or an accident. The sun shone and Jo beamed.

Her good humour lasted the entire and thankfully smooth journey into town. She felt as ready as she could possibly be as she took the last flight of stairs back up into the light. She had a vague list of possible presents in her head which, allied with a similarly imprecise impression of which shops were where, would be guiding her route. Above ground at Oxford Circus she looked east, west, north, south. There were indistinguishable retail outlets in all directions. Her first port of call would be something electrical and her memory suggested that meant... north. She swivelled, took a first half-step, dodged a tourist, and set off.

She was after a gizmo, one in particular. She had heard about it from a couple of the guys at the station. It sounded ideal for Mike. Apparently it took real-time video footage and, if you hummed at it, it would recognise the tune, download your preferred version, attach it to the video, edit for rhythm so that the music and the action were in sync, upload it to your favourite platform, label it and publish it, all at the same time and in less than a second. Or something.

None of this made any sense to Jo. It was not her total ignorance of the tech that distressed her; after all, no one 'understood' the tech. Everything was so small and so fast now that future museums were already in real trouble. She had mulled this over just recently on a visit to the British Museum. She had been gazing at a spidery device that translated the clay draft of a sculpture onto the marble that would be used for the real thing, when it suddenly hit her: what would the museums of the future contain? All the technology until recently had been visible. Tools, clocks, engines, vehicles, all big enough to peer at and, if not understand, at least appreciate. Even the computers had at one time been the size of rooms, with values you could look at and buttons you could press. Now it was all the size of molecules, avenues on silicon so small you could not even use a microscope. She had pictured crowds of people a century hence, all straining to look through some as-yet-uninvented optical device, oohing and aahing at the lovely way in which an infinitesimal line of something metallic

joined something else unimaginably tiny and shiny. She had wondered, too, how that future museum would explain 'apps' and the
cultural phenomenon of sending pictures of cats, food and genitals.

Her train of thought came abruptly to a halt. She looked around. A
breeze, perhaps? Had someone brushed against her? She straightened
her back and suddenly felt just how lucky she was. She was not battling
to maintain a decent home or struggling to save for a rainy day. She was
not bewildered about what to do with her children or her relationships
or her mind. She was not fed up with her job, she didn't have an awful
commute to work, she didn't have dodgy knees or an aching back. She
may not understand or need a gizmo, but who was she to judge others
if they wanted a new and compensatory piece of kit that was faster,
smaller, cooler, cleverer and more adaptable than its rustic cousin of
last month or the month before?

She turned from the street and focused her gaze on the window of
bristling digital delights before her. Lenses, screens and black boxes of
various sizes were draped with explanatory notes couched in incomprehensible words. Items with impenetrable functions boasted their
formidable capacities in a language of alien symbols and mysterious
code. She didn't want to judge, but everything in the window looked
suddenly impossibly complex and pointless.

Jo swivelled on her heels, a decision made: Mike would not be receiving a gizmo for his birthday. She would have to think of something
else. Perhaps, she wondered, he would one day see the gift she had had
in mind in a museum. Perhaps not.

Either way that still left two gifts: she was intending a scarf or some
other summer accessory for her mother; and had been considering a
belt for Miranda, something understated yet convincingly rebellious.
Jo could, she supposed, kill both birds with a single department store

stone; or she could decide roughly on her budget and aim for the appropriate 'price point' environment just west of the tube station.

She set off for the latter, a route that unavoidably took her through a cluster of high-end boutique retailers, a zone of luxury goods and exclusive designer brands which provided genuine spending opportunities for the wives, daughters, boyfriends and playthings of the city's ultra-rich, as well as wander-and-gawp opportunities for an assortment of tourists and lunchtime locals. It was a risk, Jo knew, to walk unprotected through such an environment: despite one's best intentions, it was almost impossible not to glance into at least one of the windows and the consequences could be severe.

And so it proved. Having managed to remain thoroughly engaged with her internal dialogue for some considerable distance, Jo had to dodge a group of window shoppers which unexpectedly changed speed and direction and she inadvertently glanced sharply left. A heavily framed thick glass frontage displayed a selection of kitchen equipment. Arranged decorously on the left, a set of knives; to the right, further cutlery, for the purposes of swiping, scooping, ladling and otherwise re-distributing items that had been sliced and diced with the knives. In the centre, describing a carefully choreographed spiral, a set of saucepans.

All the items were part of what is called 'a matching set'. Jo had once listened while Dr Miranda in full sociologist mode had explained the cultural importance of 'matching sets' and just how keen people were to have matching sets of things in their homes – furniture, screwdrivers, porcelain animals, crockery. Jo remembered such things from her own childhood: her father had a matching set of engineering text-books; her mother had three or four matching sets of coasters. Jo had failed to bring a predilection for such things into her own adulthood. For some reason, it just did not bother her enough. Her flat was not merely a superficially disorganised jumble; it was a *deeply* disorganised jumble, a thoroughly eclectic collection of items deemed useful, attractive or both, but never (unless by accident) matching.

Her initial mystification at people's preferences for matching sets – apparently widespread and entrenched – had turned into something of a hobby. Well, perhaps not a hobby so much as a diversion. Very often at work she had to deal with incredibly upsetting situations in people's homes: she had been told early on by one of the older hands that it sometimes helped to have a mental routine you could lean on when things got too tough. She had learned to lean on 'matching sets'. It did not matter where you were, there was invariably some sort of personal collection – a set of tea cups and saucers, a display of picture frames, a selection of cuddly toys by the rear window - that you could notice and mull over as some sort of emotional bulwark against the effects of whatever horrors were going on around you.

With time and experience came further questions: what are the factors that signal the 'matching'? Just how similar did things need to be before they could be called 'a set'? Sometimes it was obvious, sometimes less so.

She assumed, staring into the window at the kitchen equipment, that the underlying logic of connection would be sophisticated and subtle, elusive, perhaps even artistic. This was, after all, a retailer in the very thick of the most expensive pitch in London – whatever was in this window was going to be fearsomely expensive.

The items were, indeed, fearsomely expensive, but little that was sophisticated, subtle, elusive or artistic was going on. The saucepans seemed to have achieved their twin conditions of 'extremely expensive' and 'matching' through the blunt process of having precious jewels embedded in the handles. Jewels. In the handles. Of saucepans. It made no sense to her. What kind of people bought diamond-handled saucepans? What kind of world contained people that thought owning diamond-handled saucepans was a good idea?

Jo supposed that the kind of people who would buy such items would do so in order to impress their guests – in which case the question became even worse: What kind of people would be impressed by a host that had bought diamond-handled saucepans?

It was all appalling and proved too much. Jo's ambition of acquiring one or more humble birthday offerings had been critically undermined. For the remainder of her expedition, it did not seem to matter whether she strolled the narrow alleyways of the chic independents, the more garish but obvious offerings from the mid-market brands or, in her final effort, the concession circus of the department store. All were filled with the same exhortations to replace yesterday's perfectly lovely and fully functional item with today's more fashionable yet somehow identical alternative so that, tomorrow, you could do it again. Jo saw more and more clearly, too, that not only were all the shops equally and inevitably quiet on the utter pointlessness of buying any of the items on offer, but all were completely silent as to the actual costs and consequences of the addiction that they all embodied. Even the 'honestly-we've-been-nice-to-the-bees/whales/elephants' labels seemed like just another part of the 'brand positioning' landscape.

Tired and dispirited, and having failed to eat a proper lunch, Jo decided to have one last coffee before disappearing once again underground. She just about had time before the full power of rush hour was unleashed and any prospect of a comfortable journey home erased.

The expedition had been a mistake. It had always been unlikely that she would make the kind of purchases she had intended; in fact now she was perplexed that she had ever even thought it was a good idea. It was not as if any of her loved ones would have been expecting such gifts. Last year she had given Mike a wallet she had found in second-hand store and which she had then cleaned and polished. Her mother had received an enamelled bracelet that Jo had bought directly from the woman who had made it; and Miranda had received a couple of jars of pickle that Jo had made herself. The year before – well, that was harder to remember. Maybe her mum had received the pickle. No matter. Last year, and the year before, and the year before that, Jo had given the same things she had always given, to them and to everyone. Things that she had made, things that she had found, things that had been repaired, things that she had somehow turned from one thing into another. Things that had little or no commercial value, things that were, rather, ingots of love and care.

So why – she asked herself, finishing the coffee and heading for the entrance to the station – why had she this year tried something different? Had she just forgotten how awful she found it out there? Or was she worried that her friends and family were becoming tired of her homespun trinkets? Or perhaps she was simply in the foothills of middle-age and growing tired of the effort required to think so hard about everybody?

Empty handed and full of such reflections, she sat down in the train carriage, oblivious to her fellow passengers, to the driver's usual warning about the doors and to the innumerable advertisements around her. The doors slid shut. The train jolted slightly and there was a strange noise from her right. Two men were standing very close to two women. The men were well-built, jeans and t-shirts, white. The women, also white, wore headscarves and the long black dress distinctive of Muslims. The men were not companions of the women. One of the women rested her hand on the handle of a baby's pushchair. A small boy, on foot, clung to his mother's dress, half-hiding himself. One of the men stood slightly in front of the other. He was leaning towards the older of the women. His words were indistinct; his aggressive tone was crystal clear.

Jo scanned the rest of the carriage. The usual mix of business folk, shoppers, tourists, students. The usual mix, too, of responses to the unfolding and uncomfortable drama: some focused furiously on their electronic device; some found an important speck on their sleeve, or the shoe of a fellow traveller; some looked more or less directly at the developing scene, keen to watch the action and with no intention of intervening. The man's voice grew louder, and clearer.

"...fucking outrageous, wandering around looking scary in those fucking headscarves, fucking terrorists, my kid fucking brother can't even get into the local school cos of you lot, fuck's sake..." He was leaning ever closer, his finger now raised towards her face, both women and the boy and the buggy compressed into the junction between the carriage door and the plastic screen separating the standing area from the seating area.

Jo glanced left and right one more time to confirm the paralysis around her but, just as she was about to stand up, the gentleman nearest to the confrontation moved from his seat. Rather than standing, however, he slid directly into a crouch. He looked fifty, maybe fifty five. Crouched as he was, it was difficult to say how tall or big he was. Jeans, casual shoes, a light jacket, dark hair, balding. Almost kneeling, he began speaking directly to the small boy half hidden behind his mother's dress. Above and behind him, the pointing man began suddenly and rapidly to lose momentum.

"...bet your husband's... Oi, what you doing? Hey, mate." Simply to look down he was forced to back away a little. The older, crouching man ignored him. The entire carriage, including Jo, looked on, transfixed. "Oh for fuck's sake. Oi, you!"

The crouching man was inaudible, but he was clearly talking to the small boy with some intensity. The boy's face, visible to Jo, was rapt. He smiled, then nodded. He watched the crouching man's face carefully, then nodded again. The man reached out to the boy, grasped him with both hands around the waist and, still with his back to the two men, stood up, lifting the boy with him. The aggressive man's hand fell from the older man's shoulder and he stepped back almost involuntarily. The two aggressors were now, astonishingly, a good couple of metres away from the two Muslim women: the older man was standing directly between the two pairs; and, still, the older man had neither spoken to nor even looked at the two younger men.

Standing, it was clear he was neither small nor frail. He lifted the boy and held him suspended until the youngster had both hands securely on the tube train's hanging rail. Jo saw the older man's questioning nod to the boy, who signalled back, and the older man's hands simply moved apart, just a few centimetres, and the boy's smile of satisfaction burst through the carriage like a flood. He was hanging from the hand rail! On a train! The mother, as transfixed as everyone else by the older man's actions, made a half step forward but then just as quickly relaxed. The two younger men, by now completely sidelined, fell even further back. The train began pulling into the next station and the older man lowered the boy diagonally so that he landed directly in front of his mother. At the very moment the train came to a halt, the older man's natural motion of having lowered the boy seemed to bring him back to the vertical, and to twist, so that he suddenly and for the first time looked at the two younger men.

The doors slid open. The older man said nothing. He gazed at the two younger men. The first of the men blurted a few further words of profane confusion and both younger men got off the train. The doors began closing, and the older man rotated and descended, back into the crouch. He looked directly at the boy; and then, and seemingly for the first time, up at the mother. Jo could not see the question delivered by the upward flick of his eyebrows, but the response was obvious as the boy was once again lifted, this time with a yelp of delight, back to his improvised monkey swing.

The man let him swing a few times with the rhythm of the carriage before once again lowering him to the floor. A final crouch of communication, a smile upwards to the mother, then he swivelled and stood. His seat was now occupied: when the two aggressors got off the train, someone else had got on and, oblivious, had taken the nearest empty spot. The man glanced about and, without making eye contact with any of the spectators, took the only available empty seat. Next to Jo.

She spoke before she even had a chance to remember London's unwritten protocols of underground silence: "That was amazing," she said. "Thank you," he replied. His voice was gravelly, distant. He continued to stare into the middle of nothing.

"It looked as though you've had training, or something." A pause. "I'm a firefighter, er, we often have to deal with difficult situations, you know, people can behave very... strangely. I've been on a couple of courses." Jo felt curiously tongue-tied and hoped she would soon stop speaking.

He rotated in his seat slightly, unhurried, and for the first time met her eyes. She had the most unsettling sensation of actually being seen. As though he was looking all the way in. "My name's Daniel," he said. And she told him her name. "Good to meet you Joanna. No, no particular training. But I'm always delighted to meet someone from the front line. Fire fighting? Must be interesting breaking into a male bastion like fire fighting. How did that happen?"

And she told him. They got off at the same station and, since they turned out to be walking the same way, stopped for a brief drink in the bar she liked. Then they went their separate ways. The mid-evening springtime light gave the morning's iridescent greens a new and somehow tangential quality, which had a similar reflective and buoyant impact on Jo's mood. She felt herself almost skipping home. She realised that she had, quite uncharacteristically, spent the whole of the past hour talking almost exclusively about herself. Somehow she still knew next to nothing about him. As far as she could tell, he hadn't flirted with her at all; and she, as far as she could tell, had been cool and clever and charming.

On top of that, she had his phone number.

Part Two: This Year

Thursday

It was a Thursday. Jo was cooking. She was behind schedule: Miranda would be arriving soon. Jo's flat was in its usual state of dishevelment, sportswear strewn across the sofa, papers and magazines piled untidily in inconvenient places, bicycle repair components scattered across the solitary coffee table. The shopping, too, was somewhat out of control, this evening's meal, tomorrow's snacks and a selection of top-up items all seemingly mingled and determined to elude proper order. It had been a normal day.

Her phone rang.

She checked the display and knew she should answer. Mike rarely called, so it was either something important, possibly urgent, or something exciting, perhaps some news. She hit the green button.

"Hey, it's me."

"Hello you," she replied. "How's it going?" She hit the speakerphone button, leaving both hands free so she could shut down the cooking.

"Yeah, good. Not bad. Just ringing to say hello really."

This was unexpected and clearly a ruse. Jo set off from the rapidly cooling hob towards the sofa, bending to begin the process of clearing a space. "Great," she said. "Well, hello. I was just about to cook dinner."

"Oh, sorry, I can call back later..."

"No, no, no problem, honestly, it's lovely to hear from you. How's it going?"

"Well, I've been thinking about that stuff we were talking about the other week, you know, when we went for that walk with mum and dad." She liked the fact he called them – her mum, his dad – just mum and dad. It had been a good weekend, plenty of fine food and the now-traditional bracing walk through the low rolling West Country hills. She and Mike had fallen into a long and deep conversation about the world's troubles, about just how fast the handcart was heading towards its fiery destination and about what, if anything, he - and she - should be doing about it.

"Gosh, yes," she said. It had been on her mind too. She had opened up to him about the frustrations she had been experiencing. She had told him about the incident at the food bank, where the pallets had collapsed and she had met Abena, and how it had crystallised her feeling that she was just skipping on the surface, still not really making a difference, just picking up the pieces rather than tackling things at source. She had talked, too, about some jewel-encrusted saucepans she'd seen, and how she couldn't understand the people who bought them, and how difficult she found it to come to terms with a world in which there were some people who could spend that kind of money on a saucepan while there were other people who couldn't afford to eat.

He had talked about his own frustrations – at the world, and about himself – and his sense that too few people were able properly to affect what happened to them. He felt he was just going around in circles. She had wondered whether there was something he could do, perhaps a movement or organisation he could join, something he could get his teeth into while he worked things out.

"I've been thinking about what you said," he told her now. "I was thinking maybe I could volunteer over the summer. I looked at a couple of local charities and some of the big international ones, maybe I could do some travelling, you know." Jo could feel the 'but' coming. "But a lot of it just looks like an excuse for a holiday, you know? And even the good ones feel, I don't know, too narrow? Too focused? Like, the problems are so all-encompassing, and so joined up, and they all seem to be looking at just one piece of the jigsaw…"

As he spoke, Jo wandered back to the kitchen to check that nothing was on fire and to collect her cup of tea.

"I looked at the political parties, too" Mike continued, "to get some idea of what they're saying and doing about the environment and caring for the planet and looking after poor people and stuff…"

He spoke for several minutes, explaining what he had found out, the pros and cons as he saw them, a description and explanation that was typical of the young man, mostly clear, occasionally infused with bursts of passion, easy for Jo to follow and understand. She sprawled comfortably on her sofa, limbs at natural angles, a toe positioned so as to idly toy with the edge of a cushion. She nodded invisibly from time to time, making occasional grunts of comprehension or encouragement.

He fizzled out. She sat with the silence. "And so?…" she ventured eventually.

"And so I think we need to do something different. Something new. I think I'd like to do something with a bit of a bang. Definitely more than just clicking a button or signing a petition. Something bigger than just a one day news item, but not something that's going to take for ever. I mean, I'm supposed to start uni in October, and I still want to do that..." he trailed off again.

"Did you just say 'we'?" she probed.

"Oh, yeah, well. Yes. I was thinking maybe we could do something together. I mean, you sounded pretty fed up too."

"Something bigger than a one day news item but not something that'll take for ever," she repeated.

"Er, yes. What do you think?"

"Well, I suppose you've narrowed it down a little!" she laughed. "I mean, obviously I'll think about it." She paused. "I think, well, the way my thoughts have been going, I keep coming back to all these people who need help, here, not on the other side of the world, people who for one reason or another aren't able to look after themselves. I don't know, maybe they're too old, or too frail. Or too weak, or too poor, or just struggling to cope with the sheer torrent of life. There just seem to be so many people who need... looking after. Who need some help. Who need care."

Jo took a mouthful of the cold tea, and then resumed: "And there are plenty of people who seem to give care – you know, the nurses and doctors and the people who work at my dad's place and those people like Abena and... oh, I don't know, they all seem to be working on their own. Like you said, it's not joined up. And it's the same for me. I rescue people, but then – poof! I'm gone. No joins." She paused again. "It's definitely not a one day news item!"

He, too, laughed. The doorbell rang. "Oh, shit, sorry, that's Miranda," said Jo.

"Hey, no worries, it's been good, thanks. So you'll think about it, yeah? See if we can come up with something?" He sounded more than merely hopeful; almost desperate.

"Yes, definitely. Definitely. Listen Mike, I'd better go, but, really, take care. I'll kick it about. I'll call you."

"OK. Thanks. Love you."

"Love you too."

The buzzer sounded a second, longer time. "Yes, yes, coming!" Jo yelled through the walls, and within a few seconds she was enveloped by her friend's embrace. Amid the usual waterfall of greeting and questions from Miranda, Jo tried to explain that her delay – both in answering the door and, perhaps more importantly, in presenting supper (now at least an hour late) – was because she had been on the phone to Mike.

"Darling," soothed Miranda, "we have wine, and the whole evening. Pass me the bottle opener and tell me how he is."

Jo gratefully obeyed and, as Miranda poured the first glasses, summarised the conversation with her step-brother. Miranda's expression took on a strange hue. "Why the face?" Jo asked.

"I'm not sure," Miranda began, rather more seriously than Jo had anticipated. "I think I'm feeling a little conflicted. I still think of him as a little boy, I suppose, so it's odd hearing you talk about him as if he's a grown up... which I suppose he is now... And another bit of me is wriggling a little because he sounds... well, so earnest. Too earnest. I mean, why isn't he all girls and drugs and parties and music?" Miranda paused to make room for a big swig of wine, but resumed before Jo had a chance to intervene: "Look, I know that part of the reason we're in such a big fucking mess is because too few young people give a shit about anything serious. Yes, I know, I know, sweeping generalisation, and yes, there are probably loads and loads of really active youngsters doing stuff online that I don't even understand, and now that I think about it there was that big demo last week, but – well, just look at the numbers. For every one visible protesting student there's probably a hundred or so plugged into some on-line game supported entirely by home delivery pizza and beer." She refilled her glass, then paused a little further. "That said, another bit of me says: ooh, that sounds exciting, what's the plan?"

Jo laughed at that point. Sometimes she wondered why they were still friends – there seemed to be plenty of things about which they did not see eye to eye – but, in general, there was enough laughter to compensate for any tension; and, after all, once you've known someone for twenty-plus years, there's an ease and a comfort with a value all of its own. "I think the plan should start with me sorting out the food," she said, bouncing from the sofa towards the kitchen area. "Pasta ok, Dr Miranda?"

It was, and so was the wine. Half way through the second bottle – by which time the pair of them were very thoroughly installed on the sofa, one at either end, legs comfortably entwined underneath Jo's favourite blanket – the conversation turned to Robert Dunbar.

"So how was it?" Miranda asked. Jo had seen her ex-boyfriend a week earlier, for the second time since they split up and the first since the bizarre winter dinner at the Worshipful Company of Tanners and Drovers.

"It was nice," Jo began, tentatively. "We had lunch in that new tapas bar you told me about. Food was nice, I liked the atmosphere." Miranda kicked her below the blanket: "Enough already with the 'nice'!" she said. "How was it?!"

"Well, it was good to see him again. We didn't really get the chance to talk when we went to that dinner back in November. He's enjoying his job, I think. Still a dreamer, you know. I have no idea whether he'll stick at it or whether he'll be doing something completely different in a few months." She sipped her wine. "And we... we got on. I'm not sure what I'm hoping for. I'm pretty sure we're done as a couple. No,

I'm completely sure. And I don't think he's got a new girlfriend or anything." She stared into space for a moment.

Miranda looked closely at her best friend. "So what did you talk about?"

"Oh, I don't know. We traded work stories, I asked about his mum and dad, he asked about Mike. Just easy stuff, you know." Another pause. "No, there was one proper bit of discussion, now that I think about it. Do you remember that time when you and I were at that Italian place last year and you were telling me about how men like to compete over how much rubbish they produce? Well Robert was talking about the same thing in finance, how it's all dicks on the table and balls in the fire, all that kind of nonsense, and that he'd tried a couple of times to suggest to his colleagues that some deal or other they were working on needed to be seen in some bigger context, I don't know, that they really needed to think about some of the broader connections and consequences of the deal they were making, you know, the effects on jobs and the places where people lived and things like that. He said he was just ridiculed, told to stop being such a wimp." She gave a heavy sigh. "The whole game is about the money shot, and everything else is just..."

"...commentary," Miranda finished.

"Yes," Jo continued. "And I know we've joked for years about all these boys with their toys and their addictions to competition and testosterone, and how one day it would be lovely if people felt sympathy rather than admiration for their pathetic need to have a bloody Ferrari or whatever, but it was just really sobering to hear from Robert what it's like on the inside, you know?"

Jo paused, only to become momentarily lost in her feelings. There was something about Robert that had always been compelling. Sometimes you could see it in his eyes; sometimes it danced around the edges of his mouth; sometimes it played havoc with his eyebrows and his forehead. It wasn't just that he was clever and handsome and charming. There was something else. An unpredictability. A sense of danger. A feeling that something remarkable, something mad or inspiring or thrilling might just happen next. It was intoxicating to begin with – but exhausting over time.

She had never fully grasped why he had loved her. She knew why she had loved him; but why had he loved her? It was not the sort of thing she had ever managed to get him to talk about. Maybe her stability made him feel safe? Perhaps he just needed someone – anyone – who could keep up. They certainly used to laugh at the same things. And he had always seemed comfortable in her company whenever he just ran out of steam, something she knew he was scared of.

She was still very fond of him and she felt relaxed about that. But how did he feel about her? Was it possible he still loved her? Suddenly she felt less at ease: did she want him not to love her anymore, or was she hoping that he still did?

Jo returned to the room with a start, saw Miranda's expression, shook her head and resumed: "Anyway," she said, retrieving the thread of her thoughts, "he said that, basically, the people with the biggest status are not the ones that pull off deals that create the most jobs, or even deals that make the most money. Apparently the biggest players are the ones who cut the biggest deals, who risk the most. People who have lost millions are more highly prized than people who have made thousands. Because they've got bigger balls." Jo took a deep swig of wine. "An entire chunk of our lives dictated not by logic or 'market forces' or whatever, but by little boys competing over who has the biggest willy. Jesus."

"So, um, how is Robert doing?..." Miranda wondered - and both of them exploded with laughter.

Once they had recovered something resembling composure, Miranda resumed: "It makes me think..."

"More wine?" Jo teased, offering the bottle.

"Well, yes, obviously," said Miranda, proffering her glass, "No, I mean something else about what's going on. And it's a struggle. It's not just that there's a bunch of macho dickheads over there doing one thing, and another bunch of dickheads over there doing another thing, and another over there and so on. And it's not just that thing you were saying a few months ago when you met that woman at the food bank – what was her name? – yes, Abena, her – well, you were saying how you felt that you were just patching things up, not really following through or something."

"Yes, I remember," said Jo. "I was just saying the same thing to Mike."

"Exactly," Miranda continued. "So I'm thinking that the problem is something to do with the connections between things. That's where it's difficult. We find it difficult to see the joins, which makes it difficult to see what's the best thing to do."

"What do you mean?"

"Well. For example. We were talking about recycling in that Italian restaurant, weren't we? So – what's the connection between all the rubbish we throw away and, say, the stuff that Robert's doing? Or, I don't know, what's the connection between what Abena's doing, and food banks, and..." - the wine made a leap – "...and your dad's care home. Or between..."

"...racist incidents on the tube and the desire for shiny electronic gizmos?" Jo suggested.

"Exactly! It's not something we tend to think about." Miranda screwed up her face for a moment. "No, it's worse than that," she continued. "It's not something we're encouraged to think about, or trained to think about." She sipped her wine. "I mean, when I think about the stuff I teach, or even how I was taught, it's all in straight lines. You know, this is 'biology' and this is 'engineering' and this is 'politics' and this is 'English'. All of it in little boxes, separate. In reality – I mean, here, in this messy real world – it's all... entangled, isn't it?"

"Hmm," said Jo, slowly. "So it could go something like: Robert's business buys and sells money rather than, I don't know, buying machinery that makes things, and that means... What? That someone invents a new machine which produces less waste but they can't get the money to develop it properly because the money's being used somewhere else?"

"Maybe," said Miranda. "Or maybe it's that the people who do what Robert does have so much money – they earn so much money – that they can just afford to throw stuff away?"

Both women stared into space for a little while.

"This is hard," said Jo. "I think I may be drunk."

"And on a Thursday, too!"

"Yes, well..." Jo managed. "And what if there are no connections? What if, I don't know, it's just coincidence? Or you just pick a completely ridiculous pair of things. Like, say, this glass and, um, fire engines? Or Mike's gap year and my mum's collection of coasters?"

The conversation had clearly run into something of a hole and they climbed out by busying themselves for a few minutes with clearing away the residue of the evening and re-arranging cushions, before diverting into an unexpectedly heavy chat about babies and how they both felt about the fact that they hadn't had any yet. It was Jo who brought them back to the elusive connections.

"So," she announced, with a little more grandeur than she intended, "what we were saying is that there are connections between Robert and food waste, but that they're difficult to see, and that makes it difficult to know whether, if you wanted to make the world a better place, it would be better to tackle Robert or to tackle the food waste."

"Or to tackle something else which is in the middle," Miranda added.

"Hmm, yes, ok, that too. So we need to figure out the connections, then see if there's some sort of common denominator, then work on that."

"Exactly," said Miranda.

"Well that's that sorted then!"

They lapsed once again into silence. Minutes passed. Then more minutes.

"Got it," said Jo.

"Uh huh?"

"Care."

"Care?"

"Yes. Care. The common denominator. Whether or not you care. How you care. Who cares."

"Nope, not with you yet," said Miranda.

"Well. Food waste – do you care about it or not? Hungry people – care, or not? Climate change – care, or not? Your neighbour, your mum, your football team – care or no care? It's like some sort of universal solvent. And where it's missing, bad things happen. Big money doesn't care about small people – bad. Wealthy diners don't care about food waste – bad. People from one country don't care about people from another – bad."

"Wow. Nice. I'm going to have to think about that."

"Be my guest." Jo was now sitting upright. "Care. That's what it needs. Bundled up. If we try to work out all those connections we were talking about earlier it'd take forever, and then we'd squabble over where to start." She stood up, glass in hand. "Get a whole load of people together who need care, and a whole load of people who do care, who give care – fuck it, who just care – and see what happens!" She whooped with delight and turned to stare at Miranda. "That's it! Ha! Care to save the world, Dr Miranda?"

"Care. To save the world." Miranda swirled the thought with her wine.

"Yes. A care package," Jo concluded with a flourish. "If we got enough people together in one place, it would it be a care city!"

"A care city?" Miranda replied. "Couldn't we start with something a bit smaller? A care town? A care village? A care street?"

"OK, maybe a town. Best not to get too carried away I suppose..."

"Maybe," said Miranda. "Think over these things further we should. Let's finish that wine first."

Friday

It was a Friday. Dr Miranda Farnaby had just finished giving a lecture and was now running late for a meeting. She was not unduly flustered: her colleagues on the committee would be working their way through the procedural chaff, she still had a few minutes before the main business began. She was quite looking forward to it. The university had been invited to co-sponsor a festival. It was the sort of thing the vice-chancellor and the other cheeses were very keen on – outreach, profile, inter-disciplinary collaboration, attracting the overseas market, etcetera etcetera. Today's meeting was to hear directly from the conference organisers in advance of a final recommendation from the committee. Miranda was keen on the whole idea, and keen to be seen to be keen. Progress in academic life did not depend solely on publications and citations.

The meeting was, as Miranda had anticipated, still in its preliminary stages when she arrived. The room was one of those anodyne and anonymous academic rooms so typical of the mid-tier universities, used variously for small lectures, seminars and meetings such as this. A few desultory chairs and tables had been hurriedly and not entirely precisely arranged in an attempt to convey collaboration rather than confrontation; papers were piled haphazardly across both tables and chairs; illumination came from the windows along one wall and the low-impact lighting in the ceiling, both of which conspired to remind all those present that they were partially underground. To complete the ambience, the walls were an instantly forgettable grey.

Quite unforgettable was the tall woman clearly leading the festival team. She was wearing a vivid box jacket composed of rectangular patches of designer cloth involving, it seemed, all known colours. She wore a blouse in hallucinogenic emerald; a power skirt, in grey, skimming just below the knee; dark low-heeled shoes shaped flawlessly to acknowledge the curve of her calf; and, running through her thick dark-blond hair, a scarf that seemed to catch just that set of tones from the remainder of the ensemble to give the impression of a perfectly lit painting. She had cheek bones to die for. Her make-up was elegant and precise. Her teeth were perfect.

Miranda almost lost her footing. She felt suddenly clumsy and awkward as she struggled to squeeze behind first one and then a second occupied chair, as she fumbled to find her papers and as she stumbled into a seat that was now too small, poorly positioned and hideous.

"Dr Farnaby, glad you could join us", said the committee chair-woman, in a tone perplexingly both genuine and cutting. "The pre-sentation from..." - she glanced down at her papers – "...from Kate Humboldt and her team at Statement is just about to start. Ms Humboldt, over to you!"

The beautiful human called Kate Humboldt unleashed a dazzling smile and began speaking to the committee, looking each of them in the eye, introducing Statement plc and the members of her team, talking smoothly, silkily and without hesitation, deviation or repetition. Her voice was confident and reassuring. She used intonation, cadence and variations in pace. She used verbs, nouns, vowels and consonants. She gave an outline, hinted at detail, offered insights, administered jargon. Miranda heard every word, registered nothing and believed it completely.

Soon there were slides, and pictures of a large flat site as if seen from a helicopter, or a balloon; there were diagrams of infrastructure and temporary stadia; there was a three dimensional visualisation, with a fly through and a run past; there were colours and movement, time-lines and deadlines, interim provisions and critical paths; there were logos - so many logos! – of promoters and supporters, of Statement itself, of bronze sponsors and silver sponsors and gold sponsors and platinum sponsors, of theatrical companies and musical performers and noteworthy speakers and prize-winning think tanks and soft drink providers and cross-platform broadcasters and social media flux ca-pacitors...

"And so, to summarise," Miranda heard Kate saying, "Statement has planned a festival of music, art and culture which, in purely phys-ical terms, will, we believe, be the largest for at least half a century. Add in the virtual components and we're confident this will be one of the largest structured non-sporting entertainment events the world has ever seen. We have secured sufficient backing to be certain that the event will now go ahead, but we still have opportunities for you to become involved, at either platinum or gold level. If, as I said, you were to come in at platinum, this would ensure you had an exclusive on the academic slot – which, as I'm sure you appreciate, would be hugely powerful for you and would, I think I'm right in saying, fit perfectly with your five-year positioning strategy.

"There," Kate concluded, "That's everything I wanted to say. I am of course happy to answer any questions you may have."

Of course there were questions – but could anyone formulate them? Miranda glanced at her fellow committee members, all accus-tomed to a menu of carefully specified research grants and defendable hypotheses. She felt as though they had just been subjected to an oratorical display of molecular gastronomy from one of the world's finest restaurants: on what basis might they ask anything of the chef?

The committee chair shifted in her seat, knowing that it was her formal responsibility to break the silence. She made a show of consulting her notes. She glanced left and right to her colleagues, all of whom continued to consult their own notes.

"Well, Ms Humboldt, thank you very much for that." Ms Humboldt gazed back at the chair with a minutely crafted expression of patient interest. "And thank you, too, for the material you provided last week." Ah-ha, thought Miranda, good thinking, refer back to the documentary evidence, well done the academic. "I think I'd like to start with a couple of simple clarifications on scale." Ms Humboldt nodded, encouragingly. "We obviously need to know what sort of reach our investment would have," the chair continued, sounding steadily more secure, "and, of course, what sort of penetration we're likely to achieve with our core audiences."

Miranda leaned back in her chair, relieved at least that some sort of balance was being restored. Ms Humboldt, of course, responded seamlessly, beginning with a breakdown of audience types by broad classification, continuing with a more detailed exposition of segments deemed most relevant to the tertiary educational sector before steering assuredly to a concluding spray of key target sub-groups, each illustrated with a tantalising murmur of background detail on learning propensities, on/off platform preferences and the extent of the sub-group's dependence on income from a variety of sources.

"Which, as I'm sure you realise," Ms Humboldt pirouetted, "means both an exceptionally high ratio and an exceptionally low risk." Her eyebrows reached optimal elevation with the conclusion of her sentence, her head angled at fifteen degrees to the vertical, her hands supporting the sheer certainty of her observations and gently pouring any remaining syllables across the room. Miranda was in awe. Did it matter what the woman had said?

"May I, chair?" One of Miranda's fellow committee members broke the spell and, in response to the chair's nod, continued: "So, if I heard correctly, you're expecting to have 250,000...um... 'customers', is that what you called them? Ah, sorry, yes, 'participants', 250,000 paying participants, plus, presumably all the support staff and security staff and performers and artistes and so forth, so maybe?..."

"An additional one hundred to one hundred and twenty thousand," Humboldt answered. Miranda shook her head in slow disbelief. So did most other committee members.

"Yes, yes, so in the region of 350,000 people," the committee member continued, "present in some sort of physical capacity."

"Correct."

"That is, um, a very large number of people."

"Indeed. A modestly sized city."

"Exactly. I'm wondering how they'll all get there."

"I'm sorry?"

"How they'll get there. And leave at the end. How they'll get there, and leave. I've been looking at the map. I'm not sure I understand."

"I'm not sure I understand," Humboldt replied. She did not yet look remotely flustered, but Miranda was delighted at this admission of something other than omniscience. The fact that this line of questioning appeared to have nothing to do with whether or not the university would rise to the challenge of platinum sponsorship was neither here nor there; her colleague had espied a chink, and where there was light there might be laughter.

"Well," Miranda's colleague resumed, "could you, um, put the map up on screen?"

Soon enough, an image appeared. Others had been available –
dynamic representations of soundfields and air quality, of prevailing
winds and likely precipitation, of water systems and sewage systems
and possible interruptions to the movement of wildfowl – but, for
present purposes, a brutally simple photograph of the physical geography was all that was required.

The screen showed a roughly oval island, tethered at its south west
corner by a narrow isthmus to the mainland, with the main channel of
the Thames running to the island's north, a smaller tributary running
down the west and along its southern side, and the main estuary
leading to the English Channel to the east. The island lay in the river
east of the mighty city, perhaps 60 kilometres as the crow flies from
its centre and 25 kilometres beyond the orbital motorway. It was
still in London's gravity well but, at this distance, as the great river
relaxed into its estuary, much of it was remarkably undeveloped. The
map appeared to show little in the way of settlement; indeed, little of
anything, just an outline surrounding an area of flatness.

"There's, um, only one road," said Miranda's colleague, gesturing
towards the tendril at the island's south west corner. "Look. Just one.
The back of my envelope suggests it could take the best part of a week
to get everyone onto the island..."

Any hope that this constituted some sort of triumph over Ms
Humboldt's crystal conviction had begun to dissipate at the word
'road'. Humboldt's body relaxed infinitesimally, her head adopted the
angle preferred by nursery school teachers, her smile journeyed from
gentle via – fleetingly – fierce to its intended state of beatific wisdom:

"That is an astute observation, and I'm very sorry for not having
covered these issues in my presentation, but if you turn to page 63 of
our prospectus..."

And thus it became clear. Using techniques developed by the military - Humboldt explained - the festival organisers would be constructing an entire temporary city on the island. All the city's infrastructure – transport, food, energy, water, all of it – would be not just temporary, but functionally elastic. Early in the festival's implementation ("Remember," Kate smiled, "we'll be on site for several months before the actual festival") the city would be small; but, as time passed and the size of the team grew, the city itself would grow too: it would simply be folded out.

"A fold out city?" asked Miranda.

"It's wonderful, isn't it?" Kate responded. "Here, look at these pictures." On screen, in response to some fiddling at her wrist, Kate summoned a picture of a desert. "Afghanistan," she advised. A time-lapse sequence began and showed, incredibly, a settlement the size of a village, and then a town and then a small city literally unfolding across the desert floor; and then, even more incredibly, folding back up again. "As the number of troops varied, so too did the city," Humboldt concluded. "We're simply applying the same techniques in a civilian context."

The screen flipped again, this time to a computer generated image of the island. A festival city magically unfolded, quarter of a million simulated participants and a hundred thousand simulated staff enjoyed the party, then it all folded back up again.

Kate re-wound the image, paused, then adjusted so as to highlight some features and diminish others. "Here," she continued, "you can see the transport infrastructure at its full extent." Not only were there now four crossings ("This one dedicated for cyclists and pedestrians; this one only for coaches" Kate added) but there was an entire filigree of temporary roads and paths across the island's surface, together with an extension to the island's existing main docking facilities ("We envis-

age a number of our sponsors will want to bring their guests by boat")
as well as a new heliport ("Surprisingly easy, this bit," Kate explained).

The room returned to its strange grey silence. Kate's smile returned
to its calm and reassuring default. Somewhere in the back of Miranda's mind a small bell was ringing. She still did not know what it
signalled as she asked her question:

"Presumably a temporary city will require all the things a normal
city would require?"

"Well, up to a point," Kate replied. "For the festival we shall obviously need feeding and hydration points and medical facilities and
rest areas, and of course we'll be making provision for security and fire
protection and personal safety and so forth, and we'll have a range of
temporary buildings for administration and broadcast and computing
etcetera... The festival proper only lasts four days - we won't be building any schools or care homes!" She finished with a little laugh. It was,
Miranda realised, the first time she had laughed. It was an unsettling
noise.

Miranda responded with her own chuckle of conclusion, and stared
at the map. The little bell in her head drowned out the remainder of
the meeting.

Tuesday

I t was a Tuesday. Miranda and Jo braced themselves against the strong moist breeze that romped gaily and uninterrupted across the island and the estuary. In every direction lay the horizon. The sky was immense. The idea seemed impossible.

"This is ridiculous," said Jo.

Five months had passed since Miranda had listened in awe to Kate Humboldt's presentation about the festival and three since the university's decision to proceed with its sponsorship. The bell that began ringing in Miranda's head had reverberated through a series of conversations with Jo; and Jo, in turn, had sounded out first Mike and then, at the third of their 'post break-up' meets, Robert Dunbar.

"So," Robert had asked, "what's this idea you and Miranda are so excited about?" Robert liked Miranda. He liked her big hugs, her rambling stories, her wicked laugh. Since breaking up with Jo he held no particular expectation that he would ever see Miranda again - he didn't like her *that* much - but her details were somewhere on his phone and if Jo were ever to tell him that she was bringing Miranda along he wouldn't suddenly start looking for an excuse.

About Jo he remained less clear. He was sure he'd done the right thing in ending the relationship when he did: he had simply been finding it harder and harder to join everything up in his head. It was as if he needed some minimum amount of turbulence, somewhere in his life, and falling in love with Jo had met that need completely. *Being* in love with Jo, on the other hand, seemed to have the opposite effect. He had compensated with some spectacularly reckless behaviour at work, a couple of bouts of cocaine-fuelled debauchery and a month or two of single malt whisky. None of them worked and it seemed, eventually, three years in, that leaving Jo was the only remaining option.

Being honest with himself was not something he was good at, so he was still some distance away from fully understanding why he had reached out to Jo about the Tanners and Drovers dinner. It had seemed like a good idea at the time; and, as it turned out, the dinner had been great and Jo had been great and he'd been very pleased that they'd seen one another since. He enjoyed Jo's sense of humour, and she always seemed to have a sense of the bigger picture, something he, in occasional moments of lucidity, realised he did not always have.

The bigger picture thing seemed to be in play, Robert thought, as Jo began her story. Next summer - she said - somewhere north of three hundred and fifty thousand people would be assembling on an island in the Thames estuary half way between the city and sea. They would be gathering for a long weekend of music, dance, arts and culture. Most of them would be young, energetic, healthy people intent on having a great deal of fun. There would be a tremendous amount of positive energy, lots of generosity and love, heaps of smiling and hugging and kissing and sex.

Weirdly – Jo continued – a great many people would not be there: people who were sick, or people who were immobile; people who were looking after people who were sick or immobile; people who were too sad or too mad, people who were too tired or too anxious, people who were too poor or too huddled.

What if – and at this point Jo tipped her head forward and looked at Robert very directly indeed – what if some of those people were there? Why shouldn't they share in the positive energy and the generosity and the love?

"And the smiling and the hugging and the kissing and the sex," Robert added.

"It's not just that it would be inherently a fair and lovely thing to do," Jo continued, ignoring his facetious tone, "but all that love and generosity and hugging and fucking is exactly the kind of thing that would make all those people feel a bit better. It's a bit perverse, don't you think, that the very people who might benefit most from a giant festival are the ones that are most obviously excluded from it?"

Robert Dunbar firmly and comfortably agreed with the logic of this fine sentiment, but was still struggling with the relationship between the abstract utopian loveliness of the idea and the gritty practicalities of – of what, precisely?

"So what, precisely," he tentatively enquired, "does that mean in practice?"

"Well," said Jo, positively jumping with excitement, "it turns out that Statement plc – they're the organisers of the festival - are effectively building a temporary city on the island. They're using military techniques to build the thing in modules, almost like Lego. If you need, I don't know, a bit more water or a bit more sewage, you just bolt on another unit, so as the number of people goes up you just bolt on some more bits, and as the people leave and the population goes back down again you just un-bolt the bits you don't need any more. Apparently, once the whole thing's over, they just pack the entire thing up and there's no sign it was ever there."

"Well," said Robert, "that does indeed sound bloody amazing – but" and here it was his turn to look meaningfully down the length of his nose and into Jo's eyes, "what's that got to do with all these... these people that wouldn't otherwise be there?"

"Well," said Jo, this time with a truly thick dollop of sarcastic emphasis, "it means we can simply build an extra bit on the side of the festival, purpose built and tailored to meet the needs of all those extra people. The people who wouldn't otherwise come. Easy peasy. And..." she added, quickly, forestalling Robert's interruption, "and the festival organisers think that, if it goes ahead, it would fit with their" – and here she stumbled, just a little –"with their 'brand positioning'." Robert stifled a guffaw. "We're calling it Care City," Jo continued. "Statement think it would play really well with the other sponsors and the online audiences and all that kind of thing, and loads of people who might otherwise not have gone to the main festival because they've got care responsibilities might now think about coming! It's like a win win win win thing."

Robert gazed at her for a moment, a tumult of admiration, bewilderment and disbelief battling for control of both his features and his words. "You're proposing building a sort-of giant temporary crèche on an island in the Thames while the world's biggest music festival goes on next door?" he said.

"Umm," Jo hesitated, hearing it come back in condensed form. "Yes. Well. When you put it like that it does sound a bit ridiculous..."

Standing now on the island, Jo couldn't help herself: "This is ridiculous," she said, again. Somehow over the past few months the idea had landed, germinated, taken root and – and now, here they were.

"What did you say?" asked Miranda.

"Nothing," Jo replied. "I was just remembering that we're intending to build a sort-of giant temporary crèche on this bloody island while the world's biggest music festival takes place just over there."

"Now now," said Miranda. "Mr Tiresias will be here in a minute, I don't want you going all weird on me." Peter Tiresias was the senior chap from the local council liaising with Statement plc on the logistics and planning for the festival. As a platinum sponsor, the university was entitled to special privileges, such as today's bespoke site visit; and, as the university's lead on Care City, Miranda was entitled to special privileges, such as bringing Jo.

"I know, I know, but I'm just a bit nervous and a bit... you know, it suddenly feels..." Jo looked around at the bleak marshy surroundings, the endless horizon, the forlorn and low-rise agricultural buildings dotted here and there. "It suddenly feels pretty bloody stupid is what it feels. How in god's name are we going to build a giant bloody crèche, even a flat pack crèche, right here?" She paused, not for dramatic effect but simply because it took a few moments for the next thought to arrive. "And even if we did," she resumed, "why would anybody come?"

Miranda, whose own doubts in this regard were at least as well developed as Jo's, was just summoning a response when a mid-range saloon car in a mid-range colour swung into mid-range view from behind a cluster of farm buildings a couple of hundred metres away.

"Ah," said Miranda, "Mr Tiresias arrives."

Tiresias turned out to be charming and affable in a mid-range continental kind of way. Tall, blond and slender, his easy grip and gentle smile worked quickly to put both Miranda and Jo onto a slightly more relaxed footing.

"Welcome to our island," he said, "I hope you aren't too unsettled." His accent confirmed the suggestion of his mid-range mid-brown suit that his origins were indeed continental, but Miranda and Jo would later disagree over where, precisely, he came from. Either way, his use of the word 'unsettled' was itself unsettling: was this a translation issue?

Their uncertainty must have been evident, because Peter Tiresias swiftly explained that "I find that many of our visitors, especially those from London, can be a little taken aback when they first experience the very special sky we have here." Miranda and Jo, naturally enough, looked up; and Tiresias, smoothly prepared, continued: "Of course, the number of visitors has been a great deal higher lately."

Jo could not decide whether the man was simply weary, or whether he harboured doubts about the entire project, or whether, perhaps, this was just his mid-range manner. Whatever the reason, she had the distinct impression that Tiresias, despite his charming affability, was not entirely pleased to be spending his afternoon out in the wind. She sprang into effusive gratitude mode:

"It must be very exciting for you and everyone here, and we're so excited too and really grateful that you were able to come and show us around this afternoon, you know how hard it can be sometimes just looking at diagrams and reading reports and looking at stuff on computers and we really just wanted to get a sense of the place and think about how much room there really is and, you know, just try to decide if we're completely mad or..."

And on she went, and so did Miranda, and soon enough the wind died down and everyone got on famously. Miranda and Peter both had hand-held devices with big screens so that, as they conducted the tour, the three of them were able to compare the actual island around them with images of the prospective festival version of the island. Peter's device, it turned out, had an augmented reality function that enabled them to gaze as if through a window onto the future, and a smorgasbord of buildings, footpaths, roads pipes cables gantries speakers screens and even people appeared as if by magic on the marshy flatness around them.

"This is, obviously, merely the current version," Peter reminded them. "There's plenty of time for revision yet."

"Really?" asked Jo.

Miranda reminded them of the time line for the whole thing, checking with Peter occasionally as much to establish his view of feasibility as her own grasp of the plan. He grimaced – politely – on a couple of occasions, but it did indeed seem that, because of the modular nature of the set up there was room to modify the final size and layout until remarkably close to the actual start of the festival.

"So if we get a few more or a few less people..." Jo ventured.

"...we just take it down a notch or up a notch," Miranda affirmed.

"There are some limits," Peter explained. "I'd like to show you the sites for the crossings. It's easier if we drive. Would you care to follow or shall we share?"

Within a few minutes all three stood on the south side of the island looking across the slim belt of water to the mainland. Here, at its narrowest point, the gap between solid land and solid land was about 100 metres. At low tide, and if you were prepared to get a little muddy, the gap could be as little as thirty metres.

"As you can see," Peter pointed, "the existing bridge has a span of about 200 metres, but is relatively narrow and not suitable for all types of traffic. As you know, it is proposed that there will be temporary crossings -"

"Like pontoons," Miranda interjected.

"Well, yes and no," Peter replied. "That depends in turn on some design decisions and some capacity decisions." Jo and Miranda gazed expectantly. "For example," he resumed, "a chairlift solution has been suggested for just over there," and he supplemented his gesture with an image on his device, "and that could be used comfortably by 5,000 pedestrians per hour during the peak arrival and departure times. That would of course mean we'd need to have some sort of parking and embarkation facilities on this side of the creek and," he paused to turn and face the two women, "it might mean that access for some people might be more difficult."

Jo and Miranda nodded slowly and in unison. There were indeed limits. Accommodating several thousand people with restricted mobility, or who might need their hands held for whatever reason, was not simply a case of increasing the number of accessible toilets.

"I think we need to go through this quite carefully," said Miranda. Having stuck her neck out with the university to persuade them – provisionally, at least – that supporting Care City could be the best possible move in terms of the university's 'positioning', Miranda was especially alert to anything that had the potential either to scupper the entire idea or to spring some horridly expensive surprise.

"I agree," said Peter. "Best done in my office, don't you think?"

Jo and Miranda did indeed think this, and after another short car-borne tour of the main site they headed to the compact assembly of temporary office buildings that had clearly been relatively recently installed by Statement for just such a purpose. The lobby proffered some large-scale photos from low orbit, some hydrological and ecological cartography, a couple of screens on which unfolded a looping selection of enticing images of the festival-to-come and a machine dedicated to the production of a range of hot meeting-issue drinks. Thereby refreshed, what seemed now to be a rather efficient little working group set about the task of identifying what Miranda called the key 'pinch points'.

"You mean the things that could totally screw everything up?" Jo wondered.

Miranda, more thoroughly versed in contemporary meeting etiquette, felt the fleeting wrinkle of discomfort from Peter Tiresias in response to Jo's vernacular and sought quickly to smooth things out. "Well I don't think I'd necessarily express it that way," she suggested, "but it's important that I can reassure the university that it isn't unduly exposed."

Jo did not react well to this. Though she was enormously grateful that her best friend Miranda had managed to persuade her university to fund Care City – or, at least, to provide sufficient funding guarantees to ensure it went ahead – a part of Jo still thought of the idea as essentially hers and reacted badly whenever she ran into any words or people that threatened her sense of ownership.

Miranda, for her part, was enormously grateful that her best friend Jo had come up with an idea that had provided her, Miranda, with an opportunity to make such a dramatic mark at work: she had already had facetime with the Vice Chancellor and, if this all went well, she now stood a very good chance indeed of leaping several career hurdles (cumulatively about a decade and a half long) in a single bound. She was, however, finding Jo's possessiveness increasingly irritating.

They glowered at one another intermittently and with escalating intensity for the next hour or so. The efficiency of the working group declined precipitously. Whether by instinct or accident, Peter – who knew nothing of the pair's long-standing friendship - called the meeting to a halt mere moments before what would have been an uncomfortable and potentially very damaging explosion.

"I think," he said, "that we have covered all the major points. We have made good progress, no?" He looked at Jo. "Your vision remains intact?"

Dully – she suddenly noticed how tired she was, and how unpleasant was her headache – Jo nodded, and said "Yes, thanks, thank you, you're right, it does all seem doable." .

"And Dr Farnaby – the university will be happy?"

"Er, yes, yes, I think so. Thank you." She hesitated before speaking more forcefully: "Thank you Peter. You've done much more here than I was anticipating."

"You are kind," he replied, "but I am genuinely very keen, not just on the festival but on your Care City idea. And not just me. There are many at the council who are keen. There is a chance for something…" he gazed out of the window, across the water to the island, his eyes suddenly more distant than at any previous point in the afternoon, as if the horizons themselves were suddenly closer: "…something wonderful," he finished. "And" – he turned, with something close to a flourish, and said with a twinkle that was far from the middling origins of his car and suit, "if there is the prospect of something wonderful, then it is not a prospect to be lost!"

It was if a warm and reassuring wind had lifted them. Miranda and Jo forgot their bickering enmity and, in and for that moment, rejoined in the wonder of the wonderful.

"Cheers to that!" said Jo, raising her small plastic cup of cold cappuccino and drawing laughter from the three of them. The laughter carried them all the way home.

Tuesday

I t was another Tuesday and, this time, it was Jo's second day in her new job. She shifted uncomfortably in her chair. She did not like the chair. She did not like the office-friendly clothes she was wearing. She did not like the computer, the desk or the manicured plant. She was not at all sure that this was a good idea.

"Jo! Good morning!" It was Kate Humboldt. Jo liked Kate, but it was Kate's fault she was here, and for a moment Jo's disgruntlement was in charge of her face. "Oh dear," said Kate. "Bad commute?"

Jo had of course cycled to the prestigiously located offices of Statement plc. Statement's interests spanned all known media platforms and a bewildering variety of content types. They represented globally-successful music, video, sports and political entertainment providers; they choreographed concerts, festivals, rallies and movements. They maintained connections, facilitated introductions and organised placements. No product, personality or ideology lay outside their realm of endeavour. Only two criteria were relevant: was there scope for presentational management; and was there scope for profit. Few had ever heard of them, which was just how they liked it. They liked to think of themselves as the invisible hand, judiciously begloved and with the skills of the prestidigitator.

From here on the third floor Kate Humboldt ran the team responsible for what was now officially and publicly known as 'The Big Float', a summer festival on an island to the east of London that would be the biggest the world had ever seen. With just a few months to go before the event itself, there was a sustained air of intensity: sponsors needed to be briefed and lunched, contractors to be instructed and managed, performers to be scheduled and massaged. Great quantities of effort, time and most especially money were in ceaseless flux. Negotiations over broadcast rights were on schedule; ticket sales across all platforms were strong.

"You'll be ready for the session at 10?" Kate asked.

"Yup, no problem," Jo replied. She glanced back at her screen, and Kate was gone. The agenda shimmered. Jo tried to focus. It had all seemed like such a good idea at the time. Once the outline plans for the Care City had stabilised, Kate had simply made Jo an offer.

"Look," Kate had said, a couple of weeks after Jo's trip to the island with Miranda. "It's clear that this is really your baby." Jo gazed, a little stunned. "So I want to appoint you as the programme director for delivering Care City."

"I have no idea what that even involves," Jo managed, eventually.

"Well, someone has to be in charge of making sure it actually happens," Kate said, with another of her scary little laughs. "And I think it should be you."

"Well, that's nice, thanks," said Jo. "But - really - I have no idea what that even involves. I've never so much as organised a garden party never mind a festival."

Again the uncanny chuckle. "My experience has been that these things work when the person in charge is genuinely passionate about it. And you are definitely passionate about this," Kate explained. "My team will provide all the nitty gritty support. You're obviously smart, so you'll pick it up quickly enough. There'll be plenty of people around you. Your job will be..." They both looked intently at one another. "Your job will be to be the face of Care City. To be its voice. To tell its story, explain it. To sell it to the world."

"I'm a firefighter," Jo said, softly.

"And therefore already more trustworthy and impressive than anyone else," Kate said. "Look, my team will do all the legwork – we'll set up the meetings and crunch the numbers and work out the mechanics... but we need someone to front it, someone credible, someone whose passion will simply win people over. That someone is you."

"What about Miranda?"

"Miranda's lovely," Kate purred, "but her role is clearly to be the link to the university. I'm quite sure she'd be the first to acknowledge that you are the best person to do this job." She deployed her high-impact head-tilt-with-smile: "What do you say?"

Jo discussed it with everyone – ex-boyfriend Robert, best friend Miranda, step-brother Michael. She talked about it with her father, too, who seemed comfortable enough in his new care home, and who smiled affably throughout her exposition but who clearly understood little or nothing of what she said and who had no opinion one way or the other but who, simply having provided his daughter with the opportunity to say it all out loud without interruption, had provided a deeply valuable service. She had also discussed it with Daniel. They had had coffee a few times since they first met on the tube that time, and though she still did not really understand quite what their relationship was all about, she was glad of having spoken to him.

"What's the worst that could happen?" he had asked.

"Well, um, I suppose I could just completely screw things up and Care City doesn't happen and everything is a total disaster."

"Do you think... Kate, is that her name? Do you think Kate would let that happen?"

"Good point," Jo said.

"More importantly," Daniel continued, "Kate probably sees the same person I do – a clever, passionate woman who is a firefighter. Not many could pull that off. And the kind of person that could overcome a whole heap of prejudices and meet the intense physical demands of being a firefighter - well, that person could probably organise a wee festival." He paused. "It seems to me," he resumed, "that you've got a once-in-a-lifetime opportunity to have a go at doing something amazing. And didn't you tell me that you were fed up with just rescuing people when they'd fallen down? With always being – how did you put it? – end of pipe? Surely this is something where you get to help people before they fall. I mean, if it works, who knows what might happen..."

So she had put aside her misgivings ("They're an evil corporate empire, aren't they?" she had said to Miranda at one point; "Yes," Miranda had drunkenly replied, "but Statement don't seem to realise that they're about to give the keys to a Jedi eco-warrior"), handed in her notice with the fire service and begun tackling all the background material that Kate's team had sent through. Now, here she was, carrying not a wounded child or a dazed motorist but a manila tablet, walking not among broken glass or burning timbers but along a corridor clad in deep-pile carpet and corporate art. As she reached the meeting room door she shook her head, vigorously, as if to shake away the dream.

"Jo, great, take a seat. Everyone, Jo. Jo, everyone."

There were murmurs and nods of welcome, and Jo fell into idle chat with her immediate neighbours around the large oval table centring the room while the weekly progress meeting awaited its final participants. Once underway, the discussion moved briskly across the various agenda items with a well-practised rhythm: site preparation was underway, key accommodation and infrastructure modules had been commissioned, localised supply chain pinch points had been prioritised, recruitment and volunteering agencies had been appointed, platinum and gold sponsors had been thoroughly briefed.

"Okay," said Kate, once the standing items had been covered. "New things and tricky things." Jo straightened in her seat. "Jo's joined, as discussed, to head the Care City programme; welcome Jo." More murmurs of greeting and assurance. "The full briefing session on Care City is on..."

"Thursday," Jo offered.

"Thursday, great, yes, those of you who are in that loop, please make sure you're fully up to speed by then. We're roughly on track, but this is an experiment for us and I don't want something obvious to trip us up. Good luck Jo, good luck the rest of you."

Jo had been expecting to say a little more than 'Thursday' and had leant forward as if to make a further contribution, but a soft hand pulling her back revealed a friendly face to her right gently shaking a 'no, don't worry' head. Kate moved on without pause.

"We also have an issue with the ambulotronics that I want a view on." Jo glanced at her agenda, vainly seeking the word 'ambulotronics'. "The ethics team has raised a question about this," Kate continued. "You'll remember that absolutely everyone on site will be wearing one of these" – she held up a wristband made from hard plastic and bearing a small rectangular screen on one side – "in the run up to and during the festival, as well as in the wind down phase."

"The contractors assured us," cut in a young man diagonally opposite Jo, "that the device could multi-function in the way we wanted, so we could use it for both staff and punters, monitoring site access and hours and so forth for the former, and for the latter handling the financial transactions, the zonal access, the dating algorithms and so on..."

"And it does all those things successfully", Kate added.

"Yes," he continued. "And the real-time positional tracking works perfectly too, which means we can be re-allocating the commercial opportunity infrastructure precisely to match imminent demand and we can completely integrate the on-site actual reality with the on-line virtual reality across all the platforms."

Jo's expression of complete incomprehension caught Kate's eye.

"It means," she explained, with only the merest flicker of exasperation, "that we can do two things that have never been done before. First, we'll know exactly who is passing any given point on site at any given time, and we'll know exactly what they've eaten or drunk or otherwise bought or ingested in the preceding hour or two, so we'll be able to tailor each offering they encounter precisely to meet their needs, continuously, throughout the festival, for both on-site and on-line purchases. And, second," she continued, "our on-line participants will be able to immerse themselves completely at any location, at the click of a button, and will be surrounded by avatars of the actual people in that actual place at that actual time."

"Very good for the dating campaigns," came a rejoinder to Jo's right.

"But the problem," continued the young man, despite no change whatsoever in the expression of blank incomprehension on Jo's face, "is coming from the civil liberties research. Some of the older people in the focus groups didn't react too well to all this, and, where's that quote... oh, here we go: "If I wanted to spend a weekend with Big Brother I'd have gone shopping – I thought festivals were supposed to be all free love and stuff, I don't fancy being spied on all the time"."

"On top of that," said Kate, "our tech people are saying that the sheer number of access points means the risk of a hack is higher than they'd first thought. And a big hack would be... a fucking nightmare."

It was the first time Jo had heard Kate swear. From the reaction of the room – the air seemed to stop moving for a moment – it was indeed a rare event.

"Thoughts?"

There was a brief pause, and then the thoughts poured forth. Jo heard little of what was said: she was simply transfixed by the sheer energy on display, the torrent of gestures that Humboldt's question unleashed. It appeared utterly chaotic to Jo until, suddenly, Kate resumed control:

"So, what I hear is: we'll live with the risk of losing a few older people, but we don't want to take risks with the hack, so we'd be willing to compromise a little functionality for security. Good. I'll go back to tech on that; and we'll distribute a new demographic module..." she glanced questioningly at the young man who'd spoken earlier: "first thing tomorrow," she finished. Jo saw the tiniest gulp from the young man.

"Right, final item – the drone swarm." Jo looked again at her agenda, this time with a feeling of profound ill-ease. A drone swarm? "I think we may have to drop the drone swarm." The room made a noise that Jo found hard to discern: disappointment? Relief? Exhaustion? "The contractors came back with the revised specification, to cope with the traffic we'd envisaged, and the cost more than doubled. Given the other risks we'd heard about, ("They thought there could be twenty thousand dead birds," came a whisper from Jo's left) I'm inclined to just drop it completely. We haven't yet gone public, so there's no problem there, and there's only two top sponsors with an interest and I'm sure we could smooth that. Any thoughts?"

The room's silence echoed itself for a few moments.

"Good. Drone swarm dead," Kate concluded. "Any more for any more?"

There being none, it was no more than a few minutes before Jo found herself back at her desk. She glanced at her appointment schedule. An 'appointment schedule'? She suddenly felt sick and very far away from firefighting. Between now and Thursday lay a pitted landscape of briefing sessions with the infrastructure team, the marketing team, the sponsorship team, even the food team. Maybe especially the food team. How was she to know? Beyond the Thursday briefing session with her new Statement colleagues lay the first wave of meetings with outsiders: health care providers, specialist activity providers, nutrition specialists, nursing agencies, people who wanted their logos on every single mobility device...

An hour or so of emails later, her telephone rang: "Your visitor is here Ms Castle." Shit, she had completely forgotten – Robert.

"Hey," he beamed, as she came hurriedly down the open staircase into the reception area. "Nice digs." She laughed, and hugged him. "And nice suit, too!" he added, admiring her business apparel. "You still ok for lunch?" he asked, interrupting her mumbled response to his tease. "Yes, yes, of course," she said. "Just give me a minute to grab my stuff."

As she shimmied back up to fetch her bag and coat from her desk, an instinct caused her to glance back as she reached the top of the staircase. She saw Kate Humboldt passing through reception, slowing, stopping, and beginning to speak with Robert. Did they know one another? Jo could not hear them. She watched closely, her intuition clear that something important was happening. She saw Robert's smile, she saw Kate move her weight slightly from one foot to the other, she saw Robert gesture to the outside world with a slow arc of his left hand, and she saw Kate's head tip back slightly as she laughed at something. Fuck: they were flirting with one another! Jo took another step up, hoping to become invisible. Robert Dunbar and Kate Humboldt continued to talk, paying no attention either to the receptionist, to Jo or to the pair of Statement employees in intense conversation who wandered through the reception and across Jo's line of sight. Another gesture, more head movements, and Kate began turning, resuming her interrupted journey. As she turned, the last fleeting instant of Kate's expression became visible to Jo, and there was no doubt.

For the next few steps, to the top of the staircase and into the corridor of carpet and art, Jo's stomach clenched and tumbled. She had no right to feel this way – she surely had no claim on Robert, not after all this time – but it was still brutally uncomfortable to see him in action like that, and to see the reaction of another woman, so obviously reminiscent of her own reactions all those years ago.

Quickly, though, that feeling subsided and, in quick succession, two quite different sensations took hold. That had been the first time, Jo realised, that she had seen the astonishing, powerful, composed, beautiful and scary Kate Humboldt behaving in anything other than a manner of total and composed control. Which was – Jo found – disproportionately satisfying.

Then came a quite unforeseen rush of self-confidence. She, Jo, might not in fact be quite so unequal to the Care City task. She was, perhaps, quite as extraordinary and fascinating and capable as Ms Humboldt. Robert, she knew, did not twinkle like that at just anyone. Perhaps, after all, Joanna Castle, misfit firefighter, Ninja eco-warrior, single thirty-something resident of the maddest and most amazing city in the world might, just might be able to work with these rapacious and exploitative bastards to deliver the most insanely wonderful and caring counterblast to the utter insanity of modern life and show these fuckers once and for all that sitting around talking about it endlessly was simply not good enough and that, if you got lucky and were in the right place at the right time with the right equipment you could, maybe, perhaps, actually do something that would make a difference.

Veritably bouncing with such reflections, and having secured her coat, bag and – she was delighted to realise – her hat, she grabbed Robert's arm as she skipped through reception: "Lunch, then."

Wednesday

It was Wednesday. Jo and Mike were leaning on the railings of the Central South observation platform, ten metres up. Stretching north, east and west, the great plain of the great festival. The Big Float. Mid-morning sunshine lit the scene, a bewildering amalgam of military tattoo, medieval fair and technology zoo. Nearly one hundred thousand staff and volunteers were already on site: this afternoon, the first paying customers would begin to arrive; by tomorrow evening, a third of a million people would be making and having the biggest ticketed party the world had ever seen.

"Wow," Mike managed as his gaze swept left to right. He took a swig from the water bottle. "Just – wow."

"How are you feeling?" Jo asked him.

"Me?!" he spluttered, a spray of water arcing from his mouth. "I'm just a baggage boy!" Mike had volunteered his services at the first opportunity. "I'm fine. More important - how are you?"

Jo looked down and watched two burly men wrestling a large keg of beer as she savoured the question. How was she? She hardly knew. The past few months had been the most breathtakingly extraordinary and demanding of her life. She had done deals and thrown tantrums. She had shaken hands with politicians, diplomats and journalists. She had managed to persuade an assortment of pension funds, service providers, government agencies, academic institutions, research bodies and manufacturers of a bewildering array of equipment to support a thing called 'Care City' - the most extravagant experiment ever seen anywhere in the simple human art of looking after people. She was jubilant, terrified, exhausted, ebullient, stunned, happy, overwhelmed.

"Overwhelmed," she said.

"Too bloody right," Mike replied, chuckling.

"I just came from one of the Care City kitchens," Jo said. "Now I know what half a million free range eggs looks like."

Mike cast his gaze left, to where Care City lay. The gantry behind them obscured a fair chunk of the great care experiment – where around thirty thousand guests, carers and staff would soon be installed - but its northern and eastern flanks were clearly visible. The access routes to the main festival site ran just in front of them and Mike watched as a variety of canisters and containers were ferried back and forth. Most of it appeared to be food. He had been up since 5.30, working with a group of about twenty volunteers, all roughly his age, finalising the sleeping quarters, checking on bedding, making sure the air conditioning systems were working, looking out for loose cables and unfinished access ramps and similar snagging. Jo had brought him onto the project nearly four months earlier when he had agreed that Care City was indeed more than just a one-day news item. He was now heavily invested and, it seemed, very proud.

"I really enjoyed those kitchen training sessions," he recalled. "Do you remember when that chef lost the plot?" Jo had heard his story before and chuckled with the recollection. A number of celebrity chefs had wanted to be associated with the Care City project and Jo had seen no grounds for choosing one over the others. She had brought them all on board. She had also been talking with several different prospective suppliers of temporary kitchen staff, including a couple of charities that specialised in rehabilitating young offenders. It had seemed only natural to bring the two groups together – and only slightly mischievous not to have warned either party in advance.

One of the celebrity chefs had not taken kindly to this turn of events. A large, excitable and raucous group of youngsters, expecting to receive engaging and uplifting instruction from 'the bloke off YouTube', instead encountered a rather surly and disgruntled individual seemingly intent on minimising his contact time. The audience did not react well. Initial dismay turned into vocal mockery and something of a shouting match ensued. Only the timely intervention of a passing security guard had prevented the occasion descending into scuffles. The celebrity ego had threatened to sue someone and his mid-ranking underlings had shouted at Jo but the steam quickly evaporated and the main outcome had been to give the Care City catering slot a burst of unforeseen kudos that made everyone (celebrity chef apart) feel very pleased with themselves.

It was probably only a couple of weeks ago, Jo reflected. It felt like months, maybe even years.

"And when Miranda told those guys from the university's dementia team where to go!" Jo said.

"God, yes, she was amazing," said Mike. He was twenty now and Jo suspected he had something of a crush on Miranda. She smiled as he continued: "I loved the way she just swept them aside!" He looked wistfully across the festival plain for a moment. "Shit," he said, bringing himself up short. "Where is Miranda?"

Miranda had been as frantically busy as Jo these past few months and had, by and large, maintained her typical good humour throughout. Now, in the final few hours before the business of the show began for real, she was as tense as she had ever been about anything. At the precise moment of Mike's question, she was standing at the back of a

large marquee-like structure a couple of kilometres due east, close to
the centre of the main festival site, puffing at a cigarette. Her ambu-
lotronic wristband was complaining about this but its powers were –
in this regard, at least – limited, so she swore at the bloody thing and
carried on smoking. In a moment she would return to the inside of
the marquee-like entity and resume supervising the completion of the
university's premier marketing commitment, an art/science fusion in-
stallation whassname channelling Babel, Rosetta and Chomsky onto
a pan-platform carousel intended to signal the university's breadth,
depth and appeal to the discerning prospective undergraduate from
wherever-the-fuck. Later, she would track down Jo and help formally
inaugurate the central fountain at Care City. Right now, and for a few
more moments, she was having this delicious cigarette in a secret oasis
of calm.

"I'm sure she's fine," said Jo. After a brief pause she said: "Have you
seen my dad today?"

"I think they're settling him in at the big aviary," Mike suggested.
"Great idea that, by the way," he added. Jo silently agreed with him –
it was a great idea. Acting as a sort of rib cage to Care City's design
was a network of glasshouses (though they were made of a type of
bio-degradable plastic) containing a variety of habitats, eco-systems,
butterflies and, in four distinct zones, birds. Guests could wander or
sit, or stand and stare, or otherwise make use of the spaces as they saw
fit. The spaces provided (as Jo had been obliged to formulate for the
purposes of the marketing material) 'arched and viridian light' supplemented by 'rich and stimulating sounds and aromas'. Statement
plc had not reacted especially well when it had first been suggested, but
the numbers stacked up: 'A wounded individual able to watch birdlife
from his or her recuperative bed leaves hospital 40% more quickly'
was typical of the stylised facts that Statement's finance people found

irresistibly persuasive. Even the engineers charged with designing the thing seemed to like it: "It's like one of those runs you make for hamsters," one of them had suggested, "you just bolt them all together, make the shape you want, then take 'em apart at the end. Nice."

"I'll go and see him later," Jo said. To her right, eastwards, a distant roar went up, arriving blustered and distorted with the wind. "Huh, something good happened," she said. She glanced at her wristband: the screen showed the time, her basic physiological state, the weather, her credit level. She flicked her wrist, twice, and grunted with satisfaction. "Six more minutes," she said, out loud, but to herself. "Where are you next?"

Mike, she discovered, was looking directly at her, with a curious expression on his face. "What?" she asked. "Six minutes?" he replied. "Yes, ok, ok" she returned, acknowledging his observation. The Jo of six months ago would not have recognised the notion 'six minutes' unless it referred very specifically to the time it might take to reach an emergency incident. Now, almost unrecognisably transformed by appointment schedules and critical path planning and multi-variate logistics operations, she really did mean six minutes: this day, perhaps more than any of the others, had been precision-tooled to within an inch of its life. Busy the previous months may have been, but there had always been wriggle room, a little slack here or there, some space to catch one's breath; and tomorrow, and for the other days of the festival itself, there would of course be a million and one things to attend to, but events would by then have their own momentum, and the scope for asserting control, for wrestling each task and each moment into submission, would be reduced. Today, this final day of preparation, this last day before the barrel went over the falls, today was the last of making sure nothing went wrong. Even this moment of reflection with Mike had been factored into her timeline for the day. She had just six minutes left. Correction: four.

"I've got the final run through for the fountain switch on," Mike responded. "Should be fine." The fountain, like pretty much everything else on the festival site, was being powered by a potent combination of wind, tidal, bio and solar energies, and was using water from the estuary that had been filtered through some funky reed beds. The inaugural moment would entail a firework-style display, with dancing water and an accompanying laser show, visible not just to those directly present but also to the millions that had subscribed to the continuous digital feed or even the billions that might conceivably take a peek at the open transmission. It was effectively a small-scale version of an opening ceremony modelled on global sports events.

"There's a few things that could go wrong, I suppose," he continued, "but it seems buttoned down pretty tight." He took a swig of water. "Those boys and girls on the fountain tech have done this kind of thing all over the world, you know, New Year's Eve gigs, twenty first birthday parties for the kids of oligarchs... I'm way down the food chain – I'm supposed to be making sure that people in the audience don't get wet." He paused, briefly. "Or, at least, no one gets wet who doesn't want to get wet..." It was already warm, and everything seemed set for a hot afternoon and a glorious weekend of summer sunshine. Across the festival site as a whole provision had been made for plenty of cold water - not just for drinking but for water pistol fights, balloon bombing, open-air showers and generalised cavorting – but no-one could be really sure how the vulnerable folk of Care City might react, either to the heat or to being doused in buckets of cold water. Hydration and ambient temperature management were Mike's principal responsibilities over the next few days: he was going to be kept busy.

"What about you?" he asked Jo.

Two minutes to go. "Well I'm going to visit dad at lunchtime, and there's obviously the fountain launch later," she replied. "Right now I've got some meet and greet for half an hour, you know, some of the cheeses from the gold and platinum sponsors. Miranda's Vice Chancellor, and a couple of local politicians, that sort of thing. Then, um, a bit of on-line media, I think. Huh, can't remember." She chuckled. "Good job this thing is on the case," she said, waving her wristband. She stared at it for a moment, her perspective suddenly shifting. Funny, she thought, how that happens. She recalled looking for a birthday present for Mike, a gizmo that made instant music videos, or something, and how she had abandoned it in the face of the gleaming chrome menace of modern retail. Now here she was not merely wearing one of the awful things on her wrist but actually relying on it, glad of it. Must remember not to lose touch, she chided herself. Must remember.

"Right," said Mike, puncturing her thoughts. "Once more unto the breach?"

"Yes, yes, sorry!" she blurted. "Right, yes, um, hope it goes well and everything! See you at..."

"Four," he said. "Four o'clock. Don't worry, the wristband will get you there!"

They hugged, a big, full squeeze. "Yes," she said, again, not sure what she meant but unable to find anything else. She found herself welling up a little. "Go, grrl!" he insisted, and she did, all through the meet and greet, and all through the media slot - almost, she thought, as if she had been doing it all her life. Another memory bubble popped in her head (How does that work? she asked herself) in the few seconds between the completion of an on-line forum interview on one screen and a direct TV interview on the next, and she remembered the feeling she had had on seeing Robert chatting that time with Kate Humboldt, the feeling that, yes, she Joanna Castle could do this, and now, here she was, six months or so later, very definitely having done it and still doing it, live on air, or whatever it was called these days.

Interviews completed, the wristband guided her to the festival's central control hub, a discreet but intense amalgam of high-tech portable accommodation units tessellated with military guile so as to recede from sight, irrespective of the direction of view. Spooky what this stuff could do, Jo thought. Inside there was something very particular she needed to check. She sat in front of a bank of monitors. This was a fifteen minute slot. If all was going to plan, she should see... yes. There they were. She broke into a huge smile. This was one of her highlights, one of the things she was most proud of and most excited about. She had first heard about it when she was a child, an annual charity event, oddly old-fashioned. Seemingly without any publicity, and certainly without any fuss, each year since the war a group of London's cabbies had organised an outing to the seaside for disabled children. Each year, Jo had learned, the mantle was handed from one cabbie to another; each year a handful of schools and hospitals organised their schedules and liaised with the cabbies; each year a convoy of sometimes fifty, sometimes a hundred cabs set off from the city's poorer eastern quarters, wending their way through the old streets, avoiding the bypasses and elevated sliproads, gently and carefully delivering a few dozen unbearably excited young people together with their plushies, wheelchairs and carers to a seaside resort that last enjoyed its heyday half a century or more ago but which, for one magical day each year, became an unsung profusion of love and joy.

What if? Jo had wondered. It had popped back into her head in the middle of an otherwise interminable meeting about transport

planning. (Of all the meetings, she had discovered, transport planning set the sternest tests to those determined to remain awake.) She
made some calls, did some digging, kicked it around with her team at
Statement and – and now, look at that! The embarkation point was
a football stadium, the only place big enough. Feed from the stadium
showed dozens, scores, hundreds of black London cabs. Surrounding
them, thousands of people. Any minute now (she checked the time)
the convoy would begin: five hundred black cabs in a procession that
would stretch nearly five kilometres, together bringing the first official
guests and their carers, nearly fifteen hundred people arriving as Care
City's opening event. Jo felt the goosebumps on her arms.

The media team had turned the dial up to eleven on this one. There
were cameras everywhere: mounted into the drivers' caps, buried in
wheelchairs and mobility scooters, hanging from lanyards, swinging
from lamp-posts along the route, underneath the drones accompanying the convoy. (This was not, Jo had been very firmly told, a drone
swarm, although special features - available only to subscribers - meant
that the virtual experience could be re-constructed in 3-D from the
drone feeds.) The convoy's departure was timed to ensure maximum
coverage across a number of global news cycles. An incomprehensible
computer programme had used likely expenditure per product category per target segment, weighted by platinum, gold, silver and bronze
sponsorship, to derive the optimal transmission times by time zone,
and that time was... now.

Jo stood, almost involuntarily, as the screens showed the first cab
leaving the stadium perimeter. She checked her wristband, took a final
glance at the screens and headed back out into the sunshine. Two
hours until the convoy arrived on site: three until the fountain launch;
time now to see her father.

John Castle had arrived the night before, one of a few dozen early guests, mainly friends and family of the organisers and others working on site. He was dressed, as ever, in a smart jacket, carefully pressed trousers, an ironed shirt, a nice tie. It had been something Jo had stipulated way back when they had first agreed on Oak Heights: he should be well dressed, always. He no longer knew that he was well dressed; or, if he did, he understood it in a way that was very, very different from Jo's. But it helped, she found, to remind her – and, hopefully, anyone else that was dealing with him – that he was a full human being, fully deserving of the rights and dignities afforded anyone else. He looked at her now, seemingly aware that a fellow soul was present, but utterly unaware as to whom it was. Or, indeed, where he was, or when, or why.

It didn't matter, Jo reminded herself. The possibility of joy, if only for a flickering instant, remained; and he, like the thousands of others that would be the temporary citizenry of Care City, was entitled to the opportunity to have that instant. She chattered to him, moved his wheelchair to a slightly different angle, picked lint from his shoulder, pointed out a pair of birds visible in the glasshouse. He grunted at one point, and she wondered for a few moments, but the moments drained away, and the birds flew off and the sun moved the shade a further seamless fraction and it was time to move on.

"Love you," she said, brightly. She checked her wristband. "See you soon!"

Almost immediately she bumped into Miranda, hurrying towards Care City's main square and trailing cigarette smoke. "Yes I know I know," Miranda almost yelped, deflecting the anticipated disparaging remark before it had even been formulated. "My turn to be stressed." Jo fell in alongside her. "How you?" Miranda asked her. Jo remembered: "Overwhelmed," she replied. Miranda burst out laughing.

"Sure," she managed, "you look completely overwhelmed. Jesus girl, where does it come from?"

"Where does what...?" Jo's words tripped up on themselves as too many thoughts and a cascade of facial expressions all collided. For a brief moment she saw herself running on water, like a basilisk.

"Great, here we are!" said Miranda. "God it looks amazing." It was true: it was amazing. The fountain stood at the centre of a great civic square, perhaps a sixty or seventy metres along each side. Two of the four sides were made from the ribs of the glasshouse structure, rounded and folding, occasionally arching upwards to allow passage for either people or vehicles. One corner of the square seemed to be an entrance. A third edge was built from a mix of accommodation units, while the fourth wall had, ironically, been left more open, punctuated with gantries and supply points and low-rise seating systems. About two thirds of the space directly surrounding the fountain was filled with temporary seating: a few people were already sitting down. Soon it would be full.

The hybrid 'hi-tech historical' theme that had been adopted as the central trope for the whole of The Big Float was evident: pennants of ceaselessly mutating colours flew from the towers at each of the four corners, for example; and the fascia of the accommodation blocks somehow hinted at both fifteenth century Italian and post-modern organic, Jo thought. More generally she could not quite work out how the space achieved the effect that it did. It really did feel as though one were... floating. Were the buildings moving? Or undulating? Was it the wind?

She closed her eyes for a moment and tipped her head back, facing the sun. The heat settled onto her eyelids. She noticed the noises: a group of workers dealing with the chairs, some engines in the distance, some birdsong, the breeze. She noticed her own breathing. She noticed her arms and her legs and her feet, and her hands and her chest and her stomach. She smiled. She could smell the water from the fountain, and green things somewhere, and the plastic of cables and walking boards, and wood, and even woodsmoke. She felt that, yes, maybe, she could actually just float.

A new noise snapped her back. A deep throbbing, a rumbling. She opened her eyes. "They're here, they're here!" shouted an excited voice on the far side of the square. Jo laughed for a moment with the sheer joy of it. In a moment the first of five hundred taxis would enter the square over there, drive across to here, drop off its cargo of children and then exit over there. The whole thing was simply amazing. It was going to be amazing.

Monday

It was Monday morning. Miranda lay in her bunk, cautiously and slowly opening and closing one eye. She was trying to establish just how bad her hangover was. Jo, two hundred metres away, also in a bunk, was still asleep. She would, soon enough, have to conduct her own preliminary investigations. It had been quite a night.

The bunk that Mike was sharing with his friend Tom was actually in the main Big Float festival area rather than Care City itself. Around them the early movers were already packing up and moving out. There was still dew on the grass and the plastic and the chrome. The noises of departure were rising at the same speed as the sun. Soon the hubbub would be a commotion. For now, the boys slept on. It had been quite a night.

Somewhere on site, somewhere luxurious and exclusive, Kate Humboldt was very happy. Everything had gone very well. The final numbers, both on-site and on-line, had come in late yesterday and everyone that mattered had made a great deal of money. It had been quite a night.

Had a drone swarm been present, it would not have been able to capture either these or any of the myriad other morning afters that comprised the true aftermath of the great festival, the amazing weekend, the unbelievable party. The Big Float. The sun had shone.

The bands had played. The troupes had performed and the poets had declaimed. Psychoactive substances in great profusion had been consumed. There had been music, dance, art and culture. There had been a tremendous amount of positive energy, heaps of generosity and love, and lots and lots of smiling and hugging and kissing and sex.

On the Care City site there had been fewer psychoactive substances, and less sex, but otherwise its citizens had competed well with their brothers and sisters on the main site. They had probably mustered more smiling and hugging, and there had certainly been more generosity and love. There had also been more food: Care City had culminated with a mighty feast on the Sunday evening, thousands upon thousands of people sitting in noisy communion at long wooden tables in the central square, groaning under the weight of dishes from every cuisine known to humanity. It had been quite a night.

The sun rose a little farther. Miranda was up. She headed for the shower. Her hangover was bad, but she was pretty sure she was not going to be sick. The shower felt nice.

Mike woke before Tom and pulled aside the shutters. It was daytime out there. People were doing things. It all looked faintly ridiculous and not at all urgent. He lay back down and went straight back to sleep.

John Castle was dressed and sitting in a chair in the aviary. He was not alone. There were many people, mainly elderly and a little confused, sitting calmly in the diffuse green light. Elsewhere in Care City there were old people and young people, children and teenagers, parents and carers, believers and unbelievers, rich people and poor people, black people and brown people and white people. There were blind people and people unable to walk; there were people with dementia and people missing limbs; there were people suffering from chronic depression, people enduring terminal diseases, people shattered by terrible loss. Some of them were packing their belongings. Everyone had had a simply wonderful time.

Jo stirred. Her head hurt. She checked her wristband. She made a noise, a long low groan. Sunlight, now clearly above the fringe of the buildings surrounding her accommodation block and almost certainly now eliminating the morning dew, bludgeoned its way through the blinds. She buried her head under the pillow, promising herself she would get up shortly.

Miranda was dressing when her phone rang. The caller made her laugh, but then she stopped. "OK," she said, "Give me a moment."

A few minutes later Jo's phone rang, dragging her startled into the material world. Gosh it hurt. "Hello?" "Hey. You need to get over here. Main control room," said Miranda. "Er, I'm still..." Jo groaned. "Yes, I'm sure you are, but you need to get up Jo. See you as soon as you can get here." Jo stared at the phone.

She had long refused to give any thought to what would happen once Care City came to an end. Kate Humboldt and one or two others at Statement had asked her a few times, not so much with an interest in Jo herself but clearly with an eye on future downstream opportunities for the concept. Jo had seen a couple of emails suggesting that Statement were thinking about it anyway, presumably calculating that, if the numbers stacked up, there might be mileage in repeating the exercise in some way shape or form. The university and a few of the bigger sponsors had wanted to know about post-festival planning, too, but Jo had been as opaque and evasive with them as she had been with Statement. If they wanted to think about it, that was up to them.

Mike has pestered her about the future a couple of times, mainly – it seemed to Jo – because he was trying to figure out his own next steps and anything she might do would probably have some impact on his choice. Robert, too, had at some point tried to remind her just how much she had learned in the past few months and suggested that it might be sensible to have a bit of a plan to put all this new learning and insight to good use, but it felt rather less like supportive suggestion and rather more like uninvited interference and things had started to get tetchy and he wasn't her boyfriend any longer and the entire thing had come as close as they had in their new landscape to having an actual row.

In any case, all and sundry had been rebuffed. As she pulled on a pair of baggy shorts, a long-sleeved, lightweight and heavily faded sweatshirt and looked for her sandals, Jo still felt she had done the right thing. Beforehand she had had no idea whether The Big Float would work or whether Care City would work, indeed she still was not entirely sure what 'work' actually meant in this context. Lots of people came? Lots of people had smiled? Some big corporations made lots of money? The reviews were good? She had had no idea either about how she personally would actually feel about it all. A sense of achievement? A sense of relief? A sense of potential? How could she possibly know in advance?

So she had stubbornly refused to answer any questions about 'afterwards'. As far as she was concerned, afterwards would start on this very Monday morning, and she would find herself there, here, as she now did, and she would give herself as much time and space as seemed necessary to reflect on what had happened, and how she felt about it and then, hopefully, she would find the right shape emerging from all that and it would be completely obvious what to do next. Hopefully – she muttered to herself as she stumbled out into the really rather painful morning sunlight – whatever that next thing is, it will press all those Zen Venn diagram buttons, she could not remember the name, that funny squiggly drawing with the 'good for you' and 'good for the world' and 'something you're good at' and so on all overlapping in circles to show you the way. Or The Way. Or whatever. Bloody hell her head hurt.

She climbed the external metal staircase, flashed her wristband at the security scanner and pushed open the door. There were four of them in there, including Miranda, who had a very strange expression indeed on her face.

"Morning," said Jo. "And, yes, I know, I look terrible." Jo quickly scanned the faces, now that her eyes were adjusting to the lower light. "I see we all look terrible."

"We have some... news," said Miranda.

"That I figured," Jo replied. "Good or bad?" It really was not at all clear either from Miranda's tone or her face.

"Difficult to say," said Miranda.

"Huh."

"There's, um, a sort of committee, I didn't know about," Miranda began, faltering uncharacteristically.

"A committee?"

"Well, maybe that's not quite the right word... but I'm not sure what is. There are quite a few of them and they, um, they seem to be quite well organised."

"What the fuck are you talking about?" said Jo, her hangover running suddenly very short of patience.

"Sorry, sorry, I'm still trying to get my head around it, don't be horrid to me," Miranda replied, clearly in some disarray. "Look. Listen. They are refusing to leave."

"Pardon?"

"Refusing to leave. A few hundred of them, possibly more."

"What? Who are?"

"Um, well, it's a mix. Guests, carers. A few staff." Miranda glanced at her colleagues. "And, um, it's definitely more than just a few hundred. They, um, they don't want to go. They want to stay."

"Stay."

"Yes. Stay." A pause. "Here. In Care City."

Jo looked for a chair, found one and sat down. She stared into space for a few moments.

"Nope, I don't understand. Explain again," she said.

This time Miranda drew on the support of her colleagues and explained as best she could. Sometime earlier this morning ("Just after seven," came a voice) a delegation ("A delegation?" "Best word I can think of") had arrived with a petition ("What, an actual petition, on paper?" "Yup") explaining that the undersigned had experienced such a dramatic improvement in their life circumstances blah blah blah ("You can read the precise wording later, but it basically says they've all had the most amazing time ever and that their inalienable human rights are now finally being acknowledged and that the lives to which we would be forcing them to return would be intolerable") and that they are unwilling to return to their previous situations and are demanding ("Demanding?!") that Care City remain open and functional henceforth etcetera etcetera.

"As far as we can make out," Miranda concluded, "some sort of informal committee began canvassing views yesterday lunchtime, and by the time we started the feast last night the petition was doing the rounds. We were all so busy or so pissed that we didn't even see it."

"And it's been signed by..." Jo wondered, tentatively.

Miranda gulped and spoke quietly. "Three and a half thousand. Roughly."

"Holy shit," was all Jo could manage.

She stood up again. Her headache came with her. She opened the door and moved to stand on the small balcony. The view east across the main festival site showed an entire city on the move, a shimmering and protean being emerging from its slumbers and beginning the process of slithering away. Muted noises – shouts, clanging, engines, falling things, colliding things – had the same character as the sunlight, still coming in at a low angle but with intimations of the heat and chaos to come. Jo stared. Behind her, had she turned to look, thousands of people should be producing the same effect across the more modest but still substantial expanse of Care City.

But that was not the scene.

There was no contingency plan. Even if she had been persuaded to engage with 'afterwards', this would not have been on the list. These people cannot simply not go home! It just doesn't make any sense!

She span on her heels and looked back into the control room. "They can't stay," she blurted. "No way. It just can't be done, even if we wanted to." Thoughts and words battled between her mouth and her mind. "There's no food!" Or there won't be very soon. "The whole place is about to be dismantled and taken away!" This isn't even a real place! "Look," she said, flinging her arm in the direction of the extreme north east of the festival site, "the team's already on site! They start folding everything up in a couple of hours!" She paced into the control room, and around it, and back out again. "There won't be any water. Or sewage systems." And all the security people will have gone home. "Christ, I don't even know who owns all this stuff. Or whose land it is." And the money! Jesus, where do they think the money will come from? "No, no no no no no. Impossible. It can't be done, can't be done, they're going to have to leave. We'll just have to tell them. I'll tell them. I'll have to tell them..."

"We agree with all of that," said Miranda, more slowly than Jo had prepared for. "But... Well, I think these people are pretty determined... And they seem pretty media savvy too." Miranda looked Jo directly in the eye. "I think they have a good idea of how bad it would look if we tried to forcibly evict thousands and thousands of vulnerable people..."

"And how Statement and the university and all the others would not be at all interested in being associated with images of that kind," came a supporting voice.

"They've, um, issued something of a threat," Miranda resumed.

"A threat?" Jo was incredulous, almost shouting with disbelief.

"Well, sort of," Miranda replied, hurriedly. "They've said that, um, from lunchtime onwards they're going to occupy the fountain zone, the aviaries and the glasshouses. Looks like they know their onions on non-violent resistance – they've got a rota worked out, and we think they're distributing padlocks to the wheelchair users as we speak..."

"Oh my god oh my god oh my god this cannot be happening!" Jo screeched. "Tell me this isn't happening, please." There was a short silence. "So you're telling me that we're effectively facing a well-organised rebellion by several thousand sick and disabled people, and that they're using the world's media as leverage, since they just happen to be here. Is that right?"

"That's about the size of it," Miranda said. A small smile began on her face. She tried to suppress it, but failed. Jo saw, raised her eyebrows in a mix of chastisement and disbelief – then burst out laughing herself. The laughter grew, enveloped the whole room and took some moments to subside.

"So," Jo managed, eventually. "We can't and won't kick them out today. I'm sure we can find a way to feed a couple of thousand people for a day or two, and we can probably hold the demolition boys at bay for a while, and, hell, there's probably even a positive spin we can put on it for Statement's sake as well." She smiled broadly, forgetting her headache for a moment. "Amazing, really, when you think about it." She paused again. "Right. That's what we'll do. Comfortable?" Nods. "OK. We're going to need a full team meeting in here, in... an hour. Can you start getting everyone together? Miranda, fancy doing the call to Humboldt? Remember to tell her the solution before you tell her the problem. Tell her we're adding two extra days to Care City, that's all, as a publicity stunt or something." Miranda chortled in agreement. "Me," Jo continued, "I'm heading for the fountain to see if I can find this... this committee, see if I can persuade them to stand down with all the chanting and banners and chaining themselves to heavy objects before they even get going..." Jo chuntered and chuckled as she headed back out into the sunshine, unaware that she had already forgotten her hangover. Tom slept on. Mike peered out once again at the world from his window and noticed nothing unusual. It was the last Monday of June.

Part Three: Next Year

Robert

I t was the day before the start of the court case, late September, fifteen months since The Big Float had ended and Care City had begun. Not that it was called 'Care City' anymore, Robert reflected: these days it was called 'Visco'. He had heard the story of why it was called Visco, but could not remember quite when the change had taken place. Right now he was in the middle of London, staring down at the Thames, upstream from the estuary and that mad, mad island. His absent-minded wrist swirled the pale remaining mouthful at the bottom of the heavy crystal wine glass in his hand. He turned from the floor-to-ceiling plate glass window that formed the north-facing side of his apartment and headed for the kitchen. He replenished his glass and returned to the view.

The city looked good at this time of day, he always thought. The angle of the shadows. And from this height, too, you could see most of the major landmarks. What fine testaments they were! Sculpted residue of long ago egos, a gleaming iconography of wealth and power, a cryptographic history of the things we once believed. A message. An apology.

Yes, yes, he was sorry. He knew he should be feeling excited, glad, positive; but he did not. He felt foolish, uncomfortable and small. He had tried to do the right thing: or, at least, he had told himself he had tried to do the right thing. And good things had happened, hadn't they? Maybe he had always known. Maybe he had always loved her. He took a long mouthful of the shamefully expensive wine. When had it started?

Did it start in the middle, or at the beginning? He was not sure he really believed in the linear narrative. The things that were important at the beginning might turn out to be nothing: the things that turn out to be important might only seem so in retrospect. If it was only from the end that the story makes sense, in what sense could it have been a story as you went along? Maybe it was only at the end that it could become a story: up until that point it was just... things happening. Which of the things that had been happening were the things that were part of the story?

Maybe it was not really his story. Perhaps that was the real problem. All his life, all his white male privileged life, he had presumed that he was the lead character. That is how he was raised, how he had been educated: not strictly speaking solipsistic, but certainly egocentric. It was all about him. He had been told (and he'd believed) that it was his responsibility to be civil and wherever possible kind, but in the end – and he'd also been told this – his first duty was to himself. Unless he was looking after himself, how could he look after anyone else? Unless he was happy, how could he make anyone else happy? Unless he was the master of his own destiny, the author of his own story, what would he be but a cipher in someone else's story? An extra, a splinter in a sub-plot intended only for light relief, or misdirection, or to provide some subtle but essential leverage against the flywheel of some deep and mysterious narrative arc?

The bottle appeared to be empty. It was probably not the best idea to have drunk an entire bottle by this time of day, but – fuck it – it was increasingly obvious that his notions concerning 'the best idea' were hardly to be relied upon. He opened the second bottle, filled his glass, took a long mouthful and immediately re-filled the glass. Back at the window he decided that it had all started in his second year at university: that was when he had first realised that it might actually be possible for him personally, rather than he in some abstract way, or through sheer bloody luck, or in the form of some unrealisable fantasy, that is when he first realised that he could make a lot of money. A lot. Given what he was, and what he could do, and what he knew and who he knew and how he functioned – yes, I Robert Dunbar can leave this place and make a lot of money. A lot.

No. That was not the beginning. The beginning must have been earlier than that. Yes, that's right – he was nine. Nine years old. An old friend of his parents had come to stay. What was his name? It mattered not. There had been dinner, conversation at the dinner table, the man had asked Robert questions, had spoken to him directly, without any reference to his parents, just questions about what he thought about things, what he had seen on television or on the computer, why he had enjoyed a particular film. It had been intoxicating, to be treated like a grown up. Robert had gone to bed but had forgotten something and snuck back downstairs. The adults were talking about him. He wanted to listen, but was scared – scared of being caught, and scared of what they might be saying. And he did not want to listen – but he was scared, scared of missing something important, scared of what they might be saying.

He had listened. They were describing someone he did not recognise. He listened very hard, very attentively, and he knew most of the words they used, but much of it did not make sense to him. Why were they talking about him as if he were somebody else?

"Ha! Yes!" Robert said it out loud to the chrome and leather and electronically managed emptiness around him. He saw it now: a future from the past, a future him, described then, catapulted here, now. The boy he had been; the man he might then have become, the man he was now, the other men he might have been, if this or that or the other part of the story-that-isn't-yet-a-story had gone one way rather than another.

No, no, that's not the beginning. Not of this story. His head slumped forward. Admit it. The story started when you met Jo Castle, because that's when you fell in love, a feeling you did not understand then and you still don't understand now but which is the single most important thing that's ever happened to you because otherwise how could you possible explain – explain all this. He looked around the room – the architect-designed and niche-rich sitting environment, the hand-picked art, the conversation-piece lifestyle – but he knew that it was not the 'this' he meant. He laughed, a cold brisk bark, and turned back to the view. "Go on, I dare you," he said aloud.

He thought about Kate Humboldt. He thought about her face, her cheekbones, her body, her willpower. Her burning eyes. He thought about her laugh. He thought about the first time they met – a couple of years ago now? – that time in the lobby when he had gone to meet Jo for lunch. He thought about the first time that he and Kate had fucked, an electrifying torrent of power and control, of abandonment and peril, of mad heat and pale dust. He thought about the moment he decided not to tell Joanna.

He took a slower mouthful of the wine. An aeroplane drifted one way, a boat the other. He noticed the clouds, just a few of them, heading north and east, meandering. The clouds and the boat and the aeroplane all seemed to be moving at the same speed. He had decided not to tell her because – because it seemed like the right thing to do at the time. He lied because he did not want to tell the truth. He lied because it was a normal part of the armoury of being the person that had devised those particular coping strategies, blah blah blah. He just lied.

He had been pretty sure that the relationship with Kate was not going to become serious. No, that is not right. It was serious from the moment they locked eyes – serious in the sense of heavy, powerful, important. No. He had been sure from the beginning that his relationship with Kate would comprise mainly the fucking. That was serious enough. He had assumed – yes, looking back now, he felt this was correct – he had assumed that the fucking would burn itself out, and that the whole thing – though serious – would remain self-contained.

Yes, that's it. Self-contained.

And since it was only ever going to remain some sort of serious but self-contained fuck bubble, there seemed little point in broadcasting any news about it, especially to Jo. Jo, after all, had only just started working at Statement. And he had only just begun doing the post-relationship lunch thing with Jo, they were still in the foothills of finding a new way to be in one another's lives.

"Huh," he grunted, again to the polished emptiness of this not-quite-penthouse flat. He had been thinking ahead even then, planning where the relationship was going, too busy reviewing the past and scenario-planning the future to actually experience the now. And here he was doing it again! He laughed, a little warmer this time, and replenished his glass once more. Was it late afternoon or early evening? Was there an official boundary? Or could you decide for yourself?

He decided it was early evening. Down at street level the scurrying forms were commuters not shoppers. There would be traffic jams and incidents, excuses and lies, relief and despondency. All things that were happening right now – not earlier, not later, but right now. So, Robert – he asked himself – how are you doing, right now?

His mind refused to confront the question. He shot back instead to those first days and weeks after The Big Float, when the whole world seemed to shift on its axis, when everything went crazy, when any and all plans and anti-plans were thoroughly shredded and hurled into the swirling wind above the island's great plain. He had not been at the festival itself, but he had seen Kate just a few days before it started, and had chatted with Jo a couple of times, so he had a reasonable idea of what was going on. Christ, everyone had some sort of idea about what was going on. He couldn't deny he had an inside track, though. The pillow talk with Kate - it was pretty much the only time they did talk - had given him a rolling idea of the corporate backdrop to the whole thing; and Jo's utopian excitement about Care City had completely consumed every conversation he had with her. His recollection was that, beforehand, he had not said much about it all, he had just made those reassuring noises and asked occasional questions. That was his recollection. Maybe. Maybe not.

In any case it had swiftly been overtaken by events. Within hours of the guests refusing to leave he'd had both of them on the phone, these two remarkable women, each not so much asking him what to do as using him (ha! using him!) as a means of working out what to do. He suspected, looking back, that he had not managed the Chinese walls especially well and that had either of them been looking more carefully then they might have wondered quite how he knew this or that or the other, but quite frankly it was all so completely bonkers in those first few days and hours that nobody was paying that much attention to any particular conversation.

Or, at least, it had seemed that way to him then. Now, looking back, he was not so sure. Maybe they had noticed. Maybe they had noticed and chose not to say anything. "Huh," he grunted, again, despite the continuing lack of response from the room. He had not been that important. Maybe they had noticed but, quite frankly Robert, it's not all about you.

He drained the wine glass in a single draught. Refilling (he poured too quickly and a little of the straw-coloured liquid leapt onto the marble work surface) he remembered the first time that Jo had asked specifically about Kate. "Do you think she'll give us any money?" Jo had asked him. That must have been day three, maybe day four, when it had first started to become clear that these people were not simply going to go home after a couple of days. Yes, those first couple of days had been okay, reasonably straightforward: some excitement on the media channels, a sort of global chuckle at the impudence of all those disabled people, the various funders and agencies and whatnot had cobbled together a few spare resources so as to keep the lights on and food on the table. But then it became clear just how many people had decided to stick around, and it became clear that they seemed to have no intention of going home, and then it became clear that something more organised would be required if these people – what was it, three thousand, four thousand of them? – were to eat and keep cool and generally be looked after.

"We're going to need money," Jo had said. "Proper money. Do you think Kate will give us some?"

She hadn't just mentioned Kate, of course. In fact she had not really meant 'Kate' at all. She had meant Statement plc; and she had asked about the health care people, and the big charities and the university and the local authorities and everyone else that had somewhere along the line become involved in Care City but had done so in the belief – the quite sane, widely shared belief – that their commitment would end sometime during the Monday after the weekend before. No-one had budgeted for Tuesday, or Wednesday, or indeed any of the subsequent days.

"Look, you understand money," he remembered Jo telling him. "I could really do with a little help here."

"A little help," he said to the plate glass view, to the room, to the great city spread below and beyond and around him. Oh the irony. A little help.

It had started as a little help, he supposed. Yes, he understood money. He knew where it came from, how it moved, how it changed shape and colour. He knew how to make it appear and how to make it disappear, how to make it bigger, and how to make it seem bigger than it really was. He knew how it liked to be tickled. Yes, he understood money. So, yes, it would have been churlish to refuse to help; certainly to refuse 'a little help'. He could not tell her about Kate, obviously; or, if not obviously, then not telling her about Kate had by that point become a feature of the landscape, something inherited from the past, something with momentum and history. Like any lie. It doesn't matter whether it's a hotel bill, a road traffic violation, an affair or a question of paternity, once it's started, once it's told, it cannot be untold: there is just the endlessly repeated decision – do I reveal today, or do I continue on the basis of the amended truth, the working truth, irrespective of the consequences?

So, no, he did not say anything about his relationship with Kate. And, yes, it was through his relationship with Kate that he was able to lodge an argument, plant an idea, suggest a suggestion that – as he had foreseen – emerged a little while later as a proposition from Statement plc to Care City and which, a little while after that, came back from Care City to him, Robert Dunbar. Might it have happened like that anyway? Was it a great idea in any case? Maybe. Maybe not.

The easy bit had been to broker some short-term funding from Statement plc just to keep the show on the road – a great opportunity, he had explained, for some terrific PR. "As cause-related marketing goes," he remembered opining, "this is pure gold." But as the summer had turned into yet another warm autumn he devised and then began setting up a specialist 'financial vehicle', a form of partially-sighted Trust, a species of asset management normally relied upon only by the most esoteric financiers to ensure maximum returns and minimum comprehensibility. The solution enabled Statement plc's short-term bridge funding to taper at exactly the rate they needed, allowed Care City to begin the journey towards financial independence, made pro-vision for a range of longer-term funding solutions to be folded-in as and when necessary, made sure that all the people (there must have been seven or eight thousand by that stage) living in Care City could carry on eating and sleeping and having their bottoms wiped, and made sure too that Robert looked generally fabulous. He winced as he discovered the continuing need of his ego to seek evidence of his fabulousness, and winced further as that same ego threw, in quick suc-cession, memories of the very distinct forms of gratitude shown him by Kate (who was simply delighted at the astonishing tax efficiency of his solution, as well as the kudos lapping around Statement's ankles as a result of their tremendous foresight and generosity) and Jo (who was simply delighted).

Jo had stopped hugging him now, of course. The hugging had come to an end as soon as she found out about his relationship with Kate. He still could not be sure - damn that ego - but he guessed it was simply the trust thing. Not the Trust, capital T thing. That had gone from strength to strength. He had – he had to admit – played a game of sustained brilliance on that front. Who, after all, had an answer to the question: if a group of people wanted to build an entirely new city, big enough to house many thousands of people (it had been amazing just how many people had starting arriving as those first few weeks turned into the first few months), and this population, rather than earning money in some traditional way were intent, instead, on conducting some massive and bizarre experiment in providing care for one another and undertaking all those care tasks with, ahem, care: how could that be funded?

Well, no-one had a complete answer, obviously; but he had come close. By pooling all the budgets that people would otherwise have been drawing on - mainly the money that local councils were spending to look after people - as well as the conventional pension-style assets at their disposal, they had been able to assemble by the end of the year something remarkably similar to a sovereign wealth fund. Thereafter it was not dissimilar to the way your typical billionaire ran his or her affairs: keep the enormous asset moving around, ceaselessly swilling and swelling, and live off the froth. Once you've got the first hundred million or two under your belt, the rest is straightforward, and certainly sufficient to generate the money needed to keep a moderately-sized Care City up and running on a day-to-day basis. Chuck in a couple of innovative Bonds (in which – he had so much enjoyed this one – savings from reduced future care costs were amortized into present value, and thus comprised money now, to be frothed in the normal fashion) and – hey presto!

Such, at least, had been the plan; and, so far, it appeared to be working. The Trust's asset base had, in the months since its inception, just about kept pace with the growing population of Care City. There had been resistance to the idea these past few months, of course, as there had been to most of the Care City experiment; and there had been times when the ratings agencies or the specialist press or whoever had thrown grit in the wheels. But, compared to some of the other stuff that had happened, the Trust had got off lightly. Unbidden, his ego again offered its congratulations and, again unbidden, he felt the burning flush of shame.

He still had not decided whether to attend the opening of the hearing tomorrow. Jo would, of course, be there. They had not spoken for months, not since... not since she found out about Kate, about him and Kate, not since she had had to confront the possibility that her dream might have a dark centre, not since she had realised she had been kept in the dark, not since she had realised that he, Robert Dunbar, had done a Good Thing in a Bad Way. Not since he had lost the trust thing, small t.

He looked down at the almost empty wine glass and realised that his eyes were misty and his vision blurred. "Fuck," he said. The room, once again, did not react.

Jo

It was the day before the start of the court case, late September, fifteen months since The Big Float had ended and Care City had begun. 'Visco' Jo corrected herself. Visco. She repeated it a few times in her head. She was out jogging the perimeter of the site, pushing the blood around her system, the air into her lungs, the light into her mind. This route was the shorter of the two she had settled on: it was also better at this time of day. Running clockwise, she turned into the rising sun as she ran and found herself blurring with the rippled beams of light coming in off the estuary where it met the sea. It was like being in a famous painting.

It had taken a while to come to terms with the jogging. Back in the day - it felt like another life entirely - everyday life had been enough to keep her fit and healthy. Since she had taken up semi-permanent residence on an office chair, a rather more disciplined effort was required. She had tried 'going to the gym' during her first few weeks at Statement, but it was too contrived, too crowded. The gym at the fire station had been well-equipped and was focused on the necessities of keeping well and staying strong: the three commercial gyms she'd tried out in London seemed like weird hybrids of hydraulics, cat walk and night club. Better, she eventually decided, to buy a few weights and a decent pair of running shoes.

Sometimes she ran in order not to think; sometimes she ran to do the opposite, to get away from the endless electronic interference and give herself room. Sometimes, like today, she did not know until she hit a rhythm whether she wanted to think, or not. Her thoughts were jumping up and down like startled pebbles, rising briefly into view with each landing stride before falling and rolling away again to rest. Left, right, left, right, this, that, this, that. Nothing stuck, nothing grew, images and dream fragments and memories and possibilities and beliefs and conclusions were indistinguishable, all a gentle shimmer of nothing in particular and everything at all.

Her father's smiling face broke free from the background and did not subside. For a moment she could not place it: was it from before, or after? She held the image in her mind, looking into his eyes. From her childhood? From those adolescent years when he had seemed so distant and disappointed? From her twenties? Her thirties? From before the dementia, or after?

She was still not used to this. He had died in the spring – Jesus, was it nearly six months already? – and for the first few weeks life had been like trying to move through a sort of syrup, as though the air itself had become viscous and was no longer fully transparent. The fact that it had been foretold, almost ordained by the diagnosis, seemed to have no ameliorative effect on its impact. She had discovered an untold purpose to what were still euphemistically called 'the arrangements': they gave you something to do at a time when you were reeling and bewildered and had no idea what to do. But those arrangements – appointing funeral directors, contacting relatives and friends, liaising with sisters and brothers, arranging and then having a funeral - all were experienced through the same gelatinous lens. Everything seemed real, but not quite; present, but a little further away; happening, but at the wrong speed.

She had expected the feeling of loss to have a different shape. He, after all, the man that he had been, had largely disappeared by the time the man he had become – who happened to look exactly the same as the man who had been her father – by the time that man died. Died. That word. Another word, she had fiercely noticed, more conspicuous by its absence at such times, invariably obscured as it was by an entire thesaurus of euphemisms. He had passed away, passed on, gone to a better place, often simply 'passed' or 'gone'. No, she had said: he's dead. But had he 'gone' before he died? That is what she had heard from others, that dementia steals the person long before they actually die. Some, she had heard, even found the eventual death something of a relief. Perhaps, she had speculated, that might make sense if it had been a protracted process. Perhaps, if the person you loved disappeared years ago; perhaps, if you have been visiting some sort of facsimile month after month, year after year, then the final demise of that being might free you at last to recall the one you had once loved.

But John Castle had died more quickly than that. Yes, he had been warned of 'rapid onset' and 'swift deterioration'; and, yes, she and the rest of her family had been fully party to the diagnosis, as well as his brief yet stoical clarity on that diagnosis. But – well, it had still happened brutally swiftly, and her grief had very definitely not been mollified by some zombie hiatus. Her dad had died, and it was awful.

The thickness of life around her had eased, of course – goodness knows there was plenty of life around her to be getting on with – and it was only then that she began seeing him. His face, just as now while she jogged, had simply loomed into view. That first time had been doubly upsetting: not only was she suddenly seeing him; she suddenly realised that until that point she had not been seeing him. She had been sitting in a meeting at Statement and had simply burst into tears.

Everyone had been very sympathetic, on that occasion and the two or three subsequent occasions when the grief had simply ripped its way through her innards and out through her throat.

Dead dead dead. She looked into his eyes. They were smiling in concert with his face and she knew, then, that this was her dad from before. There was recognition, and engagement, and love. She realised her chest had become tight. She made an effort to relax, back into the rhythm of the run, and promptly lost his face. This was normal, she now knew. It hurt each time, but not so much. She knew that she could not, or should not, chase the image, but she allowed herself to continue wondering what time the image came from. Many, she had heard, found that their memories of loved ones that had died after a long sickness were only of the sickness: it was very hard to bury back before those times to find the light and the joy of that person in health. Her experience had been different, she did not know why. He appeared to her: and, each time he did, he came from somewhere that seemed random.

This time she felt as though there had been a sadness in his smiling eyes. Or was it disappointment? At himself? The failure of his marriage? Or at her, his daughter Joanna? A pang shot through her, somewhere from her midriff then along her spine. Had he really been disappointed in her? How could she ever know? Was it just that she did not follow the same stellar academic path as her brothers and sisters?

It was a question that had bothered her more when she was younger but it still nagged now and again. The newer question, and the one to which she still did not have an answer, was about propulsion, or drive. She still wasn't sure what the best word for it was, that thing inside that obliges you to make an effort, which some people seem to have in buckets and some people seem to have in no more than spoonfuls.

Buckets and spoons? Was it like some sort of liquid? Or was it like a switch, on or off? Or perhaps several switches, like a mixing desk.

It didn't seem linked to intelligence or education or even things like happiness or contentment. It seemed more like... more like having hair of a certain colour or being a particular height. She, Joanna Castle, seemed to have been born with a lot of whatever this stuff was and it was the stuff that made her decide to become a firefighter because for a woman to do that was obviously going to be incredibly difficult and her 'stuff' needed 'difficult'. And the same stuff – a mix of stubbornness and determination and hunger and craziness, her jogging thoughts seemed to suggest – the same stuff had persuaded her that something called 'Care City' made sense, and the same stuff had propelled her to join Statement so that she could make this thing called 'Care City' actually happen and the same stuff had, somehow, fuelled her through the past year and a half of unbelievably demanding madness.

Sometimes she felt like a passenger in her own life. As though she didn't actually have a choice. Maybe her father saw that and was simply perplexed, as she was. That's it: it's not disappointment on his face; it's perplexity.

Maybe, she thought, sharply, as the ground beneath her feet changed angle slightly and threw a firmer than expected jolt through her ankle and knee, maybe she was just slightly crazy and the craziness of the past eighteen months was in some sense inevitable, something she had caused to happen rather than the other way around.

Of all the craziness, she found herself thinking, the most interesting and exhausting and, in the end, revealing, had been the people. She liked people, generally; and she liked helping them, especially. But she had discovered that she preferred to keep them at a distance and – she had finally acknowledged – there was something about being a firefighter that worked for her. Arrive, save people, leave again, don't get too involved. You worked closely with a small team and that was it. She had never worked as part of a big team and had certainly never been in 'management'.

She had never given anyone a job, either. Well, that was not completely true, she had interviewed a couple of people for a job in the days before she joined the fire service, but that was completely irrelevant to the events of the past couple of years. Visco – the Visco whose perimeter she was jogging – now had something like forty five thousand people living in it. Forty five thousand! The number barely made any sense. When it had been Care City and no more than an adjunct to The Big Float festival there had been twenty thousand guests and ten thousand staff. All the staff had been supplied through Statement - well, more precisely, through a myriad of sub-contractors reporting to Statement - and the guests had all applied on-line to buy tickets to a festival. Straightforward. Easy peasy.

As soon as people refused to leave – an episode in Visco folklore now generally known as 'The Sit-In' - everything began getting a lot more complicated.

The simpler issues were those connected with people who were very obviously 'in need of care'. People with dementia, people with serious physical disabilities, people whose mental health was in such disarray that they could not really function on their own – not exactly 'easy' but nevertheless straightforward in terms of deciding the basis on which they resided in Care City. At the beginning there had been about fifteen hundred people in this category. A lot, sure, especially when they were all in the same place at the same time, but compared to the mêlée of the preceding few days of the festival it had seemed quite manageable.

Their carers were more complicated. There had been about a thousand in this category who refused to leave, a higgledy piggledy mix of parents with disabled children, partners of broken adults, children of elderly parents and so on. For the duration of the festival weekend these people had been paying guests. They had been expected to play some role in the care of their charges, but had been in large part free (that was partly the point!) to have a bit of a break and join in with the more general revelry. As soon as the festival ended and the bulk of The Big Float was folded up and away, their status changed. Were they now supposed to return to their caring duties, as if they were back at home? Or were they expecting to continue in party mode? Or was some entirely new arrangement required?

More complicated still were the people who had up until that point been called 'staff'. The short-term deal that Robert had brokered with Statement – Jo almost lost her footing for a moment as this recollection came to mind – meant that for what turned out to be the first couple of months or so there was a corporate mechanism in place to handle things, but the sheer variety of people and tasks was breath-taking. There were people required to build, maintain and disassemble the buildings, and the rest of the fold-up infrastructure; there were people needed to clean the buildings, clean the toilets, clean the site itself; people to deal with electricity and cables, computers and transmission equipment, food delivery and storage and cooking and serving, security staff, administrators, health care professionals, the list went on and on. Most of them had, quite reasonably, been expecting to go home, if not on the Monday then shortly thereafter. With Statement's help it had proven possible to retain quite a few of them for a few more days, but not enough, and not for long enough.

It was sometime during the first full weekend after the official end of the festival that Jo had abruptly asked herself: Hang on, what am I doing here? Everyone seemed to have assumed or decided, she couldn't tell which, that she was in charge. She seemed to have decided or assumed that she was in charge. "Someone has to be," Miranda had said. "Yes, yes, but I only signed up for a few days!" Jo screeched. Miranda had looked at her with a cool level gaze, before slowly raising her eyebrows into a flawlessly quizzical and ironical arch.

Jo's formal status had, by the second week, settled into something like 'Chief Administrator'. With the managerial resources of a Statement team at least temporarily at her disposal and the basic provisions of life more-or-less in place – the buildings were stable, the power was on and food was being served – two issues rapidly became Jo's top priorities: dealing with the people who began arriving (or returning) once it became clear that Care City had not gone the way of the main festival; and dealing with the offers of help that began pouring in as the news spread.

The early offers came mainly from well-meaning charities, well-meaning individuals and, occasionally, well-meaning businesses. Dealing with them was a process of ruthless juggling. Most of the initial approaches came directly to Jo since she had spent so much time 'doing the rounds' in the months preceding The Big Float. Over the space of just a few days she grew accustomed to a rather harder-edged exchange than had prevailed during the 'before' period: time and focus were now of the essence. What sort of help can you offer? How many? When? Yes please, no thank you.

One call during that second week – Jo broke into a complicated smile as she recalled it, and noticed too the gatepost marking the mid-point of her morning jog – one call had been different. Pivotal.

"I don't know if you remember me," the speaker had begun. "My name is Abena Tsibirin. We met a couple of years ago..." Of course she remembered her - "The food bank!" Jo exclaimed.

"I hope you don't mind me calling you," Abena continued. "I have something of a confession to make." It turned out that Abena had been in Care City for the festival. Not only that: it turned out she had been one of the main organisers of the petition that had led to the sit in.

"I didn't know it was you," Abena had explained. "I thought you were a firefighter."

Abena had signed up early for the festival, for Care City. She had brought nearly a dozen people along with her, people she had collected during her years at the food bank, people struggling with the world, people she thought would enjoy a few days' respite, people - she was wont to remind anyone listening - with the same rights as everyone else and people entitled to the same dignified treatment, the same life, as anyone else. She'd brought a couple of helpers, too.

All of them – she explained – had had the most amazing time. For most of them, it was the first time they could recall feeling 'normal'. "Normal?" Jo had wondered. "As in, feeling like they weren't different from everyone else," Abena had explained. Ordinarily, her guests lived in a world where it was hard to get on or off a bus, hard to ask for what you wanted in a shop, hard to make sure a friend or relative was on hand when you needed them, hard to navigate the websites and paperwork and administration and transactions that the world is made from these days and which, if not second nature, are at least routine for most of us.

"Being in Care City," Abena went on, "was a revelation. One of my ladies was weeping on the Saturday evening, weeping with the joy of it. She was in one of the glasshouses, watching the birds. She is in a wheelchair, and she has trouble speaking, she had a stroke some years back and most of her family live elsewhere. Whenever she gets out, she told me, she can feel the world looking at her, frowning. Everything is hard. Everything is an effort, just going to the shops." Jo remembered the damp heat in her eyes, listening to Abena's story.

Abena continued: "This lady, she said to me, she said that she'd never been so comfortable. In Care City. They all said it. All the people I brought with me, and everyone else I spoke with. All of them. The beds they slept in. The food. How easy it was to move around." Abena had paused. "Most of all," she continued, "every time they looked around, they saw people like themselves."

Jo's conversation with Abena had long since moved from the telephone to one of the Care City cafés. It felt, Jo remembered, as though her disorganised feelings about Care City, about what it meant, about why it mattered, were being brought into focus.

"We were having breakfast on the Sunday," Abena told her, "when we began thinking that we were like refugees. Refugees from the world, from ordinary life. But it wasn't as though we'd been evicted from our homes and were somewhere temporary. It was like we'd found a new home. And we didn't want to go back."

It had been – Jo savoured the word again – pivotal. For the first time, she had really understood why the petition had happened, why the Sit-In had happened, why all those hundreds and thousands of people had refused to go 'home'. She began to understand, too, why other people, people who had not even been at the festival, had begun to arrive. She had quickly persuaded Abena to help her with the overall administration of the place and she remembered sitting in a meeting a few weeks later as Abena told her about some of the people who had arrived the previous day.

"This couple," Abena said, pointing at the photo heading an A4 sheet of paper, "they arrived in their car, back seat full of their belongings as though they were going on holiday, except the lady is just exhausted from looking after her husband, he's paralysed from the waist down. They simply left their retirement home on the coast because," and she glanced down so as to get the words right, "'We just can't stand it anymore'. And this one," she said, waving another piece of paper, "this one is a mum with three children, all under ten. Two of them are autistic. She says she has run out of money. They all got on a train and headed our way."

"You were right," Jo remembered saying, "it's just like a refugee camp."

"Yes, it is," Abena said, "but there's something else. The line between the refugees and what we might call the aid workers is becoming more and more blurred. Many of the people who need care are also providing care; and many of the people who stayed on to provide care are also receiving it." It had been a crucial insight, and it crystallised into a phrase that, though first uttered by Abena, soon became an authorless and guiding mantra for Care City as a whole:

"Those who can, walk; those who can't, we carry."

Miranda had not reacted especially well to this piece of phrasing. "It sounds a bit communist to me," she had said. "You know, 'from each according to his abilities, to each according to his needs' and all that."

"Huh," Jo had replied.

"Is that what you're doing now?" The barbed undertone was not especially under. "I thought you were running a sort of extended holiday camp for distressed care workers."

"Oh fuck off," Jo had said, immediately regretting it. Once upon a time, and not that long ago, when they were younger and closer, telling Miranda to fuck off would have been fine, even if it had not been a joke, because it would have been said within their broader frame of love and friendship. These days, things were more strained, and the fuck off was both despatched and received with venom.

"Sorry," said Jo, hurriedly. "I didn't mean it like that. Really. Look, you know how tricky it's been." This conversation had taken place face to face, Jo remembered, towards the end of August, maybe early September, when Care City was a couple of months old and still pretty rickety. "I'm basically running a freeform refugee camp here. The first few weeks were just mad, and we're trying to work out some sort of way of organising ourselves on a steadier basis, from first principles, you know?" There was method in the madness: "So we say that everyone living in Care City needs care; and everyone can give care. It's just a case of how much. So as long as everyone mucks in it should work. We're trying to set up a sort of brokering database at the moment, everyone lists what they need and what they can give and then the tech boys and girls are working on some sort of algorithm which shares everything out fairly." Miranda still did not react. Jo continued. "I don't know how long it'll work for. The deal we've got with Statement means we've got money for a little while longer yet, so we can keep the lights on and feed everybody and buy detergent and stuff, and Robert seems to think that this Trust thing he's come up with might keep things going for a few months after that. So maybe we'll be ok..." She had drifted off at this point, no longer sure whether she was trying to convince Miranda or convince herself.

"And," Jo resumed, with some force, "the whole 'care' thing is embedded. Or it needs to be. It's not just about giving care, it's about taking care, it's about being careful, it's about doing whatever you're doing with care."

"Care, carefully given," Miranda echoed.

"Yes, something like that," Jo agreed.

It had also been around that time, Jo recalled, when the new arrivals began to change. For the first couple of months everyone who had turned up hoping to join whatever was happening on the island in the estuary was in some way disabled: all were fleeing a world in which they were marginal through no fault of their own. But as the summer ended and autumn began, a new type of person began to arrive. People not with disabilities per se but people who, simply, rejected the world as it was. Idealists. Refusniks. Rebels. People with an alternative perspective and ambitions for an alternative lifestyle.

To begin with this new group of people – what Joanna and her colleagues came to call 'the second wave' – fitted in easily and well, and they joined in the emerging pattern: everyone was a carer, and everyone received care. The great computerised time bank allocated janitor duties and physiotherapy duties and electrical repair duties, and there seemed to be enough money trundling through the Trust to buy the food and provisions that Care City's citizens needed, and whilst no-one bought a new car or a new watch or a new television, and no-one bought a new pair of designer shoes or a fancy shirt or a sexy new top, it did not seem to matter. Whatever was happening seemed to be preferable to whatever was the alternative. At least that how it seemed to Jo.

Or, at least, that is how it had seemed then. Here, now, as she reached the end of her run and stood gently warming down, her limbs swinging back and forth, her breathing returning slowly to normal, here and now it was all a bit more complicated. Things had become a great deal more serious. It was a big week. Court tomorrow.

Mike

I t was the day before the start of the court case, late September, fifteen months since The Big Float had ended and Care City had begun. Mike loved its new name Visco but had no intention of accompanying his step-sister to court. In fact, to make sure he could not change his mind at the last minute he had left London, the island and the estuary completely and travelled to see his mother. He had not seen so much of her lately. That was probably normal. As in, normal for someone of his age rather than normal for someone who lived in Visco. No one who lived in Visco was normal.

It was not as though he was disenchanted with the idea, although he was, in truth, disenchanted with the idea. The point was – he told himself as he threw the soggy twig for his mother's dog to yet again chase across the field at the back of her house – the point was that the very fact of it being a court case was, as far as he was concerned, a dismal concession to the very system that Visco existed to reject. Visco stood apart from the patriarchal, oppressive, exploitative, destructive and empty model! Visco and its citizens represented the future, a future that - at last! - acknowledged that reform was impossible. The only way forward was to start again. Why on earth were they engaging with the dying system in this way? Engagement was concession. Concession was weakness. Weakness meant defeat.

The dog placed the repulsively soggy stick once again at his feet. It was more saliva now than wood. Mike picked it up gingerly and once again hurled it away. The haplessly jubilant hound, a portly Labrador, bounded off. His mother fed it too much and exercised it too little. He could hardly blame the animal. He thought of those people he had watched from the balcony in the shopping centre in London – how long ago was that? – and the way so many of them seemed to waddle rather than walk. A bit like the dog. He thought about the notion of 'blame'. He kicked out at a piece of turf and resumed his walk. He found himself looking back at the nineteen year old boy that he, now twenty-one, had recently been.

He did not feel so confused any more. He could remember the intensity of his bewilderment whilst he stood on that Christmas balcony, his sense of impotence, his inability to summon either the focus or the strength even to know what to think, never mind what to do. What an extraordinary couple of years it had been. He remembered those conversations he had had with Jo. What had he said? 'Something bigger than just a one day item, but not something that will take forever.' Is that how he had put it? Something like that. Huh. Well that had worked out.

"No, time for a new one boy," he said to the dog. It really was just too disgusting. He found a new twig – more of a small branch, really – and hurled it as far as he could. Should keep the dog busy for a few moments.

Bigger than a one day item. Well Visco had certainly been that. Of course he had stuck around once the festival was over and the new world began. Of course. Where else could he possibly have gone? And it was, he had to admit, incredibly exciting. He found it hard to recall a previous state of mind. Now, tromping through this late summer field at the back of his mother's house, he felt... yes, cantankerous. And perhaps chastened. Maybe even dismayed – and definitely disheartened. It was a powerful combination, he felt, making it very difficult to remember with any conviction his emotions in those first few days and weeks of the new world. Yes, he could remember the words – excitement, anticipation, exhilaration, curiosity, a sense of power and possibility – but he could not actually re-feel the feelings.

The thing he remembered being most excited about was the fact that there was nothing to buy. Well, it wasn't exactly like that. People needed things, obviously, like food and shoes and toilet paper, but most of that kind of thing had been provided through the refectories and Care outlets and you simply went and helped yourself to whatever you needed. He had never properly understood the workings of the Trust that Robert had set up – the phrase 'semi-autonomous sovereign wealth fund' had been bandied around – but Jo had explained on a couple of occasions that no-one really understood the Trust that Robert had set up, possibly not even Robert, and that was partly the point.

Then there were things like televisions and beds and armchairs and the like, and they all came with the buildings, or at least they appeared to, so you didn't need to buy those. And then there were things like clothes, where there were certainly donations from the outside world that came in handy (some of the Care outlets were a bit like old-fashioned charity shops) but mainly what happened was that people either repaired clothes or re-made the donated clothes by cutting them up and sewing them into new shapes. Some people had even made their own clothes seemingly from scratch. Mike remembered his incredulity on seeing this for the first time.

Then someone set up a repair shop for the tech, and then another one and – hey presto – everyone seemed to have pretty much everything they needed and there wasn't a single multi-national locally-branded retail chain outlet in sight.

It was too good to last, Mike ruefully conceded, screwing up his face as he changed direction slightly and the wind picked up. He was a bit higher up now - how odd it was to climb a proper hill after all those months on the flatland - and he was tempted to use his next throw to send both moist branch and slavering dog as far back down into the valley as he could, but that seemed suddenly a little cruel. It was not the dog's fault it was overweight. It was not even really his mother's. She lived on her own, she went out to work, she was finally building a bit of a social life, it was hardly surprising she didn't get to take the dog out as often as she might like for the long walks that would be really good for him. He still wasn't sure how he felt about his mum. No: that wasn't right. He wasn't sure how he felt about his mum's life.

No, that wasn't quite right either. He had the odd feeling of something distant, out of sight, as though there was something that he might have known, or would one day know, but could not know now, in fact he could barely savour the not knowing of the not knowing of it. And he felt awkward, perhaps even a bit guilty, about the balance of his time and affections since his dad had married Jo's mum. His dad had always been the funnier, cooler parent; and his new wife was, well, new, and different and interesting; and her children – well, what was there to say about Jo? Mike's mum was a working class woman who had married a minstrel musician when she was a little too young and he was a little too old, who had had a single son and who had then seen the man slip slowly away and who had seemed for most of Mike's life either to be dreary or tiresome or restrictive or all three. Only now, as he entered adulthood proper, was he beginning to glimpse the rest of her. It made him uncomfortable.

He stomped in an effort to shake off the discomfort brought on by his train of thought, but it served only to stun him into a new and even more uncomfortable reflection. He found himself remembering the period when 'Wave Two' started, a year or so ago, a couple of months after the end of the main festival, when the new people arriving at Care City began changing. To begin with everyone had been the same: disabled people, people with dementia, poor people, people who needed lots of care - and, of course, the people who cared for them.

Once the summer had ended, new people started arriving. It was almost, Mike remembered thinking, as if they had finished their summer of music and travel and revelry and were heading towards the island for the winter. Like a form of migration. Just like the birds that began gathering in the estuary before heading south. Only these new people – grungy students, wannabe anarchists, political activists, hardened eco-warriors – these new people had no intention of heading south.

He had found it quite exciting to start with. It was as though the hidden potential of Care City – its underlying radicalism – was beginning to come to the fore. Up until that point he had not really thought about a bigger picture; it already seemed quite big enough. Getting ready for Care City had been amazing; The Big Float festival itself had been amazing; and it was amazing that people had refused to leave and something new and remarkable was happening. But when Wave Two started he suddenly found himself having entirely new kinds of conversations and began to see Care City in a new light. Rather than being some sort of wonderful bubble, destined surely to pop, it began to look more like a direct challenge to the mainstream system. It was the time he'd started to learn what words like 'patriarchy' and 'exploitation' really meant.

He'd been due back at university at the end of the month and he was desperate to squeeze as much in as possible. Sitting around a campfire one evening he suddenly thought it would be great if his friend Tom could see this. He hadn't seen him since they'd shared a room during The Big Float, and although he knew Tom was a pretty cynical guy – that was partly why he'd liked him – he genuinely thought that Tom might be persuaded.

Maybe, Mike reflected, once again throwing the stick for the dog, maybe I wanted to show off, too. A sort of 'Look what I did'. A sort of 'See, I told you things could be different'. A sort of 'Fuck you'.

So Tom turned up one weekend, all boisterous cynicism and machine-gun delivery and almost immediately Mike began regretting the invitation and wondering once again why this person was still his friend. He quickly decided that this was the final act of the friendship and that the only thing to do was to grit his teeth and get through the weekend. There were plenty of people and plenty of things to do – how hard could it be?

It turned out to be very hard. Tom was caught stealing a laptop from one of the repair shops on the Sunday morning.

Mike had been mortified. Embarrassed. Ashamed. He felt as though he was personally responsible for tarnishing – destroying! – the very essence of Care City. This wonderful, beautiful, amazing place, a place of trust and love and care – and he had brought something malignant into its heart, a friend who wasn't even a friend, someone so utterly unable to grasp what was going on that they thought it would be entertaining to steal a computer.

But when Mike joined the meeting that had been quickly convened to decide what to do about Tom, something even stranger happened. It turned out that quite a few things had 'gone astray' in the past few weeks. A couple of bits of tech had gone missing; a few cases of food; some expensive cabling. All had been ignored, initially – it appeared – because people were assuming mere error: a mistake in the stock control, perhaps, or a mislabelling, or someone having simply taken the wrong piece of kit when they came to collect their own. In fact, it soon became clear, people were unwilling to admit to the possibility of theft. No-one in Care City wanted to admit that the idealism was failing so quickly – and no-one wanted the police involved.

Mike had reacted with fury at the revelation that theft had been going on and no-one had bothered doing anything about. His feelings of shame and culpability about Tom propelled his outburst and he still felt himself flush at the recollection. The flush kicked him out of the memory and back into the world, where he noticed the dog, once again awaiting the next opportunity to chase the stick. "Hey, sorry," Mike said to him. If the dog shat in the neighbour's garden, Mike noted, it would be the owner's fault. He, Mike, had brought Tom into the garden.

The discussion had become very heated. It all became very confused, too. Jo may have been 'Chief Administrator', and that was fine as far as it went, but she was administrating logistics and resources and money. Care City did not actually have mechanisms for dealing with this kind of thing. Even deciding what they meant by 'this kind of thing' proved complicated. A crime had been committed, that much seemed to have been agreed, and if it had taken place in London or on the mainland that would mean contacting the police, and then an investigation and maybe a prosecution and all that sort of thing. Then someone suggested that Care City should simply deal with this itself.

"We can't do that!" Mike shouted. "We're not above the law here! What if someone had been raped or murdered?"

The temperature rose still further. Everyone was shouting. Mike remembered thinking that, any minute now, someone will throw something, a fit, or a plastic cup maybe, or a fist. Jo got there first and threw her weight.

"OK, OK, enough," she yelled, until the room descended into a sullen silence. Sometimes her quietly spoken power was not so quiet. "I have a suggestion," she said, once the silence had stabilised. "And I'll make that suggestion in a moment. But the first thing I want to say is that this is above my pay grade. I think it's probably my duty to be speaking right now. But we're talking here about... about politics. Look, we're all grown-ups, let's not kid ourselves. We've had our heads in the sand. Who's even in the room? Who has a right to be here? Why should it be me or you or you or Mike or anybody in this room that deals with this? This isn't some independent fiefdom. Mike's right. We may all feel special and that we're working on something new and amazing, but we haven't left the real world and we haven't left behind the law. We aren't a government. No-one here represents anyone. No-one here speaks on behalf of anyone else." The room carefully absorbed her words.

"Maybe the time's arrived for that sort of thing, but we're not going to deal with that here and now. Right here and right now," she paused, scanning the room, alerting them to the fact that she was about to make her suggestion... "right now I suggest we call the police and -" she raised a hand to quell the sudden swell of murmuring "- and we let them do whatever it is they're going to do. It would surely," she said with emphasis, "be far worse for us – far worse for Care City - if people were to find out that we'd not called the police when we should have done." She let it sink in. "People need to feel safe here. We can't do that on our own. Not yet, anyway."

Mike threw the stick one last time and headed back down the hill. His mum was out at work but she would be home in an hour or so. He had offered to cook the dinner. He had cooked for his dad and Jo's mum a few times, and he'd cooked for Jo, too, and even Miranda once. He knew what kind of food they liked. He wasn't sure about his mum. He was a bit nervous about cooking for her tonight. He was a bit worried that his cooking was a bit middle class, that it would make her uncomfortable. "Huh," he said to the breeze. So many things to be uncomfortable about.

He had never cooked for Tom, and he never would. The police had arrived, they were nice enough, a little fazed by the Care City set up but they'd seen the news just like everyone else and – Mike assumed – someone somewhere must have discussed security and suchlike with them at some point. They left with Tom in the back of the police car, but he was never arrested or charged, just warned. Someone put him on a train back to London and Mike hadn't seen him since.

Mike had been in tumult the next day as he walked around Care City fulfilling whichever duties the rota had allocated. Looking back he could see his emotions chasing and colliding with one another like wild stallions. He was excited, but disappointed; angry, but dispassionate; curious, yet numb. It took weeks for his insides to settle down, and even then it felt like the stable door had been bolted insecurely. It just felt too paradoxical. He had come to believe in the vision, idealistic though he knew it was, and he believed in it so much that he felt he had to protect it. Protecting it had meant calling the police, uniformed emblems of the very system that Care City, he had come to believe, stood against. "To cure you they must kill you," the old song had said. Was that what he had done?

He was stomping the last few metres of the field. Tomorrow they would all be in court, fighting for Visco again, believing, like he did, like he had, that the only way to protect it was to accept the basis of the prevailing powers, powers that, as these past few months had made awfully clear, had no intention of allowing Visco to threaten the status quo. They were walking like Christians into the Colosseum – and, even if they won, surely Visco was emasculated.

Disheartened? That wasn't the half of it. Calmer, yes. He had learned a lot. Standing on the worn mat at the back door he began pulling at his boots. Did a bit of him still harbour hope? The dog, trundling and dribbling and gently barging into him, appeared to think so. "Yes, ok, dinner time," Mike said, breaking into a soft, uncertain smile.

Jo

I t was the day before the start of the court case, late September, fifteen months since The Big Float had ended and Visco had begun. This time tomorrow she would be in her glad rags in London's highest court, litigant in a case that could change the world. Jo tried not to think about it. She could think of nothing else.

Since her morning jog she had showered, dealt with some low grade correspondence and managed a couple of inconsequential calls. She had wandered around the Visco site, saying hello here and there. She sat down for a while, then stood up. She went looking for her friend Abena but could not find her. She had a cup of tea on her own. She went back to the sea wall and stared to the horizon, as flat and distant as ever beneath the enormous and unblinking sky.

She decided to go and help in one of the kitchens. There were always vegetables that needed chopping. Everything in Visco was cooked from scratch. The place was a long way from self-sufficient – they had only begun growing their own food in the spring – but most things were brought in from local suppliers and whilst the algorithms made sure that everybody had their turn on the peeling and the chopping and the serving and the washing up, they also made sure that the best cooks did the most cooking. Cooking, as everyone either already knew, or remembered, or came to realise, was almost as good as eating, if not better: the careful deployment of skill, the craft of making best use of ingredients, the knowledge that one's efforts would be giving pleasure to others, that one's efforts were essential to Visco's vitality. After that first remarkable feast in the final hours of the festival, when it was still called Care City, collective eating had had a remarkable hold on the evolving culture of the community: there were regular large-scale meals, often with a celebratory or festive air; and new arrivals were always introduced early to this aspect of life on the island.

"I don't think it's an accident," Mike had said to her one day whilst slightly more drunk and slightly less hesitant than usual, "that all the ancient universities and schools and clubs invest so much time and money in dining." Jo's mind had been momentarily spun back to the ridiculous magnificence of that dinner in the Worshipful Company of Tanners and Drovers. "Yes," he continued, slurring slightly, "they're a show of power, of opulence or whatever. But they're the occasion where you break bread. You sit down, doesn't matter, and you break bread. All the same. Levelling. Everyone sits at the same height, eats the same food. Bonding. You know."

It certainly seemed to have been true for Care City and continued to be true for Visco, Jo reflected. It had, after all, been at that very first feast that the petition had been passed from one pair of hands to another, a very physical metaphor for the linkages, the connections, the bonds that seemed to hold the place – the people – together. It had been at a similar occasion, too, not long after Mike's friend Tom had been arrested, that the first formal steps were taken to instigate some sort of accountable administration for Care City, steps that led inexorably and inevitably to tomorrow's court case.

Jo sought permission from the kitchen manager to squeeze into the roster, permission that was easily granted. Jo felt sure that anyone offering to do a few chores would have been welcomed as quickly as she had and that it was nothing to do with her status. She found herself stationed at a large stainless steel vat with several sacks of root vegetables to one side. Tonight's dinner, it seemed, started here.

As she began tipping the vegetables into the vat, her mind returned to that evening – not quite a year ago? – when the discussions that had been rustling through Care City for weeks seemed to begin crystallizing of their own accord. She had been sitting next to Daniel. He and she had become very close by that point. He had not been at the festival itself, but had visited shortly after the Sit-In, and then again, and then again. Ever since watching him deal with those racists on the tube train, Jo had been intrigued, energised, a little wobbly. He made her feel as if she were on tip toe – excited, to be stretching up and peering at something enticing, but a little off balance and at risk of falling. They met for coffee and chatted; they had been for a couple of drinks; they had had lunch. It all seemed very grown up, or something.

Things changed a little when he began visiting Care City in the summer, and changed a lot when, early in the October, he announced his intention to stay. They progressed from coffee and lunch to the occasional walk, and quickly from there to sleeping together and hanging out doing nothing.

On the evening she was remembering – sometime in November or December? - they had spent a couple of hours doing not very much between the end of the day's tasks and the beginning of dinner. Or – Jo grinned, emptying a vat of freshly peeled and diced carrots into a series of metal trays, ready for whatever was happening to them next – whatever they had done was no longer available to her memory. She knew they must have spent some time together in the hours before eating because by the time dinner started they were already in something of a groove and she felt sure, looking back, that things might have been different otherwise.

A couple on the opposite bench and a couple of seats along had been talking rather loudly about the pros and cons of representative democracy versus participative democracy – essentially whether some sort of council should be elected to act on behalf of Care City's citizens (as they were now commonly known) or whether the citizenry should regularly, perhaps even continuously, be formally involved in all the decision making. In the time since Tom's arrest there had been many conversations like this.

Jo had found some of the conversations alarming. They were invariably earnest and passionate, and they tended quickly to become technical. It seemed as though much of the energy was coming from Wave Two citizens and Jo became anxious that Care City's original inhabitants were getting left behind. "Not everyone," she had said on some occasion or other, "is as bothered about this sort of thing as you are." This had been like throwing kerosene. Not bothered?! To some, it seemed, the very idea of such indifference was anathema. It is your general responsibility to participate in political processes, ran the argument; such a responsibility is tantamount to a duty in a setting like Care City. Jo's defensive response was grounded in Abena's mantra: "Those who can, walk; those who can't, we carry." There were plenty of people in Care City, she reminded people, who already put their trust in others to look after them; allowing others to deal with the island's political life was a perfectly legitimate extension of that trust.

Many of those most heavily engaged in these discussions - and this included the couple diagonally along from Jo and Daniel - had experience of protest movements. There seemed to be dozens of techniques for including people, for legitimizing decisions, for appointing representatives and then, if necessary, getting rid of them. There were models based on workers' co-operatives, political parties, on-line communities, governing bodies, post-modern virtual deliberative enquiries, there was even something called liquid democracy. "Sounds like my kind of party," she remembered Robert quipping one evening in the early days of setting up the Care City Trust, when he and Jo had still been friends.

"I just don't see why I should have to do it," she had said to him when he wondered why she was not just setting up a council and organising an election.

"Because you're in charge," Robert had grinned back.

"No, not like that I'm not," she said. "I'm strictly admin. See, there's a clue in the name. 'Chief Administrator'. If people here want a council and if they want some elections then they can have some. That's fine. I'll help set it up if that's what people want. I'll do the admin. But I don't see why I should have to do anything beyond that. Christ, have you seen how many people there are here? The place must be crawling with leaders…"

Robert continued grinning, Jo almost laughed and then she ploughed on. "Besides," she said, "there already is a council, for chrissakes. A proper council, official and elected, over there on the mainland. It's been looking after the island and the rest of this bit of the world for donkey's years. There are processes, procedures. We can't just declare UDI. We're not throwing off the colonial yoke here."

Robert's smile slowly lowered and a single eyebrow slowly rose. Jo had begun to splutter some sort of 'No no no…' but suddenly the bag of vegetables fell from her hand and her reverie tumbled across the floor with the potatoes and she was furious with him because once upon a time she had loved him and here he was being charming and clever in her memories and now she knew that at the very moment he was being charming and clever and raising his eyebrow in that sexy and insightful way he was actually bullshitting her because although he had every right to be fucking Kate because he had every right but he should still he should still he should still have had the bloody guts to tell her and then maybe they might still be friends and she wouldn't be standing here throwing fucking root vegetables at the fucking floor.

She had made a bit of noise and a couple of colleagues – who had assumed she was stressed about tomorrow's court case – came over, collected the spuds and offered her tissues.

"Sorry, sorry," she mumbled. "I'm just stressed about tomorrow."

Daniel did not do the eyebrow thing. At the dinner back in November or December, having listened for a few moments to the discussion further along the table, he had turned to Joanna:

"I don't think it's about models and voting and representation," he said. "I think this is about leadership. All new adventures need someone to go first, someone to show the way. They're not the same kind of people that will be in charge once everything is up and running. Later, for sure, you'll need elections and terms of reference and all that stuff. But that's not what you need right now."

He paused, but Jo held onto her questions. He continued.

"There's probably ten or twenty or thirty people, already here on the island, and you're one of them. You're the pioneers. The founders. The founding mothers and fathers and brothers and sisters." It was still called Care City at this point, and the population was a little above 10,000. A few others on the table began to listen in. "It feels to me," he continued, "as though you need to think ahead a little." Jo reacted, a little stung, but he continued speaking. "Look, I know that the Trust you've put together is going to be important for the future, so you must have thought about the future from that perspective, but mostly what I see is hand-to-mouth stuff."

"So what sort of thing do you think we need to think about?" Jo asked him.

Daniel held her gaze for a moment, then looked around to notice the other faces turned his way. There was a curious static. He hesitated. "I'm not sure I ought..." he began. "We're asking you for your view," Jo told him.

"OK," he said. "It seems to me that, whether by accident or design you find yourself with an opportunity to do something that hasn't been done for a very long time. I've been thinking about that time a few hundred years ago when people were so sick of what was going on in Europe that they got up and left. They left the old world to go and live in the new. They were refugees and visionaries. They were convinced that the stuff they were leaving behind was broken. They gave up on the idea that it could be fixed. They were determined to start from scratch, to do it better." He took a sip of water. "It wasn't easy. And, let's face it, a lot of the things they did were pretty awful - the things they did to the people that already lived there were horrific." He paused. "But the pioneers fought for what they believed in. It was not certain they would win. In fact," and at this point he swept his gaze across the full arc of his audience, "there are other stories where they didn't win. Where they tried and they failed. The powers that be don't want this kind of thing going on, either in their back yard or anywhere else. They have too much to lose.

"But in the story I'm thinking of the pioneers won, they defeated the old powers and they really did start from scratch. The United States of America. They sat down, those few dozen founding fathers – and, yes, in those days they really were all men – and they started from first principles. They started by expressing what they understood to be inalienable rights. Things they thought were self-evident. They wrote them down. They declared their independence in a document and took it from there.

"They didn't look to the future and try to work out every possible option, every possible scenario, and then choose the one they wanted. Given some of what's happened since, if they'd done that they might not have bothered! But they simply said: here are the basic principles, the operating rules, now let's run the tape and see what happens. If the rules are solid, they thought, if the rules are right, then only good things, only right things can happen."

All those sitting within immediate earshot of Daniel's soliloquy had fallen quiet, and others from further away had left their chairs to stand and listen.

"And a Declaration of Independence," Jo almost whispered, "gave birth to the wealthiest and most powerful nation the world has ever seen..."

"I'm not suggesting that Care City is in exactly the same situation!" Daniel replied, a distant chuckle in his tone. "And I'm not for one moment suggesting that the United States of America isn't deeply flawed. But the parallels are intriguing, no? A group of people starting again, however humbly, with a powerful sense that the old way is finished? A group of people who are muddling through, with a feeling that something important is going on but who don't quite understand it and who haven't yet got a plan. Who seem to be getting on with things, and doing them well, but who don't have a proper mechanism for making decisions for deciding who's in charge?"

"So what, exactly," Jo asked, "are you suggesting?"

"I think what I'm saying," Daniel said, a faint and ambiguous smile on his lips, "is that you – we – should not be worrying about elections just yet. I think we – you – should be drafting a statement of intent. A statement of principle. A document that sets out what Care City is all about. That, as simply and clearly as possible, declares to yourselves and the world what the point is. If you – we – can agree on that, then everything else will follow. There's no point in electing a leader, or a council, unless and until you know what it is you're actually doing."

What a beautiful question it was, Jo smiled, picking up the last of the spilled vegetables and returning her attention to whatever it was she was supposed to be doing before her recollection of Robert had thrown food everywhere. What are we actually doing? So simple. She may have fallen in love with Daniel at that point. The gentle gleam in his eye as he led them all to the obvious question, a question that everyone had managed to miss. What were they doing?

As she had discovered, doing something elemental with your hands changed what happened in your head. She still did not know why, but it seemed to work. Perhaps some older deeper bit of your brain was activated when your fingers were busy doing something ancient. She was standing in a clean, modern industrial kitchen, she knew this; and yet she felt as if not only the feast being addressed by Daniel but the whole of what had followed was fully present, here, now. As though she was merely the three-dimensional shadow of all that four-dimensional time. Her hands held the vegetables; her mind held the moment. The moment was now, yet contained all of the past. It shimmered slightly.

The words had appeared slowly at first, awkward phrases and fragments sketched partly by committee and partly by moments of individual genius. A statement of principle. A statement of intent. Some worked on digital versions, some worked on printed copies, some carried scraps of paper. What are we doing? What is the point? Such wonderful questions! A first full draft stabilised, almost, then collapsed. Rather than being the cause of dismay, or anxiety, it seemed merely to confirm the importance of their quest in the ever-more-numerous minds of Care City. A second and even more energised draft emerged – and held together. There was debate and laughter, incredulity and commitment. They seemed to be proposing some sort of new state. They seemed to be on the verge of proclaiming a departure from the old world. It was ridiculous.

The same debates saw the emergence of the new name, too. Jo could not remember precisely when or where it had happened, but someone had started talking about the way in which everyone was coming together, perhaps even sticking together. Someone else started getting technical about it, talking about 'social networks' and degrees of separation and the frequency of social interactions being an indicator of the health of a community, and then Mike had talked about the feeling he'd had watching a crowd in a shopping centre, the way it flowed, like a thick gas, or maybe a liquid. And then someone had used the word 'viscous' to describe the way a crowd moved, and then it became 'viscosity' and then someone made a joke about 'visco city' and there was lots of laughter and someone else said 'hang on a minute' and the word Visco floated into the ether and even though it was ridiculous it seemed no more ridiculous than anything else they seemed to be imagining and everyone loved the idea.

Suddenly it was Christmas, six months since The Big Float and the birth of Care City, and everything began happening quickly. Jo told Daniel she loved him for the first time and, just two days later, learned from Kate about the relationship she had been having with Robert. The provisional Care City council – a loose assembly of the willing and the able - issued a final draft of what had come to be called the Declaration of Care and formally proposed that Care City rename itself Visco. Both the Declaration and the new name were overwhelmingly endorsed by the thirteen thousand registered citizens of Care City.

Jo remembered that the provisional council had also formally endorsed her as leader and had wanted, in homage to a famous peasant revolutionary movement, to give her the title 'Sub-commandanté'. This was a title, it was explained to her, that signalled both leadership of, and subservience to, the will of the people. She thought it signalled incomprehensible silliness and was glad that, in the end, all discussion of job titles had been overtaken by events.

The events in question comprised the beginning of the resistance to the whole idea of Visco. Early in January the first documented criticism of Visco appeared on a major news platform, alleging that the whole thing was some sort of cult; several local politicians held a press conference to condemn the Declaration of Care as a threat to democracy; and letters from 'senior business figures' appeared in the mainstream press, criticising Visco for not offering the same level playing field as the rest of the country and demanding action. The national government announced a committee of enquiry, to be chaired by an individual rumoured to have been attempting to destabilise the financial Trust that Robert Dunbar had set up.

Her emotions in tumult about Robert, about Daniel, about Visco and the Declaration of Care, and her mind reeling from a sudden and novel succession of media and political attacks, in mid-January Jo took a call from someone called Tanya Golding:

"Hello, this is Tanya Golding, of Golding Associates." The voice paused, perhaps expecting a response from Jo. With none forthcoming, the voice resumed. "I represent a consortium of retail businesses with interests in and around London," it said. "We thought you would want to know that we shall tomorrow be submitting a planning application to build and open a set of five retail units on land currently occupied by the south eastern section of Care City. I suggest you contact your lawyers: our legal team has advised us that arrangements in Care City at present are restrictive, anti-competitive and therefore illegal and that we have an extremely strong case to have the right to offer alternative retail options to the consumers both resident on, and living near to, the island. You'll have six weeks from tomorrow morning."

The soft click signalled the end of the call; and a rather louder clunk nearer to home told Jo that her last batch of root vegetables were peeled and ready. She glanced at her wristband. Gosh. Lunchtime. She wasn't hungry, but something told her she should move on now. For neither the first nor the last time she followed her instincts, and began removing her kitchen overalls.

Miranda

I t was the day before the start of the court case, late September, fifteen months since The Big Float had ended and nine months since Care City had become Visco. Dr Miranda Farnaby was looking south from her new offices in the university. Here in the older and central part of London the buildings tended not to be as tall as in the financial districts or the newer residential areas along the river, so even from this fifth floor window she had a decent view. Had she looked in the right direction, and with sufficiently powerful binoculars, she might have been able to see Robert Dunbar as he looked from his not-quite-penthouse flat on the south bank of the river.

Both, of course, had Jo Castle in common. Whilst Robert – rich, drunk, brilliant and fragmenting – was completely estranged from Jo, Miranda was still in regular contact. Almost all of that contact was, however, and for want of a better word, professional: the demands of Visco and the build up to tomorrow's court case had become all-consuming. The girlie lunches and wine-fuelled evenings had joined their childhood and adolescence in the past.

Miranda looked around her new room. Compared to her previous office, this was bigger, lighter and better equipped. Best of all, she no longer shared the space with anyone else. In academic terms, these were the trappings of success. There was a nice new (ish) sofa, and a decent coffee table, and there was sufficient room for her to pile a few bits and pieces in one corner without it jeopardising her ability to move around. She felt so comfortable that she even hosted meetings here. She had installed two pot plants, willowy bundles of green drift that made her feel cossetted every time she saw them.

Yes, success. Just as she had hoped – nay, predicted – The Big Float had proven to be the perfect springboard for her career. The sponsorship deal had given the university exactly the kind of profile it had been hoping for, the Care City initiative had been well received, the Vice Chancellor had been delighted. Miranda had made innumerable new contacts during the run up to the festival and, on the back of them, was suddenly enormously useful in a whole panoply of grant applications. With a rapidly growing profile and a surge in her cash value, the university was absolutely delighted (according to each of the successive contractual upgrades) to offer her a new and more exciting challenge. Now she had fewer teaching responsibilities, a small research team AND a small administrative team, as well as a budget to attend the kinds of top-end conferences in exotic locations that make up for the interminable administrative meetings along the way and which are the sign of serious academic status.

So engrossed had she become in her own progress that for the first few weeks after the festival she paid little or no attention to events on the island. She barely thought about Jo, either. Things had, she knew, begun getting tense much earlier: Miranda recalled the occasion when they had their first site visit to the island with Peter Tiresias and their clash over the ownership of the Care City idea. That had persisted for a while, but then Jo had become more and more absorbed after joining Statement and Miranda's work at the university had accelerated and, insofar as she gave it any attention, Miranda simply assumed that she and Jo were in one of those 'don't see one another very often' phases because other things were in the way. They had, obviously, worked closely together during the festival itself – they had both been at the opening ceremony at the fountain – but even then, Miranda reflected, the distance between them had felt as though it was an outcome of circumstances rather than anything deeper.

That belief came to a sharp and definite end, as far as Miranda was concerned, when she made her first visit to the island a couple of months or so after the Sit-In. Care City by that point was up and running in very striking fashion. Having been shown around by Jo – in what felt like perfunctory fashion – she was then introduced to Abena, with whom Jo was clearly developing a close relationship. It had been something of a jolt. Then came the moment when Jo had told her to fuck off. Suddenly it felt very difficult to call her a friend.

Her best friend. Since primary school. These things go up and down, for sure: and not many people maintain friendships from that far back; but it really had felt terminal at the time.

Miranda turned from the window. On her desk were the papers for tomorrow – well, not just tomorrow, but for the whole case. Funny how things worked out. As she left Care City that day, a year or so ago, she had felt firm in her conviction that it was the last time she would have anything to do with either Jo or the stupid little quasi-communist nonsense she was involved in. She would probably have been persuaded, had someone attempted to do so, that she would in due course be reconciled with Jo and that at some point in the coming months or years they would once again crack open a bottle of fine red wine and resume their deep mix of speculation, reminiscence, gossip and giggles. But she would not have believed – again, had someone had the opportunity and the foresight to suggest it – that she would, instead, become completely embroiled in Visco's landmark legal case to establish the very essence of its right to self-determination.

It had all started back in January, just a few hours after Jo had been called by Tanya Golding, of Golding Associates. The transition contract with Statement had by that point come to an end, so Jo had not been able to call on their legal team. In any case, as the full extent of Visco's radical agenda became clearer, Statement had been judiciously distancing itself, sending progressively denser clouds of evasive informational chaff into the mediasphere, and would probably have refused to make any support available even if Jo had asked.

Jo had asked Miranda instead.

"I've just spoken with someone called Tanya Golding," said Jo's plaintive voice over the telephone. "They want to build a shopping centre in the middle of Visco."

Four or five months had passed since the 'fuck off' incident and Miranda's memory initially summoned the longer, deeper past rather than its more recent cousin. For a few moments she had simply felt a huge desire to administer one of her trademark hugs. Her friend sounded genuinely lost as she explained the call she had received, the dire consequences now apparently in play and how suddenly very exposed she felt. The woman on the phone, Joanna Castle, was simply her best friend, small and far away and needing help.

The hurt and the distance nevertheless came flooding back.

It had been too much simply to be discarded; but now was not the time to fix things. Miranda clicked into professional mode. She may not be getting on with this person right now, but they still had history; and, rude though she may have been about what Visco seemed to have become, she was still on board with the idea at some level. Somewhere in her brain, too, was a thought that, given how fruitful the whole thing had so far been for her, yet more opportunities might lie ahead.

"Sounds like we'd better meet up," Miranda said.

And so they had. It had not been comfortable, but there had been just enough love and just enough will to see them through. They managed to sketch a provisional way forward.

"OK, leave it with me," had been Miranda's parting words, "I think I need to talk with Peter."

Now, standing in her office, Miranda glanced over at a file of correspondence marked 'Peter Tiresias'. She was going to be a witness in the case. She was not a lawyer or a planner, but she had led the university's work on the Care City project since the beginning and she had continued to lead it over the past few months as things became ever more painful. She was not going to back away now.

The first steps had been relatively straightforward. She spoke, as planned, with Peter Tiresias. He had been consistently supportive since she and Jo had met him on the island – two years ago, Miranda realised with a shock – and it had proven un-necessary to explain why she was calling. He had been expecting her call, he told her: the planning application had been received and the formal process was underway. There were statutory timetables and procedures to follow. Evidence and arguments would be gathered, there would be meetings and inspections, there would be planners and environmental impact assessments and so on and so forth.

"I should tell you," Peter explained, in a low voice, "that the support for Visco from within the council means that there is almost no chance that the Golding application will be successful." Miranda had emitted a noise somewhere between laugh, yelp and cough. "However," he had continued, with little pause, "that will merely be the beginning of the process." He gave a longer pause. "If my experience is anything to go by, Golding and those behind her will already have planned for this eventuality. They will, I'm sure, appeal, possibly more than once. They will have, I suspect, considerable resources."

Soon afterwards, Miranda secured a crash course in planning law from a colleague at the university. The easy bit, apparently, was what happened if you wanted to build something: a tower block, a house, an office, it didn't matter. You applied for permission to the local council and they said either yes or no. You had to supply drawings and diagrams and details of what you wanted to build, but essentially you just had to fill in a form. The council then said either yes or no depending mainly on whether or not your new building was 'in accord' with the various rules and regulations that the council was legally obliged to publish from time to time. This meant – for example – that you couldn't usually build tower blocks in the middle of low-rise housing estates, or housing estates in the middle of the woods, or offices where there are supposed to be shops. The council's official documents would have a big map somewhere saying 'This is a wood' and permission will not be given to build anything in this wood, because it's a wood.

From time to time, someone would apply for permission to build something just on the margin – maybe a slightly taller building, or some houses just on the edge of the wood, or a small office that looked very like a shop because it had a big glass window. If the council said no, you can't build that small office, you might disagree with them: after all, what's the difference between a small office and a small shop, really? And if you decided to challenge that decision, this was called 'an appeal'.

The interesting thing about an appeal, Miranda's colleague explained, was the change in the people involved in the decision. When you first asked for permission to build your tower or house or office the people making the decision were 'officers' of the local council – people who worked for the council – and the local politicians. If they said no and you appealed, she learned, the next step of the process was a legal one: a court, with lawyers and a judge, would decide – and they would decide not whether your tower was too tall or your house too near the woods or your office insufficiently like a shop but, rather, whether the council had the legal power to have said no. And, just like many other areas of law, if your first appeal didn't result in the outcome you were hoping, you had the right to appeal again. And again. And maybe again.

Which is where the considerable resources come in, Miranda came to understand. Once it becomes a squabble between lawyers it starts to depend on just how many lawyers you've got, and how good they are, and how much time you can devote to making your case and so on and so forth. The big boys and girls could simply outgun the small fry and either blast or grind them into submission. Out on the island, on the one side, a small and cash-strapped local council together with a rag-bag of make-it-up-as-we-go-along idealists; and, on the other, Golding Associates, backed by an unknown but probably sizeable group of big businesses apparently intent on extinguishing an emerging alternative to their preferred way of doing things.

It seemed a little unbalanced, Miranda remembered thinking. This turned out to be something of an underestimate.

Exactly six weeks after the planning application had been submitted the council issued its decision and, as Peter had foreseen, formally refused permission to the consortium represented by Golding Associates. Precisely twenty four hours later, and again as Peter had predicted, Golding Associates formally appealed against the decision.

As soon as the appeal was lodged, Golding Associates played their next card: representatives of Visco, they said, had no legal basis to be involved in the appeal. Visco was, after all, no more than a short-term tenant on the land it occupied. It had the right to submit its opinion to the appeal, but that was all, they said.

This turned out to be true. Visco's permission to be on the island at all was in the form of a short-term lease, initially negotiated with the landowners by Statement for the purposes of The Big Float. Robert's transitional arrangements had included an extension to that short-term lease, but only an extension. Come the end of June – just four months away by this point - the lease would expire and, in theory at least, everyone in Visco could be evicted. The land might have to be returned to low-grade agriculture and marsh – and then turned into shiny new shops.

The university's senior cheeses had initially indicated a willingness to help – it had, after all, sizeable faculties in both law and land-use planning – but this willingness began swiftly to evaporate as the true nature of the challenge became apparent. The challenge was not merely to summon sufficient mental and financial resources to ensure a fair fight in court; it became to withstand the wider manoeuvres of the more generalised backlash against Visco.

It would probably be impossible, Miranda reflected as she continued to idle through the various files and folders on her desk, to know exactly how much of what happened was co-ordinated. The critical news items and opinion pieces that had made their first appearances in January became, as February went by, more frequent and more hostile. Individuals that claimed once to have lived in Care City or Visco spoke of a cult, and of lawlessness, and of abuse. Businesses claiming to have been evicted, or to have had their livelihood jeopardised, appeared from the ether. Emboldened politicians spoke on television and on-line about the Declaration of Care and the threat it posed to democracy, to the local wildlife and to the right of people everywhere to go shopping whenever and wherever they liked.

Then, a couple of weeks or so after Golding had initiated the appeal process at the end of February – and at this recollection Miranda suddenly found herself wanting a stiff gin – one of the university's largest grant applications was unexpectedly turned down. A week or so later, it happened again, a different department. A week after that – it must have been late March, Miranda reckoned – a paper she had submitted for a prestigious conference was rejected. It became apparent that more-or-less everyone involved in the Visco case was suddenly finding almost every aspect of their life more difficult. There were instances of credit card fraud, minor traffic accidents, difficulties obtaining insurance. An alarming and astonishingly varied list began to accumulate.

"You're just being paranoid!" Mike had said on one occasion. He had come to see her in her offices on some pretext or other, superficially to do with the appeal proceedings, but mainly – Miranda suspected – because Mike had a bit of a crush on her.

"Inducing paranoia appears to be their plan," Miranda had replied. The pressure took its toll. The senior cheeses at the university became more and more anxious and began to row back from their previous commitments to the Visco project. A handful of the bigger charities, which until then had been happy to be seen contributing, were suddenly not answering calls. The Trust, upon which the entire long-term viability of Visco seemed to depend, began to see finance houses and ratings agencies whispering of possible weaknesses and hidden risks.

Miranda opened the second draw of her desk and pulled out a half-bottle of gin. The third draw revealed tonic, glasses and a bottle opener. There was no lemon and no ice. No matter. She threw a mouthful down her throat.

With the appeal case due to be heard towards the end of May, April saw the noise level ratchet up still further. Across all social media platforms minor battles raged between Visco citizens and non-resident supporters, on the one hand, and a slippery army of trolls, bots and belligerent aggressors on the other. Two minor political parties and one rather bigger party issued documents essentially critical of the Declaration of Care and calling on the judicial process to protect the rights of ordinary citizens by allowing the retail outlets to be built so that hard-working families could visit the inaccessible and unattractive island in the middle of nowhere to go shopping. Some of the agencies that had, up until this point at least, been happy to see their costs of care transferred to Visco began to find their own financial status undermined in the markets. With just a few weeks to go before the appeal, the university formally announced its intention to continue to provide support to what they still called the "Care City initiative" – but only, and in acknowledgement of its previous commitments, up to the appeal case. Thereafter it would be disengaging completely.

Miranda suddenly stood rather straighter at the window. The university's decision – against her expressed wishes and judgment – had been the point at which, for her, the whole game had changed. Up until then she had been committed and serious, yes, but perhaps not completely invested in the project itself. Not passionate, in the way she knew that Jo was passionate about the whole thing. But from that moment she had become seriously pissed off. She did not like being pushed around. She disliked losing even more.

In one respect, the timing turned out to be serendipitous. Although Visco itself had continued growing as winter had turned into spring – the population by late April was up around the 20,000 mark - many on the Visco side of the argument were exhausted and many others were scared. Jo, especially, was struggling: on top of the months of hard work, her father had only just died.

Looming especially large was the lease on the land. Irrespective of Tanya Golding, irrespective of the appeal, irrespective – if one's skin was thick enough – of the ever-fiercer backlash, the one thing that could categorically kill the whole project was if the owners of the land refused to extend the lease any further. Eviction was a real possibility. Finding an alternative site even at the best of times would have been tough; doing so in a climate of surround-sound hostility would have been simply impossible.

Scheduled for the very day after the university announced its decision to disassociate itself from "the Care City initiative" was a meeting with the land-owners. Jo and Miranda were both going. They had taken advice from Robert (well, Miranda had taken advice from Robert; Jo was still refusing to speak with him) as well as from Peter and a variety of lawyers and other specialists at the university. But Miranda went into the meeting armed not merely with a wealth of technical and legal detail; she carried, too, a weapons-grade fury at the bastards who were trying to bring Visco down. Said bastards had, needless to say, been making voluptuous offers and enticements to each of the landowners through the medium of Golding Associates.

Miranda was quite certain that the financial offer made to the three landowners by Golding Associates would have been astronomical and far in excess of anything that Visco could muster. But the landowners were not disembodied financial objects made of equations and electrons; they were not third-party representatives of distant portfolios and internationally mobile capital; they were not even middle-tier entrepreneurs eyeing a once-in-a-lifetime opportunity to make a fortune. They were farmers, three farmers who had spent lifetimes with the big sky and the sea-wall, with the flat-horizoned island and its mystical birdlife, its peculiar winds, its eerie night noises, its long-embedded marsh myths. Yes, they were glad of the incomes that The Big Float had brought them; and, yes, they were bug-eyed at the golden fortunes being dangled before them by Golding Associates.

But they were also receptive to the blazing passion that poured from Miranda that day as she burst into the room and their souls. Miranda talked not of rates of return and capital accumulation and diversification opportunities and life-changing wealth but, instead, of future generations and custodianship and the growth of the soil and love and – and care. Standing in her office, her spine tingled at the recollection, how she had abandoned her notes and talked of the thousands of lives on the island and the dreams these landowners held in their hands, how she'd moved beyond mere story and begun weaving a genuine mythology. Despite the piles of paper and the months of stress and the daunting prospect of the morrow, she straightened and grew. Who does not succumb to true myth? The landowners had barely hesitated. She stared from the window, a steely smile breaking across her face. She downed the rest of the gin.

A deal had been struck and Visco's tenure was secured. They agreed a lease for a hundred years. For a few glorious hours Jo's smile had returned and Miranda was exultant and they were friends again. For a few glorious hours, the whole of Visco seemed to lift into the spring air rising from the island around them. For a few glorious hours, they felt as though they'd won.

It had only lasted hours. Miranda shook her head ruefully. How naïve she had been. Golding Associates barely flinched at the setback. The media attacks intensified, the disruption of daily lives continued, the lawyers sent ever more complex and burdensome material deemed relevant to the appeal. The lease on the land meant Visco had secured the right to be present at the appeal; but the prospect of defeat in court simply grew more overwhelming with each passing day.

Miranda refilled her glass. She gazed once again at the file marked 'Peter Tiresias'. In the end, he had saved them. Or, perhaps more accurately, he had pointed them – he had pointed Miranda – in the direction of safety.

"Hello Dr Farnaby," he'd said. It had been the middle of May, only a couple of weeks before the appeal was scheduled to begin. She could still recall his soft tone, that slightly quirky accent, the sense it induced of not being sure whether this was good news or bad news. "Do you have a moment? I wanted to share something with you."

What a share it had been. Law, as Miranda's university colleagues had made clear, is based on precedent. Like a great tributary system, its various channels are all ultimately connected; but sometimes what is the case over there has not yet become the case over here. Sometimes we need merely to notice that a precedent in one case could equally apply in another case. Sometimes – and Miranda congratulated herself a little on this metaphor - we can use the land to skip from one tributary to another rather than sticking to the waterways.

"Listen," he said, "we want to make sure you're aware of a couple of very interesting historic cases where a branch of government has, as it were, handed over its powers and duties to a new and separate agency." Miranda noted but did not query the 'we'. He continued: "For example, there was a case some forty or so years ago – you may be too young to remember – where London's government was temporarily abolished. In its dying days the outgoing administration simply gifted a piece of land in the middle of the city, right by the river, to a local community group. The transfer probably had a book value of hundreds of millions, perhaps billions, but it was done for pennies. The community group suddenly owned housing and offices and a small park and so on, but also took on responsibility for waste collection and street cleaning and a few other bits and pieces. It was not perhaps fully appreciated at the time but the departing authority had effectively created a small-scale local council, right in the heart of the city." Miranda recalled learning about this, perhaps as an under-graduate. She began to feel a little weak-kneed.

"A few years later," Peter continued, "perhaps thirty five years ago, central government itself did something not dissimilar, but on a much bigger scale, in London's Docklands. Perhaps you recall? Several hundred hectares of land were handed over to a consortium, not of residents this time but of businesses. And the consortium – they called themselves the Vertical Infrastructure, Regeneration, Growth and Investment Network, I believe – were not only given the land but also pretty much the fully responsibilities of a local council. Despite having no democratic accountability at all, they were given control over business rates, over local utilities, waste collection, that sort of thing. Most particularly," and here Peter very definitely paused for effect, "they were given control over planning. Control over the decisions about what could and could not be built."

Miranda remembered simply slumping into her chair at this point. Was he really about to say what she thought he was about to say?

"Myself and colleagues here," Peter resumed, "believe that we may be able to transfer our powers in a similar way. Assuming certain conditions can be met, we believe that Visco could assume control over planning on its part of the island." Miranda's eyes had begun to well up. "Such a move would, we believe, fundamentally change the situation. In the immediate term, the appeal process would have to be suspended." Why? Miranda silently asked. "This is because the relevant planning authority – that would be you – would have to have its own planning policy against which the appeal could be judged. Even the sternest judge would have to accept you might need a little time to formulate a planning policy..."

Fundamental change indeed. Miranda drained her second gin and tonic. Her smile was broad. Using an ancient legal manoeuvre, a relic from times of war in the Middle Ages, Peter's local council had indeed and swiftly transferred its planning responsibilities to Visco. Since Visco had no planning policies in place, there was no means of assessing whether the decision to refuse permission to the Golding consortium was or was not legal. The appeal process came to an immediate halt. Golding Associates – that shiny veneer on the dark disguise of the massed forces of the vested interests – had not reacted well. This had very definitely not been in their playbook. Out of desperation they launched an entirely new – and altogether more substantive – legal challenge, far bigger than a mere appeal against a planning decision to refuse permission to build some shops.

And now, here they were. Tomorrow, in court, the case would be heard. Could Peter and his colleagues legally grant such powers to Visco? Was Visco, with its rudimentary democratic processes and its scary Declaration of Care, an entity capable of bearing such responsibilities? Would Visco, if it did carry such powers and responsibilities, be obliged to accede to the Golding demands that all citizens, everywhere and everywhen, had the right (perhaps even the duty) to go shopping – or could it genuinely step out and onto an entirely new path?

Miranda straightened the pile of papers marked 'Peter Tiresias'. She picked up her coat and her bag. She recalled the glorious moment when she had persuaded those wonderful farmers on the island to grant a future to Visco and she felt that same iridescent passion filling her limbs and her torso. She and her smile walked out of the office and into the future.

Jo

It was the day before the start of the court case, late September, fifteen months since The Big Float had ended and nine months since Care City became Visco. Jo was in bed, her limbs entangled with Daniel's. After some slow, quiet, intense sex, they were lying silently with their thoughts. Daniel's fingers drew little circles with her hair. She could feel the heat from his torso. She rested her hand on the side of his chest, rising and falling.

"What do you think will happen?" she asked.

"I don't know," he replied.

"Yes, I know you don't know, but what do you think?"

A pause. "Nope. Nothing. I have no idea."

She dug a gentle finger into some soft part of him.

"What if we lose?" she tried.

"That would be very sad," he said.

Her turn to pause. "Would you cry?"

"I don't know," he said, twisting slightly to avoid a digging finger, should it come.

"OK, OK. What do we do if we do lose?" she asked, for the first time with a little urgency.

He swivelled to lie on his side, gazing at her now, legs still entangled beneath the duvet.

"What would you like to do?" he asked.

"Why are you avoiding my questions?" she responded.

"Because this isn't really about me, is it?"

"It's not really about me either."

"I'm pleased to hear you say that sub-commandanté Castle," Daniel teased, "but on this special occasion I fancy you may be permitted an indulgence..." He had to move quite quickly to avoid an incoming finger jab.

"Seriously though..." Jo said.

"Seriously what?"

"Seriously. What's going to happen if we lose?"

"Well, I suppose we have to shut up shop."

"And then?"

"And then we'll have to decide what to do next."

Jo made a noise that was part moan, part laugh and part shriek and sat up. She began adjusting pillows and pulling at the duvet and fending off Daniel's apologetic limbs.

"OK, OK," Daniel laughed. "How about this: Honey, don't you worry, everything will be just fine. Even if we lose, we'll find a nice little place of our own and start on over..."

She looked at him. His eyes danced. She loved him. She wanted the meaningless reassurance. She didn't want the meaningless reassurance.

"You still have no idea how fabulous you are, do you?" he said.

She turned from the gaze with a half-hearted harrumph. His hand arrived on her thigh. His fingers idled. She wriggled her toes and watched the duvet move accordingly.

"I don't know what I'll do," she said. "A bit of me thinks I'll be so bloody furious if we lose that I'll just start a new Care City somewhere else. Might do a better job this time, too. The thought of that bitch

Tanya Golding actually winning. Jesus." Jo could feel her muscles tensing, and the pressure from Daniel's fingers increasing to match. "I wonder which bit of me that is?"

Daniel seemed to be manoeuvring beneath the duvet, his intent unclear. She ignored him.

"The other bit, or bits of me, however many that is, those bits just feel knackered and if we lose they'll be glad, I'll be glad, and I can have a holiday somewhere nice for a few weeks and then get back to normal."

"Normal?" came Daniel's muffled reply.

"Yes, normal," she said, obstinately. She knew that normal had long gone and would never return.

"And what if we win?" he asked.

Jo had a bit of a scratch, under her arm, down the side of one breast and then at the back of her left calf. Daniel seemed to have stopped moving.

"Do you think we might win?"

"I don't know."

She turned her head and glared at the thinning hair on the top of his head.

"If we win," she began, slowly, "I shall banish you to the far eastern wastelands for all eternity..."

His under-duvet attack was swift, but not as swift as her shimmy with twist, nor her counter-attack direct to the soft flesh on the underside of his upper arm. They wrestled for some moments until she secured victory, sitting astride his stomach and pinning down his arms. He was in pretty good shape for a guy in his mid-fifties; but she was still a lean mean fightin' machine, capable - should it prove necessary - of throwing him over her shoulder and carrying him down a ladder.

"I think," he said, struggling through the giggles, "that you should organise a party."

"What, now?"

"No! If we win. If you win."

"A party."

"Yes." He stretched his neck, hoping to kiss her. "A big one."

"A big party."

"Actually," he continued, "I've been thinking about this for a while."

"Eh?"

"Well, not so much a party. More of a celebration. A carnival."

"A carnival."

"Yup. Carnival. What do you know about carnival?"

She reflected while she released his arms, slid from his stomach and lay alongside him. "Nope, next to nothing. Floats, marching bands, late night cavorting, rum, that's about it. Tell me more." She liked it when he thought out loud.

"Carnival," he began, "from the Latin, 'carne' and 'vale'. Goodbye meat. It's a festival, Christian, though I dare say the Christians borrowed it from someone else, a festival that takes place at the beginning of Lent. It's a celebration of survival. You and your tribe worked hard last summer and stockpiled loads of food, which you've been eking out all winter, and winter is just about over. You've survived. Spring is coming, and the big spring fertility thing is just a few weeks away, and your tradition is to honour the gods and prepare for the coming bounty by fasting. You're going to fast for several weeks. It's a big thing. You've survived." Jo was rapt, and wrapped around him. "So you throw a big party, several days' worth, in which you eat all the remaining food, everything. All the meat that's made it through winter. Good bye meat; hello carnival."

"Wow," Jo said.

"It's mutated since it started, of course," Daniel continued. "The wild partying, in particular, became steadily more important. And there's less meat. But the partying has an interesting dimension. It's not just excess booze and food, it's a certain wildness, a certain lawlessness. To survive the winter everyone needs to work together, everyone is in the same boat, so the rules are tough. And you're about to fast for forty days and forty nights or whatever, and that's going to be tough, too. So for a few days, just for a few days, between the end of one set of rules and the beginning of the next set, the rules go. Jettisoned. Anything goes."

"And," Jo interjected, "the people who set the rules?"

"Exactly," said Daniel. "They disappear. Or they join in. That's one of the reasons you see so many costumes at carnival – everyone is in disguise, everyone is suddenly equal. Want to spend a few days as an ostrich, or a skeleton, or a doughnut? Want to have sex with your neighbour? Want to get lost in the dodgy side of town in the company of dangerous criminals? Carnival."

"Sounds scary."

"It is. Lawlessness. No-one's in charge. And everyone's in charge. An anarchist's dream. The semioticians love it too. Normally someone somewhere lays on the entertainment and the rest of us are the audience. In carnival, there's no difference: the audience is the carnival, and the carnival is the audience."

"Sounds exciting."

"It is." He paused. "And I think it would be just perfect for Visco. If you win. If we win."

"Because," Jo said, completing his argument out loud, "because we'd have survived, and we're all in charge, and a time of abundance lies ahead."

"Something like that."

"Wow," she said again.

They lay staring at the ceiling. It was dark outside and few noises arrived from the island around them. Jo and Daniel were still touching one another – their hips, an ankle, a finger or two – but neither moved.

"A creative time," Jo ventured.

"What do you mean?"

"Well, all those costumes, and the music, and having to think how to use up all those leftovers. All very creative."

"Yes," he said. "I hadn't thought about it like that."

"People love it when they're free to be creative," she continued.

"Yup."

"And we don't exactly live an agrarian existence anymore, do we?"

"Where are you heading?" Daniel asked, the merest goosebump beginning its journey along his neck.

"And there's no way Visco could be described as Christian. So I'm just wondering," and the fairy dust in her voice was almost audible, "what scope there is for us having our very own version of carnival..."

Daniel very deliberately did not interrupt.

Jo resumed: "I can definitely see that – if we win, and only if we win – a celebration would be the right thing to do. And modelling it on carnival sounds right, too. But you know what? We could do much more than that." She sat up. "We could invert the whole thing. Turn it on its head. What if..." she trailed off. "Imagine. With the Trust up and running, and the land secure, we don't need to spend all spring and summer breaking our backs to grow all the food. And there's a million and one things that get dealt with by the tech rather than the humans, so apart from actually looking after each other there isn't really that much to do.

"What if," she said, eyes blazing, "what if we turned it on its head? What if we spend two weeks a year doing all the work, and fifty weeks a year doing carnival! Fuck. We could probably do a few deals on the Trust and make all the money we'd need for a year. We could do any upgrades and overhauls on the tech, and any major maintenance on the buildings or whatever. Maybe it would take a month, but still. And robots! The robots can handle all the routine stuff. One month working hard, and eleven months looking after each other, and following our creative instincts. We'd have to have a few people on maintenance and cleaning and cooking, sure, but..." She went quiet again.

He looked at her. "See. That's why you're –"

"I'm not in charge!" she barked.

"-the person we need," he finished. Before she could apologise he moved on: "It seems to me that what you've just said fits perfectly with the Declaration of Care."

She smiled. The Declaration. The basis for a new way. How had Daniel expressed it all those months ago? A statement of principle? Yes – but more than that: a statement of what the point is. "Everything else will follow," he'd said. And here it was, following. She pounced on him, hugging and kissing with gratitude and love and – suddenly – passion.

"It's getting late!" he yelped, weakly. "You've got a big day tomorrow!"

"If we win," she purred, "I've got a big day the day after tomorrow, and the day after, and the day after that..."

Part Four: The Year After That

Dreams

There were unsettling dreams during the night.

Robert Dunbar dreamed he was driving a sports car. The car was going very slowly and the steering wheel was melting. He got out of the car and people threw toothpicks at him. A boy with a wooden sword was hitting his legs, above the ankle. He tried to grab the sword but his knees gave way.

Miranda Farnaby dreamed she was on a catwalk. Everyone was applauding, but when she looked at them they were empty husks. She began to tear at the fashionable items she had been forced to wear, but they turned into glutinous sods of oil. She threw the sods and they hissed and steamed when they landed.

Michael Smith dreamed he was lost in a housing estate. He ran up and down and left and right and back and forth. The building was suddenly very high. It was full of helpless people that he could not find. He found a broken bottle, and a shoe that did not fit. The corridor was dark. He could see light at the other end, but not how to get there.

Joanna Castle dreamed she was on a beach. It was hot and crowded. She was travelling very quickly on some sort of flying skateboard, weaving between the towels and families and sunscreens. She did not hit anyone. She kept not falling off. She felt exhilarated.

The court case is not a dream. It is a nightmare.

There are cameras and journalists everywhere, all of the time. There are expensive lawyers, sleek executives and menacing officials. Giving evidence is terrifying; being cross-examined is worse. The court room is austere and the clerks are chilling. The public gallery is intimidating and the judges – all five of them – are scary. It goes on for four and a half days.

Jo and Miranda go to the pub as soon as the judges retire to deliberate. The judges are deciding whether Visco can legally be given its new powers; they are deciding whether Visco can continue to exist.

"Cheers," says Jo, clinking her glass of white wine against her friend's gin and tonic.

"Cheers," Miranda replies.

"Well, at least we tried," says Jo.

"Indeed we did," says Miranda, "indeed we did."

They sit in exhausted silence. Miranda nudges Jo's elbow and signals to the window. Tanya Golding, together with a dozen corporate lawyers and executives, is laughing and chatting goodbye across the street. They exude confidence and victory. They have the air of those accustomed to winning. They know they set the rules: how on earth can they be beaten?

"Cunts," proposes Miranda.

"Cheers to that," says Jo.

The two women watch as the group slowly disperses: some call cabs, some step into their chauffeured vehicles, some leave on foot to their nearby club.

"I just kept looking at the chief judge," says Jo. "I'm sure she winked at one point. Straight at that one." She indicates a tall and expensively-dressed man in his mid-sixties at that moment kissing Tanya Golding on the cheek. "They probably went to the same school."

"Cunts."

"And I can't believe that all that evidence we had about the coercive behaviour was dismissed as inadmissible. For chrissakes, the things they've done to us. To you! And they decide it's not relevant to the case!"

"Cun-"

"Yes, yes, I get it," Jo cuts across. They look at one another – and burst out laughing.

"Fuck fuck fuck fuck," Miranda machine-guns.

"Thank you for that contribution, Dr Farnaby," says Jo, mimicking the chief judge's polished vowels, "but I think you'll find it's time for another drink."

They drink heavily that first evening, and again the second. They drink a little less on the third evening and barely at all the fourth. On the morning of the next day, the message arrives: the judges have reached a decision.

The area outside the court is like a rugby match between a dozen teams at once, a crushing pulsing heave of noise and bodies, bristling with shouts and cameras as if the whole world is watching. The whole world is watching. The drones reel like starlings overhead, the cables sneak endlessly along the ground, the media vehicles and transmission dishes block the light. Simply reaching court is a trial.

Inside, the atmosphere itches with anticipation. Both sides huddle and whisper, check devices and papers, smile at friends and avoid the gaze of enemies. The clerks summon order, everyone stands and the judges file in. Jo feels sick.

The chief judge begins speaking. Jo can hear the words but as though they are coming from far away down a long tube. She listens hard but hopelessly. The words make no sense. The judge is explaining their reasoning. Jo glances at the corporate faces to her left. She learns nothing from their blank power. She glances right to the faces of inexperience and anxiety.

The tone of the judge's voice conveys some sort of crescendo, progress towards a peak, towards the words that will actually announce their decision. Still Jo cannot force her mind to hear the words. She is glad she is sitting down. She can hear only the thunder of the blood in her ears.

And then a new thunder. It doesn't make sense. Simultaneously she hears the words the judge had uttered a few seconds earlier, and feels the roar from around her, and the shriek of delight and disbelief leaving her own throat. Someone grabs her, and someone else, and there is hugging and shouting and noise beyond comprehension and the judge calling order and mayhem and the tiny bleached and disbelieving faces of Golding and her associates and HOLY SHIT WE WON.

Holy shit. They won.

Carnival

T here is a short debate about whether it is appropriate to start a carnival in September, but only a short one. The new and now legal Council of Visco agrees unanimously that the carnival will begin in ten days' time. Even as they agree this they know that their decision is almost arbitrary: the celebrations began within minutes of the court judgment and show few signs of abating.

The official population of Visco at the start of the court case stood at 44,833. It has a hospital, three schools, eight health centres and eleven places of worship or meditation. There are dozens of refectories, cafés and restaurants. Most of the town is still made up of the click-and-play accommodation units installed when Statement was in charge: there are blocks for those that wish to live on their own, blocks for families and blocks for those that prefer to live more communally. There are offices and workshops and warehouses and repair shops and food stores and sprawling all-purpose halls where people can play or paint or pad about. There are benches and ponds. The glasshouses made out of plastic still surround the main town square, and many of the plants that used to be in the glasshouses now surround the city's many smaller parks and squares.

People move around on foot, mostly. Some are in wheelchairs or make use of other mobility devices. The original grid layout remains evident in the middle of the settlement, but there is an increasingly higgledy piggledy network of roads and pathways where the town is expanding onto the former festival site and more generally out across the marsh. There are two electrically-powered minibuses with a top speed of about 20 kilometres an hour. Many people cycle. Most are able to traverse the roughly oval Visco site in less than fifteen minutes on a bike and those that occasionally cycle the boundary of the entire island do so in just over an hour. There are no lorries or cars in Visco, although there are car-parks and depots on the periphery. There is almost no traffic noise and the horizon remains ubiquitous.

Miranda and Peter are sitting in a café watching the world go by. It is a warm and sunny day, a week since the end of the court case. They see a group of children, perhaps twenty of them, perhaps aged 10 or 11, with their teacher and a couple of other adults. They are carrying reams of coloured paper, and staplers, and cardboard and scissors and boxes and glue and bags full of plastic and string. The teacher seems to have made the wise decision that they can make their carnival costumes while sitting outdoors. Everyone is smiling.

"How long do you think it will last?" asks Miranda.

Peter is slightly taken aback. He thinks she is asking how long Visco will last. She sees the expression on his face.

"No no," she chuckles. "I mean this... this feeling. This atmosphere." Neither of them are resident on the island, but they are frequent visitors. In the days since the conclusion of the court case Miranda has been staying in one of the guest blocks. "Isn't it just amazing? Not just the smiles – I mean, it's always been a pretty smiley place. A weight's been lifted. Everyone seems to be open. Floating."

Peter makes a throaty, almost tuneful noise of wordless agreement. It is, he agrees, amazing.

"I suspect it may last quite some time," he answers, eventually. "The sense of relief must be exceptional." Miranda enjoys the way he pronounces 'exceptional'. "I wonder," he continues, "if this might even become normal."

"Normal?"

"Yes. Normal. Every day." Miranda looks about her. It is difficult to say: in some respects, the scene about her looks 'normal'. There are people moving this way and that, getting on with their day, chatting with friends, thinking their thoughts, making their plans, working on their projects, big and small. In other respects, nothing is normal: many of the people in the vicinity are frail or disabled; there is no traffic noise; there are no advertisements. Not a single surface is emblazoned with a promotional message of any kind. "When I think of other places," Peter continues, "and I think of what is normal in those places, I cannot help but think 'normal' is shaped by the history of the place, and the people there, and all their myths and stories, and it changes incrementally, slowly, and one day people wake up and find that normal is noisy and hurried and stressful and they don't even know how it happened."

"That's what most sociologists would say," Miranda affirms, "in one way or another."

"So if the myths and stories and histories start with..." Peter casts a hand about him, "with this, then an entirely new normal begins. Don't you think?"

Miranda is thinking about the marvellous melting pot that Visco has become. The first wave of citizens – the conspicuously damaged – and the second – the rebels and refuseniks – stuck it out through those months when the whole of Visco was under attack and the entire project seemed likely to collapse, and they've forged something new. The care has grown and deepened, a sense of mission and belonging has strengthened, and now there are children running around for whom this will indeed be 'normal'.

"It'll take time," Miranda almost whispers, "but, yes, I think perhaps you're right. A new normal."

Miranda nods at Peter and slowly returns her gaze to the passing world. An elderly gentleman pushes a woman his age in her wheelchair. Two young men stroll, arm in arm. A group of people, perhaps seven or eight of them, mixed ages, genders and ethnicities, enters the refectory opposite. Two women in overalls, one carrying a bag of tools, head in the direction of the facilities block. Three teenagers, at a nearby table in the café, are crowded around a laptop screen: monitoring the world? Finding where they are on the rota? Writing some code?

Visco has several websites – for speaking with the world, for organising the duty roster, for dealing with suppliers and so on – as well as its own radio station and a small press office. There are two big libraries and seven smaller ones. Discussions on whether to set up a local currency, on hold for some months, have begun again since the ending of the court case.

"I am not sure about the idea," says Abena.

"What don't you like about it?" asks Jo.

Abena and Jo are eating in one of the refectories.

"Well, I like not having the money," Abena begins. "It means everyone is the same. At the foodbank people did not have money, and we just gave them food, of course. But that made them different. They were different from the people with money. People with money, and people without money. Awful. People with lots of money – even worse. Here, no-one can have more money than anyone else, because no-one has any money." This was not strictly-speaking true, of course:

people living on the island might very well have money, there was just no way of using it in Visco.

"I tend to agree with you," Jo replies, carefully. "And it's worked really well so far. But things are changing again and we need to be ready for that." Abena looks at her quizzically. Jo continues: "Mainly it's to do with the number of people. The more people we have here, the harder it gets to make things work without some sort of money. It's not that things will cost more, or people won't be able to have things. It's just that, at the moment, we have to keep track of absolutely everything on computer, and we have to rely on trust. Remember those thefts we had? There's bound to be more of that as we get bigger."

"We're getting bigger?"

"I think it's inevitable. We're getting applications from all over the world. There's been a big surge. Most people on the Council want to let pretty much anyone come who wants to come. We could easily double in size over the next few months..."

"Goodness," says Abena. "Refugees from all over the world."

"Yup."

"And they're going to need money?"

"Well, it's not that they're going to need money exactly," Jo replies. "I mean, a lot of people pretty much give up their money in order to come here in the first place." One of the criteria for entry for most people is to invest their pensions or savings into the island's Trust. There are ways to get your money back if you decide to leave – Robert was very careful to make sure that Visco could not be accused of being a predatory cult - but few people have so far wanted to leave. "But just think about it. At the moment, you walk into the café and ask for a cup of coffee and it's just given to you, whether you live here or whether you're a visitor. Walk into the repair shop and – hey presto, we'll fix your device. No charge. Need some new bedsheets? Some toilet roll? A new blouse? Head for the stores, pick the ones you want – no charge." Jo pauses, takes a sip of water, then resumes: "And no choice, either. Well, not exactly no choice, but you know what I mean. People have to have what's available. If there was money, then people would be able to say – I'm prepared to pay a bit more for that rather than this, which would mean we'd know that people wanted more of that than this, and we could make more of that than this…"

Jo loses momentum. Abena's face has shifted from quizzical to mystified. Jo realises she does not believe her own argument. Suddenly it just sounds… ludicrous.

"I'd been thinking," Jo says, attempting to explain herself, "about if everyone in Visco had the same basic income. If everyone was just given, I don't know, 10,000 buttons at the beginning of the year, and then they could spend it on the things they wanted to spend it on, and that would provide incentives to the people making things. I don't know. Let's say I make ceramic tiles. No. Let's say I enjoy making ceramic tiles. Well, if I was in London I'd have to buy my equipment, wouldn't I? I'd have to buy blank tiles, and paints and paintbrushes and things like that, and I'd need access to a kiln. And I'd have a job, and I'd earn money, and I'd use some of that money to buy the things I needed and I could get on and happily paint my tiles."

Abena is listening intently. She has finished her lunch. Jo's food has gone cold.

"Well, maybe I put some of my tiles on sale in the corner store, and a few people like them and they buy them and I get a few buttons from the sales and I can use those buttons to buy some more equipment, some more paint and blank tiles, and I sell a few more and I get a few more buttons and so on and so on. So the money isn't just money, is it? It sends a signal. It tells me – it tells everyone – people like this rather than that. So it makes it easier to decide to do more of this rather than that." Jo is hurtling along now, at risk of tripping, possibly even falling, but relaxed that – in present company at least – it will not hurt. "Here in Visco, it doesn't quite work like that, does it? I can paint tiles if I want to, but there might not be any tiles available to paint today because we're having to guess how many tiles might be needed. And there's no real incentive for me to make more tiles, because no-one buys them. People might like them, and take them from the store, but I don't get anything from that. I don't have an incentive..."

Abena lets her trip again; then speaks. "We are leaving all that behind," she says, compassion and conviction mixed in equal measure. "That is the old way of doing things." The enveloping warmth Jo remembers from the first time they met is embracing her. "If you love making tiles, make tiles. That is your incentive. Anything else is... a tyranny." Jo smiles, weakly. Abena continues: "And if we have to work hard to explain that to each new person, then that's just part of the care we have to give." She pauses again, and the warmth – the love – is almost numbing: "We have come so far; let us not go backwards. Individually we are penniless; together we are billionaires. We are a refugee camp for the world, a refugee camp that people choose to come to. No-one else is going to do this. We have a job to do..." and she pauses one last time to find the necessary idiom: "and we must not fuck it up."

Jo's weak smile dissolves into laughter and tears, and Abena comes around the table to comfort her. Jo sobs quietly for a little while, until her thoughts return: how will they explain so much to so many? How can a nebulous concept like 'care' triumph over huge and hard ideas like 'progress' and 'success' and 'money' and 'possessions'? How can a tiny experiment on a small island save the world?

"How can a tiny experiment on a small island save the world?" Michael asks Daniel. They are standing on the same gantry where Michael stood with Jo, almost a year and a half ago, just before The Big Float festival started.

"I don't know," replies Daniel. "You tell me, captain."

Michael is dressed as a pirate, a buccaneer from a re-imagined version of the seventeenth century. About half his carnival costume was made by children who live in Visco; he made the other half himself. He looks fabulously dishevelled.

"Well I don't know either," Michael responds. "I suppose all change has to start somewhere. So why not here?" He looks across the scene of glorious mayhem beneath and around them. "I'm glad I was wrong," he continues. "I really thought we'd lose."

"Most of us did," says Daniel. He is dressed as some sort of crustacean. He seems to be made mainly of re-used plastic. The costume does not look especially comfortable.

"Jo tells me that you think we should keep the carnival going forever," says Michael. Daniel sways his head from side to side, indicating ambiguous dissent. "Are you now permanently crab?" asks Michael.

Daniel laughs heartily, which Michael enjoys. He does not know him very well. Michael finds Daniel slightly mystifying, and the laughter is reassuring.

"I may experiment with other sea creatures," Daniel musters. "Depends how long the nautical vibe continues." It does seem to be something of a trend: many of the costumes and decorations and floats that are being made for the carnival have a sea-going air. It was not decided, it just happened.

"Tell me about it though," Michael presses. "How could a carnival go on forever? It sounds exhausting. And we'll all have permanent hangovers. I don't get it."

"The drinking won't be compulsory," Daniel begins. "In fact, I have a sneaking suspicion that most of the drinking we've been doing so far has been because the rest of our lives is so rubbish. People drink to forget, to escape the trials and tribulations of their day. If the day isn't so awful – if your life isn't so awful – then maybe you won't need to drink so much."

Michael looks at him while he pauses. He decides not to interject. He has heard from Jo how, if you let him, Daniel will sometimes just start talking, and the words go for a walk, and you can follow the words and you become lost in the story and Michael relaxes and Daniel continues:

"We have become so accustomed to things being hard, to life being a struggle. Happiness happens in little bursts, moments of relief. We eat a fine meal. We enjoy our family at a celebration. We see a wonderful film. And then we return, to the desk or the dishes, to the compromises and the mediocrity. We have so much technology, so much wealth, so much wisdom, and yet we have allowed ourselves to stay miserable." He pauses, his gaze drifting along the horizon.

"Disease! Imagine! On this very island. The history is fascinating. For centuries we didn't know how to cure the sick. They built a huge sanatorium here, thousands of beds. They simply rounded up the sick and brought them here to die. Not just here of course, but this was one of the biggest."

For a moment there are no words. Michael can hear amplified music, and muted birdsong, and the muffled shouts of excited children.

Daniel resumes: "Everything became frantic, no? In all the excitement. We learned how to cure diseases, and we built sewage systems, and people started living longer, and we invented supermarkets and colour televisions and budget airlines and suddenly we all just ran around in a frenzy – must buy this, must do that, must visit this place

and that place, must see this and do this and read this before I die."
Michael is transfixed. He is hearing his messy, confusing thoughts
turned into things he can believe. "And all the while, we hurt, we hurt,
and we hide it. We drink and we take drugs and we numb ourselves
with television and gambling and pornography. Everyone works and
works, mostly doing something we dislike, making ourselves stressed
and miserable so that we can have a few minutes of happiness at the
weekend. Or for two weeks in the summer."

Daniel turns to look at Michael, a sparkle in his eyes. "So we have
lots to unlearn!" he continues. "And then lots of new things to learn.
Or re-learn. I don't know. We have to learn how to be, how to play,
how to enjoy ourselves. How to care for ourselves as well as everyone
else. How to live a fulfilling life without the tyranny of goals. How to
feel that we are a good person without always striving to be better. Or
to have more. To sleep at night knowing that we gave love to someone
who needed it, and for that to be enough. To be good enough. For
enough to be enough..."

"You think this is the place where we can learn these things?"
Michael asks presently.

"I hope so," Daniel answers. "Yes, I think so. Yes, it has to be.
Where else is it going to happen?"

Michael feels goosebumps across his arms and neck. His eyes well
up. He isn't sure what to do or say or think or feel.

"In any case," Daniel says, coming to the rescue, "it was your sister
who decided that the carnival could go on forever, not me. I was just
suggesting a big party. She was speculating on what would happen if
we turned the world upside down."

Michael nods, slowly, the daze fading and a new freshness about his
face. He feels enveloped by sounds of music and laughter, of excited
yelps and animated conversation, of generators and ball-games. From

here on the gantry he can see the milling people of Visco and the settlement's ever-more organic buildings extending ever further across the island, and beyond that the ever-present horizon, flat and infinite.

"I did some back of the envelope calculations," Daniel says. "The Trust – it's a thing of beauty, by the way, you should really try to get to understand it sometime – it generates enough money each year to pay for pretty much everything we need to bring in. Food, medicine, materials, that sort of thing. Making sure the Trust actually works properly doesn't require a team of people working on it every day, or even every week. To be honest, you could probably spend just a few days each quarter, adjusting the portfolio, making sure it's all working as it's supposed to, and that would be enough." He looks closely at Michael, checking he's still with him. He is. Daniel continues: "And obviously we'll need food every day, and cleaning every day, and the actual looking after of people who need looking after every day. And between those two extremes we've got building work and maintenance work and repair work, and making clothes and so on, things that don't need doing every day but probably need doing more than one a year or once every few months."

"And on the back of your envelope..." Michael begins.

"...the average person on the island only needs to 'work' for about four weeks a year."

"Wow."

"Wow indeed."

"And if you're only working for one month a year," Michael extrapolates, "then you can party at carnival for the other eleven months."

"Well, perhaps not quite. Carnival becomes something of a metaphor. As I said, partying hard is something we only really do as some sort of escape." Michael suddenly remembers how cold and empty he felt that morning after the party in the warehouse with Tom. "If you're only working for a few weeks each year," Daniel continues, "then I'm not sure what there'll be to escape from. So it isn't so much a party as an opportunity to have fun, to live convivial lives, to explore our creativity..."

"So we might spend our time making costumes rather than wearing them?" Michael chuckles.

"Why not? Or writing poetry, or painting, or studying butterflies, or playing games, or researching liverworts or having deep conversations with new and interesting people..."

Michael looks sharply at Daniel and meets his dark, warm, smiling eyes. He can see why Jo loves him.

"I think you'd look good as a squid," says Michael.

Their laughter drifts out and down and merges with the laughter of thousands of others, lost yet never gone. The Carnival of Care has, officially, begun.

Diversion Ends

"I have to admit," says Kate Humboldt, "I do admire them." She is dressed, as ever, with impeccable and unsettling elegance: loose fitting pantaloons from an élite London boutique, imported mauve pumps, a one-off scarf from a prize-winning artisan called Moonshift. She is sitting in the contoured driving seat of her luxury automobile. Her deep maroon jacket, sporting a genuine eighteenth-century gold brooch, is on a hanger above the rear passenger seat.

Beside her – and, though less so than most other mortals, still somewhat intimidated by Humboldt's gestalt – sits Tanya Golding. They are parked on a low hill on the mainland, a couple of kilometres south of the island where the Carnival of Care has, officially, been going on for about a week. Erratic trees and intermittent copses obscure their line of sight in a couple of directions but, in most respects, they have a good view of the entire site. If they were to open a window they would be able to hear it, too, despite the prevailing wind. The windows are, however, shut, affording both privacy and effective air conditioning. Both of them are very fond of air conditioning.

"Admire them?" Tanya responds.

"Yes. I think they've achieved something astonishing."

"Astonishing," Tanya repeats, more to feel the word in her mouth than to endorse it. "Yes, I grant you, it is astonishing." She gazes forward, towards the tens of thousands of happy and invisible souls. Towards the labyrinth of predominantly low-rise and increasingly multi-coloured buildings. Towards the physical manifestation of everything she and her associates fought so hard to stop. "Yes, I'll grant you that. But it doesn't mean I don't want to stop them. Admire, yes. Support, no."

Kate Humboldt is wearing the smile that so unsettles Jo and Miranda. It is the smile of an emperor. She is not an emperor, but she is now the chief executive of Statement plc and, as such, almost unimaginably powerful. She enjoys power. Very much. She enjoys benevolence, too; there is a special kind of benevolence that only the truly powerful can administer. She enjoys the prospect of benevolence, the process of deciding whether or not to be benevolent. It makes her smile.

"What are your next moves?" she asks.

Tanya shifts almost imperceptibly in the seat. What she says in the next few minutes – and how she says it – will have a very considerable bearing on the future not only of the programme to subvert the Visco project but the future, too, of Golding Associates and, obviously, Tanya Golding.

"Well the consortium was obviously very pleased to have had the support of Statement during the spring and summer," Tanya begins. Given Statement's skills and reach, they had been able to play a vital role in the dissemination and diffusion of a whole gamut of rumours and counter-rumours, through a myriad of channels, as well as providing access and briefings to innumerable politicians, journalists, opinion formers and 'influencers'. Awkwardly, Statement's participation had been the decision of the previous CEO. The position of the new CEO, sitting next to her in this leathered cocoon, was not known

- though her involvement with the festival, as well as with a selection of named individuals integral to Visco, was a matter of public record. "Some of those initiatives are still underway," Tanya continues. "We have recruited some islanders to work on our behalf; and we have a few dozen people on the waiting list for residency, too, who will also act as disruptors, low level crime, freeloading, that sort of thing."

Kate Humboldt remains silent. These are the small fry; she waits for bigger news. Tanya clears her throat.

"Our strategy now is twin-tracked. Track one focuses on the island itself. Low level disruption on site, yes, but also supply-chain disruption, power breakages, on-going news chaff, hacking, general black ops. We want to maintain the impression that Visco is poorly organised, possibly even dangerous, and certainly that day-to-day life on the island is pretty ghastly. We'd like to think that we can make it fizzle out within a year or so and everyone can get back to normal."

"And your second track?"

"Is international. You'll have seen it just as we have. The attention was obviously high in the summer of last year when you guys were running the main festival, but it ebbed away sharply. It's spiked hugely since the court case went against us. Suddenly there are enquiries coming in from all over the planet. And this isn't like the 60s, all hippie-dippy stuff, none of those anarchists with their free love and peculiar bicycles and fondness for marijuana. We've monitored dozens of proper officials – health people, planners, people from Mayoral offices, you name it – getting in touch with Jo Castle or one of her acolytes. A well-meaning and naïve firefighter? Ha. She's a player and she's bloody dangerous."

Kate slowly rotates her head so as to be able to look more carefully at Tanya Golding. She does not know the woman especially well but has been briefed about her fiery side. It is interesting to see it on display;

and interesting to see it become so readily enflamed by Jo Castle. Kate
Humboldt, of course, has a complex relationship with Jo Castle. She
is reasonably confident that Golding does not know the full nature of
that complexity.

"So the consortium remains of the view," Tanya resumes, "that our
original analysis is correct: Visco represents a much more profound
threat to our collective interests than has been generally appreciated.
One of our members ran a couple of scenarios, looking at what might
happen if more of these 'care cities' were to develop, and how big they
might get, and whether there are tipping points."

"Tipping points?" Kate enquires.

"Yes. Tipping points. Situations where, rather than simply continuing to grow as satellite entities, a care city causes its parent city to
suddenly transform. You know. A few million people in London start
grumbling that life is so much better on that bloody island, and there's
not room for them all on the island, so they start demanding genuine
change from their politicians and – hey presto, suddenly there's a
candidate offering that kind of change – Jesus, probably some emissary
from the island who's been sent back to the city to spread the word! –
and before you know it the whole ball game goes haywire."

"Ah, yes. Tipping points," says Kate, still intimating nothing, and
everything.

"So," manages Tanya, realising she has not so far made the best fist of
this, "so it's clearly imperative that we tackle the international dimension. Some of that comes from the localised disruption in strand one,
as I've said. Emulating Visco will look much less attractive if the place
is increasingly known to be problematic, obviously. But there'll need
to be additional dedicated effort at the macro-level. Political pressure,
comms, targeting particular individuals and so on. Effectively an international version of what we ran here."

"So successfully," Kate adds, twinkling.

"Well. Yes. No." Tanya blurts. This really has not gone very well. "Most of the consortium is of the view that the legal position here is idiosyncratic. And, of course," she adds, recovering a little, "we can learn lessons from our mistakes."

Kate watches a seagull arc across her field of view. She watches the seagull's shadow and wonders if she can deduce the time. She ponders mistakes and how to learn from them. She decides to allow the silence to continue for a few moments. This will make Tanya Golding uncomfortable. Kate thinks about the capacity of the engine in front of her. She wonders where Robert Dunbar might be. She sees smoke rising from various points on the island.

"Are those fires?" she asks. As Tanya scrambles to adjust her view and her mind, Kate activates the in-car screen and logs into the feed from the spycams she has on the island. Images of a great feast scroll by. Magnificent cauldrons sit atop smouldering fires, their contents bubbling invisibly, their delicious odours imaginable but inaccessible. There are tripods of various sizes, and spits, and long tables sagging beneath bowls containing dishes from every cuisine on earth. It is a scene of collision, of glorious reconstitution, where east and west and north and south and young and old and ancient and modern and holy and secular are melting into the unimaginable new. It is a scene redolent of the very viscosity after which the settlement was named. Kate likes the name 'Visco'. It is part of why she admires the whole endeavour. A clever name. Sticky. Viscous.

Kate is startled by how swiftly and easily she has been transported by her reverie. She snaps back to the air-conditioned present, the leather seat, the deep strategic options in flux about her. Just as Tanya seems about to speak again, Kate cuts in:

"Statement's interests have always been clear," she begins. "We were very happy to be part of the consortium. I supported the decision completely. Statement prospers when – and only when – our clients prosper. A victory in the court case would certainly have been in the interests of many of our clients. It was a straightforward decision." Tanya Golding suddenly feels cold, despite the climate controlled cabin. "Things are no longer so straightforward." Tanya suddenly feels hot, a rush of – of embarrassment? Or anger? It is anger – Humboldt is surely making an emotional decision, not a business decision!

"This is not an emotional issue," Kate continues. "Or, at least, the role of emotions in our analysis has not been given undue weight. We all know, do we not, that decisions always have an emotional dimension? What is important is to appreciate the emotional quotient and to reach one's judgments in an enlightened fashion. Don't you think?"

Tanya Golding is not entirely sure what she is thinking at the moment. Or feeling. Kate Humboldt, chief executive of Statement plc, continues:

"We have of course run our own scenarios. And what I personally found interesting," she says, turning so as to look directly at Tanya Golding, "is that there is a very real possibility that the Visco model of care will win. In our scenarios these 'tipping points' could come about quite quickly. I have some analysts who tell me that a goodly proportion of the world's population is heartily sick of how things have been going and may be just a few nudges away from flipping. These same analysts have suggested to me that there may be little or nothing we can do about it. Even in scenarios where we throw our full weight behind the kind of plan you're suggesting, we delay the tipping points only by a few months."

Tanya is cold again, and very pale. She has begun to imagine the experience of reporting this conversation to the rest of the consortium. She is picturing the bosses of large property companies, of giant food retailers, of media businesses and clothing entrepreneurs and electronics and pharmaceuticals and gambling and alcohol and manufacturers and financiers and lobbyists and... She does not represent everyone, of course. And it would be ridiculous to think that every single business in every single sector was of a single mind. But there is no doubt (and not just in her mind) that the consortium she represents wields a collective influence on a breath-taking scale, and that the system they comprise, and cherish, and thrive on, is a system that serves their ends so comprehensively that they will go to quite extreme lengths to protect it.

So she knows, as Kate Humboldt's inference sinks ever-deeper into her being, that her associates will not react at all well when they learn that the world's foremost spin machine, Statement plc, is not playing ball. It may be even worse. If Statement plc is changing tack, then a more general doubt may begin to permeate. Tanya begins re-running some other recent conversations – with a retailing supremo, with the director of a property company, with a captain of industry and a master of the financial universe. She now sees previously invisible scintillas of doubt, as though through a lens of a different colour: a word here, a phrase there, a conditionality where before there had been unwavering conviction. A catastrophe is unfolding in slow-motion horror in her mind.

"These are only scenarios, of course," Kate continues, her voice as silky and refined as her scarf. "And there are, of course, other scenarios, scenarios in which the care model is not victorious, scenarios in which we - we the bastions of the prevailing order, the great beasts of our beloved capitalist system - successfully crush the insurrection." Tanya is feeling more and more uncomfortable. Kate's metaphorical flourish feels like a weapon, raised and ready for use. "But that's not the most interesting thing," Kate says, narrowing her eyes and lowering her voice and leaning a fraction closer to her victim. "The most interesting thing – and here I hope I can trust you with a confidence – the most interesting thing is that almost all of the scenarios have something rather surprising in common." She pauses, if not for effect then to ensure that Tanya feels the slow entry of the blade: "The basic mechanisms for measuring value, the very idea of money – or, at least, money as we have understood it for the past few centuries – those mechanisms appear doomed." A final, lethal pause. "Something entirely new is going to evolve over the next few years, Tanya. And it is going to be in our clients' interests to be very closely involved with whatever emerges. As I said, our interest is our clients' interest. Choosing the wrong side right now would be very costly indeed. Now, in my view, is a very bad time to be a dinosaur."

Kate rotates calmly and slowly back into the embrace of her electronically-managed seat, resumes her imperial smile and returns her gaze to the island's gently rising smoke. Tanya can feel the blood pumping in her ears. Her worst-case scenario for this discussion has been left far, far behind. She is in entirely uncharted territory. She focuses on her breathing. She battles to regain her composure, even as her thoughts continue to run wildly through dense thickets of bewilderment.

"I, um," she manages, eventually, "I had been thinking of Visco as some sort of diversion, you know. A distraction, a little piece of entertainment. At worst, like a detour, like when there's a problem with the main road and you're sent down a side road for a mile or two, and then you re-join the main road."

"Where you see that sign," says Kate, "which says 'Diversion Ends'. Yes, I know what you mean. But what I've concluded," she says, still gazing towards the thousands of admirable and invisible carnival-goers en route to the horizon, "is that we've been on an altogether bigger detour for decades, possibly even a couple of centuries. I think we are witnessing the end of an era, the era of hyper-consumption and billionaires and mega-corporations. It's nearly over. What's happening over there on that island is a path we might have been on, but we went a different way. And now that way is done. So, yes, 'Diversion Ends'. But I think it was an altogether bigger diversion than the one you had in mind."

Hilltop

A few days later Kate Humboldt leaves a voicemail for Robert Dunbar. She has not seen him for several months, and has not thought about him either, but he had popped into her head while she was meeting with Tanya Golding and it seemed right to get in touch. Their relationship had – as both of them had foreseen – comprised a self-contained fuck-bubble, and jolly nice it had been too. Since it ended – though the word 'end' did not feel entirely precise, since there had merely been an un-named final fuck, followed by no more fucks – Kate had been very thoroughly immersed in the process of ensuring she became CEO. As she leaves her voicemail message, she reflects on the experience of even allowing room in her mind for a concern about Robert, however fleeting. It feels benevolent. It makes her smile.

Robert smiles too as her listens to her message. He is far away. In the aftermath of the court case, while Jo and Michael and Miranda and no doubt many others piled down to the island, he headed in precisely the opposite direction. He is now sitting atop a small English mountain, far to the north of London's teetering madness. He has been walking and climbing and climbing and walking. He has almost decided what to do.

It is past equinox, so he has to be alert to the prospect of darkness. It took him nearly five hours to reach this particular peak. He chose it because he has read that the view is particularly spectacular; and it is. To the east, a great city, sprawled in its bowl; to the north, the rest of the mountain chain, chomping its way into the misty distance; to the west, gambolling hills, rolling towards the invisible Irish Sea; and, to the south, the valley and beyond it the plain that leads, eventually, to London and the Thames and the estuary and Visco itself. It is, as he had hoped, a perfect place to decide.

He is surprised there was a signal and is a little cross that he failed to ignore the message from Kate. Hey ho. She said nothing of consequence. It is nice to have heard from her.

He has been contemplating and rejecting the idea of suicide. At a minimum, he feels, it is the kind of thing that warrants occasional and serious thought. There are, after all, philosophers that have argued it is the only serious question we ever actually have to answer. He does not like himself very much; he seems to hurt people he cares about; he can see nothing to look forward to. He read recently about a man called Silenus who lived a couple of thousand years ago and who pointed out – apparently - that the only truly effective way to avoid the trials and tribulations of life was to have never been born in the first place. As a result, suicide was only second best; and Robert has never been very keen on second best.

Less philosophically, Robert has concluded, suicide would permanently remove even the possibility of there being a beautiful day, a moment of insight, a feeling, however insubstantial, of having helped to make the world a better place. He is a romantic, he admits it now. He is willing to stay alive just in case he will one day stand in front of a painting (he suspects it will be by van Gogh or Monet) and for some infinite, fleeting instant experience true connection with the world. He has read about it. He believes it can happen.

He believes, too, that the writings of mystics and magicians, though misguided, may contain truths. He believes that decades of tutored meditation can lead to enlightenment. He believes that transcendentalism, absolute faith, sensory deprivation, LSD and the insertion of specialised rods by neuro-surgeons into the correct areas of the brainstem can all produce subjective states of sublime insight. He believes in the good and the bad, the up and the down, the yin and the yang. He has ambled the broad supermarket aisles of philosophical and faith-based belief systems and he has sampled widely. He wakes up each morning and discovers that he is Robert Dunbar, as perplexed in the face of modernity as any other self-described iconoclast.

He has narrowed his choices to two.

One possibility is to offer his undying love to Jo. He will join her in Visco. He will commit his energies to the extraordinary Visco project of care and his love to that extraordinary woman. They will have babies. He will be a caring and devoted father. He will donate all his money to the Trust he invented. He will develop warm and mutually respectful relationships with a wide variety of interesting and capable people. He will support his mother and father. He will read stimulating texts. He will love and be loved. He will be happy.

The other possibility is – he acknowledges – just as preposterous. He is a wealthy man. He need never work again. He will never work again. He will walk around the world. He will visit rivers and cities, valleys and kings, suffocating peaks and desiccating deserts. He will communicate in new languages and none. He will go hungry and eat feasts. He will teach young children in a village and receive instruction from monks in a cave. He will sing until his lungs ache as he walks a ridge above the broiling waters of a torrent; he will wait silently in a huge crowd until he sees a tiny bird catch a moth. He will be clear and alone. He will be happy.

He looks west. The sun, low and heading lower, casts provocative shadows across the hills as they tumble and cavort their way to the sea. Robert feels... cossetted. Yes, that is the word for his feeling, he decides.

He looks north. The mountains glower at him, a glorious menace, enticing and intimidating. He feels... suspicious. He looks east, across a city that is not London, hundreds of thousands of perfectly ordinary people getting on with the heroic business of everyday life. He feels aloof, until he looks south. The valley falls away into the plain as if physically dragged by the distant gravity well. London. Once you've lived in London, nowhere else will do.

Unless someone invents something better than London. And calls it Visco.

He loves her, he's sure of that. But he's not convinced by his own conviction.

He stares south, as hard as he can. He feels steady. He is holding a few pebbles. He throws one, then another. He notices how the wind is strong enough to shape the arc of a pebble's flight. He can do something about where the pebble is thrown, but not where it lands.

He throws the remainder of the pebbles. He loves her, but not enough. He will leave. He will walk. What a fine thing walking is! It costs nothing, unless you're intending to give everything up, which he is. He feels... calm. Yes, calm. That is how he feels.

He feels a sudden and strong urge to let someone know – and the person who leaps to mind, and to his surprise, is Dr Miranda Farnaby. For a moment he ponders this before making an active decision not to think about it further. He is not interested in why he has decided to call Miranda; she is, evidently, the person to call.

He calls her immediately.

"Hey, Miranda, it's Robert," he tells whatever device is recording his voice on her behalf. "Hope you're ok. I, er, wanted to let you know,

I'm, um, I'm leaving town for a while. Well, the country, actually. Taking a long walk. You know, one of those 'go find yourself' long walks. Actually, I think I found myself already and I'm rather hoping to get away from myself, ha ha, but, well, anyway, I'd be really grateful if you could let, um, well, if you could let Jo know. Please. It's nothing dramatic or anything, I'm just going off grid for a while and I don't want you, um, her, well anyone really, I don't want anyone worrying. It's all fine. Really. I'm fine. Hope you're fine! OK, thanks, um, yes, that's it really. Take care. Bye."

Miranda picks up the message only a short while later. It is still late afternoon. She rings him back but gets no answer. She decides not to leave a message. She rings Jo. Jo is visiting London – can they meet up? Of course, that would be lovely.

"When were we last here?" Jo asks a couple of hours later as they settle into their chairs in the small Italian restaurant. They begin guessing, struggling to locate that distant occasion within the turbulent and swollen stream of disconnected events. Two years ago? Three? It was autumn, wasn't it? Definitely this time of year. Wow. Three years ago.

For a few moments they simply look at one another. Miranda sees a lean, muscular woman in her mid-thirties, slightly dishevelled and tired around the eyes. She sees the strong hands and the sinewy forearms, the amazing cheekbones (she has always been envious of Jo's cheekbones), the dark brown eyes that seem sometimes to be looking so far into the future, sometimes deep into your soul. The woman emanates a disconcerting power.

Jo sees a woman in her mid-thirties, still a little overweight but poised and elegantly dressed. She has astonishingly blue eyes. She looks sexy and strong and smart. She has a firm jaw: there are small lines from when it is firmly set. There are small lines around her eyes, too, from where she smiles.

They both smile.

"How are you?" they both say, and laugh.

"Thirsty!" says Miranda, quickly, and a bottle of wine is soon summoned.

"I heard from Robert," says Miranda after the first quaff. She watches Jo's expression stiffen, then relax again. "He left me a message this afternoon. He said he's 'going off grid' for a while. He wanted you to know."

Jo creases her brow for a moment. "What do you suppose he meant?"

"Well he sounded... odd. And it was windy so the message wasn't exactly clear. But he seemed excited. As though he'd made some sort of decision, you know, a decision he actually believed in."

Jo laughs. "Not too many of those, if I remember correctly."

It is Miranda's turn to laugh. "Do you think..."

"It seems that way, doesn't it?"

"Does he know about Daniel?"

"I've no idea! Honestly, I haven't spoken to him in months." She pauses. "I still don't understand why he didn't tell me about him and Kate." Another pause. "Why do you think he didn't tell me about him and Kate?"

Miranda looks into Jo's eyes and feels the warm glow of her friend's slow return. "I don't know," she says. "Maybe he's just a dickhead."

Jo laughs loudly and they clink glasses.

"How is Daniel?" asks Miranda.

"Yup, good. Good." Jo glances sideways, then back to Miranda. "I think I love him."

"Think?"

"Well, you know. I'm hanging back a little, just in case. Everything's been so intense. Maybe he'll disappear. Maybe I'll disappear. I don't know." Her eyes are shiny. "Yes, I love him. Which is scary shit, of course."

"Of course."

"But he is amazing!" Jo bursts, and suddenly she is telling the story of the other night when he told a really funny story and she just got the giggles and how sometimes he seems to understand her without her even saying anything and then there are other times when he is all sort of mystical and wise and, yes, she does worry occasionally about the age gap but then there are other times – like the other night, oh it was so strange, she suddenly felt like she was older than him, it wasn't as if he suddenly became younger it was just that he seemed lost, as though he had just awoken and discovered he was somewhere unexpected and she had the most amazing feeling, looking after him like that, and then there were other times...

And on and on. The wine flows. The starters come and go, the main course arrives, the eating happens but neither of them really notices the food.

"And the sex?" asks Miranda impishly.

Jo's response is a noise - a hybrid sigh, groan, gasp and squeal – that also contorts her face and upper body.

"Wow, that good?!" laughs Miranda. Jo widens her eyes in affirmative disbelief, and the pair of them giggle for a few moments. "Congratulations Jo Castle," says Miranda, raising her glass once more. It is nearly empty; and so, it turns out, is the bottle. She asks the question with her eyebrows – and Jo answers with mock horror.

The second bottle is underway within a few minutes. "What about you?" asks Jo. "How's things?"

Miranda begins tentatively. Her main concern is work. Things at the university have been very complicated since back in April when they announced their intention to cease their support for 'the Care City initiative'. Miranda had been furious, of course, but had channelled that fury into the court case. On the occasions when she had had time to reflect on things, she explains, she could get no further than the sheer irony of the situation: she had been promoted - twice! - because of Visco, and then they expected her simply to accept a decision that fundamentally undermined her.

Jo listens intently to her oldest friend. Just as she remembered, Miranda tells a story like no-one else. Yes, somewhere there is a central thread, but it is so embellished, so decorated with anecdotes and parenthetical remarks, so prone to prolonged and achingly funny diversions that it is often very difficult to remember what the thread is. This, thinks Jo. I've missed this. This matters.

"So I sat on it, basically," Miranda is saying. "I figured there was simply no point in deciding what to do until the end of the court case." Jo flickers the obvious question. "So, yes. I resigned. Yesterday."

Jo yelps with delight and excitement and stands up from her chair and tries to move around the small table, colliding with both her own table and, on the rebound, with the middle-aged woman sitting at the adjacent table. Amid mumbled apologies and checking whether anything has fallen to the floor, Miranda stands and the pair embrace, a full and joyous hug of wonder. The other diners, certainly disrupted, instinctively detect that nothing threatening is happening and quickly relax.

"So what's next? You coming to Visco?" asks Jo, once they have settled back into their chairs.

Miranda pauses for a moment, wondering if Jo is expressing a hope. "No, I don't think so," she says. "At least, not yet." Jo's expression reassures her. Miranda continues: "I've been offered a new post. Head of department. Looks like I'm joining the big league!" Jo laughs again with delight, and again they chink glasses.

"Still in London?" Jo asks.

"Oh yes," Miranda replies.

"I'm glad about that," Jo says.

"I'm glad you're glad," says Miranda.

They look at one another for a moment. Their desserts lie untouched on the table in front of them. The second bottle of wine is almost empty.

"What about the sex?" asks Jo.

Miranda laughs uproariously, once again disturbing their fellow diners, who this time seem a little more uneasy. "The sex is fine," Miranda manages at last. "Well, I say that. To be honest, there hasn't been much sex lately."

"Implying there might have been some?"

"Well, I did get a little carried away with Peter during carnival..." Miranda admits, sheepishly. "I have to confess that I can't remember too much about it," she admits.

Jo's chortle slowly fades away. "Funny which things we remember and which we don't," she says. She knows she is a little drunk. "I remember getting really upset a few weeks after my dad died when I suddenly realised I hadn't been seeing his face. Now I go for a week or two or three without thinking about him and then suddenly a memory just pops back into my head, something random, a smell or a noise, I don't know, and then he's there, or I'm somewhere with him." She pauses. "It doesn't make me cry so much anymore," she says.

Miranda doesn't know what to say, so says nothing. Her mood seamlessly matches Jo's, a function of the alcohol, mainly, but not just that. Miranda continues saying nothing.

"And I wanted to say sorry," Jo says suddenly. Miranda looks startled and perplexed. "For telling you to fuck off that time," Jo continues. "Sorry."

Miranda wells up and immediately decides that more drink is necessary. "Two brandies please," she calls, rather loudly, to the waiter.

"Your 'Fuck Off'," Miranda says, grandly, "can fuck off. It is gone. It is past. Is it... no more." She reverts to her normal voice. "Jesus woman, the stuff we've been through over the past, I don't know, year, two? Bloody hell, we've been saving the world!" The brandies arrive. Miranda announces the toast: "To Visco, and care, and to Jo Castle, and to good sex, and to..."

"...to becoming Head of Department!" Jo interjects.

They down the brandies in one and, again wordlessly, agree that they need just one more. Miranda gestures to the waiter before, with a start, saying: "But what about you? We haven't talked about your plans! What are you going to do now?"

Jo looks blearily at Miranda and screws her face up in a way that conveys a mixture of resignation, doubt, excitement and even a little guilt.

"Tell me tell me tell me!" Miranda screeches.

So Jo tells her.

Home

Miranda is taken aback by what Jo tells her and it is not for several days that she is able to summon a response she feels confident about. Abena – who learns the same news a couple of days later – becomes very upset and will spend minutes, then hours and eventually days trying to persuade Jo to change her mind.

Jo does not change her mind. She wants to be a firefighter again.

"Why?" asks Daniel.

"I keep thinking about my first morning at Statement," Jo begins. "I sat in front of a computer screen and it told me I had appointments. Appointments! And by the end of the first week I'd dealt with about 200 emails. And I'd been in, I don't know, 20 meetings? And it was weird, sure, but it was exciting, too. New, you know. Novel." Jo sips at her mug of tea. They are sitting in the kitchen of her – their – apartment on the island. "And for a while – I don't know, a few weeks, a few months maybe – it stayed exciting. I mean, really exciting. Every day was different. Every day I had to talk to someone different, persuade them that the festival was a good idea, persuade them that Visco was a good idea. And I really believed – I still believe – that Visco was a good idea. Is a good idea. Is an amazing idea..." She drifts off, momentarily overwhelmed by the turbulence of her thoughts.

Daniel remains quiet; Jo continues: "I remember standing with Michael in a shopping centre in London a few years ago. It was just before Christmas. I'd taken him there because I thought he'd enjoy the spectacle of the place. I thought... I don't know... that he'd get a fresh perspective. It's not the kind of place he'd ever have visited of his own accord. Funny that, don't you think? How many people never even visit the kind of place they claim to hate? How do you know, if you've never been? And how can you possibly hope to understand the people who do go? Anyway. I'm pretty sure it just made him more confused than he already was – but me? Me, I just found myself thinking – where does all this come from? It's all connected, somehow, but I just can't see it." She takes another sip of tea. "And the more I thought about it, the more I thought – well, I'm not sure what I thought. Maybe I felt. Maybe I just felt that whatever I was doing at the fire service was always a bit too late. Too 'end of pipe', or – yes, I know, shut up, ok – end of hose."

Daniel smiles, with pride and love and admiration and tenderness and – and anxiety. Jo continues:

"And that's what Visco – Care City - was for me. Is. Proof. Proof that it's possible to tackle all the nonsense before it becomes nonsense. You know. Keep people well rather than waiting until they get sick. Think about the stuff that makes people happy and do that rather than waiting until they're miserable and giving them pills or supermarket psychotherapy. Minimise the waste before it's even waste; learn how to walk rather than just stumbling to your car; care about the things you care about - and discover that's what you have that in common with everyone else!" Her passion makes her sound as if she has been drinking alcohol, but she has only been drinking tea. Her tea is getting cold. "And it's amazing. Jesus Daniel, we fucking won. We won! We took on the big boys and we fucking won!"

Daniel raises his own mug of tea and offers to chink it against Jo's
– but she grimaces as she sips the tepid liquid.

"Another?" he asks. Yes please, she nods, watching him move from
the table to the kettle.

"It's an amazing feeling," she resumes. "And I wouldn't change it
for the world. And I'm so proud – so proud – that I had anything at
all to do with it."

"It wouldn't have happened without you," he says.

"Well, maybe," she replies. "But me? In charge? It never felt right."

"You're a leader," he says.

"Maybe," she says, again. "Maybe…"

They say nothing for a while. The kettle boils. Daniel pours
the water into the mugs, fetches the milk, squeezes and removes the
tea-bags, adds the milk, hands the steaming mug to Jo. She thanks
him.

"Look, I understand that I have to accept what's happened to me,
and that some of that has to be down to me being me. It feels weird,
but I have to accept it. I think about dad, what he would have made
of it. I always felt that he didn't really get me, or that I was a bit of
a disappointment to him, but maybe he just realised that I don't run
along the same lines as him. I was never going to be an academic. I've
never been just a brain on legs. I don't know. Maybe he was envious."
Her voice quietens. "I wish he'd seen this." She swings her head to
indicate the apartment, the island, the miracle of Visco lying outside.
"He'd have been impressed, I think."

"No thinking required," says Daniel. "He'd have been impressed."

It is Jo's turn to smile with a mix of pride and love and awe and
anxiety. "Yeah. Probably." They laugh, comfortably and gently. "But
how would he have reacted if I told him I just can't stand it anymore?"
she says with exasperation. "I just can't stand it anymore. I love the

people, sure. And I love what it is, what it's become. And I feel so passionate – so passionate – that it survives and lives and goes onto to become – oh, I don't know, the biggest and bestest thing it can be – but I can't spend the rest of my life in meetings!" She almost shouts. "Meetings! And appointments! And sorting out logistical problems and sitting in board meetings to look after the Trust and schmoozing with prospective funders and having photos taken with politicos and trying to decide who should be allowed in next week and talking with people from this country and that country about how they can set up their own CareCity..."

He reaches out to take her hand, and she lets him, and he squeezes, and she squeezes back.

"I remember something you said," she says, looking directly into his soul. "When we were first talking about the Declaration. Do you remember?" He does, but his face remains neutral; he wants her to keep talking. "You talked about this all being an adventure. You said I was a pioneer. You said that the kind of people who get things going in the first place are not necessarily the kind of people who are any good at actually running things." He nodded, silently, staring at his tea. "And you were right. I've done my bit. I got it going. I was in the right place at the right time and I helped get something going that... that stands a fighting chance of changing the world." Her eyes are glowing, dark brown coals of fire and belief. "But I'm not the right person to take it to the next level. I'm not the right person to take it to 100,000 people. I'm not the right person to develop the Council. I'm not the right person to negotiate with London, to build bridges with the other countries, to make sure the whole thing lives and breathes and sustains and..." She pauses. "I still care, of course I do. And I'm not going to just disappear." She thinks suddenly of Robert, and wonders fleetingly about the shape of his decision and the shape of hers. "But I need to accept who I am and what I am and what I've learned, and I need to hear what my guts are telling me. And they're saying – go and fight fires."

She looks at him for one final moment, then takes a big gulp of tea.

"I love you," says Daniel. Miranda had said the same thing. So had Abena.

"I love you too," says Jo. "Nice tea," she adds. "Fancy a walk? I need to decide how I'm going to tell everyone else."

It is unsympathetically fallacious outside: a chill north-easterly wind is carrying squalls of light rain and trampling all over the island. Jo sees Daniel's grimace at the prospect and she shoves his shoulder playfully. "Come on," she says, "let's go."

Away

Michael Smith is wearing a heavy jumper, a big raincoat and waterproof trousers. He is tromping about Visco's streets and avenues in the rain. It is cold and unpleasant but he is determined to have a careful look around. He needs to see the place, not as it is in the misleading idyll of summer but at this time of year when the hatches are battened down against the worst autumn storms; and not when autumn is all stunning colours and bleached skies and swirling clouds of migrating birds but now, late November, when the bleakness peaks and Christmas is still in the planning.

He is twenty two years old.

He is at the north east edge of the site. He clambers onto the sea-wall and gazes across the estuary, the rain stinging his face a little. On a clear day he could see all the way to the northern bank on the other side of the great river; today the low grey cloud seems to merge with the sea and it is impossible even to tell how far one is seeing. He rotates clockwise until, a little further along the sea wall, he sees a newly-built bird hide, positioned to allow a fine view across the mudflats where the oystercatchers and plovers and godwits and gulls will wheel and cavort and fly and feed. He remembers seeing a murmuration a few weeks ago and remembers, too, the disconcerting sense of elation elicited by the swirling and elusive profusion of starlings.

There, behind the hut and below the sea wall, protected from the worst the sea can throw, what looks like an allotment. He wanders towards the recently-tilled rows of soil. There are pieces of string suspended between small wooden sticks; there are pieces of coloured paper in waterproof wrappings attached to the string. There is a tiny shed. It probably contains tools. There are small stakes driven into the ground just over there, and there, too, markers for where the vegetable garden will be extended when people and the weather are ready.

Michael wonders which of Visco's citizens are responsible.

He wanders on.

It is more difficult these days to know the precise limits of the city. It is not exactly sprawling but in the couple of months since the court case a variety of new buildings has been added to the complex. With one or two exceptions the new buildings are the kind of high-tech self-assembly flat-packs with which the town was founded. Like an ever-growing number of the original buildings, many of the new ones are being decorated, and in ever-more remarkable ways. That one over there appears to have been completely covered in wildly-coloured sea-shells; this one here has been painted to look like a boat. He walks towards a large building that looks like a cross between a bird's nest and a scarecrow. He peers through a window.

Inside he sees forty, perhaps fifty people, most sitting at long benches, a few sitting cross-legged on large mats. They are mainly older people, perhaps a few in their thirties or forties. There is a hotchpotch of skin colours and ethnicities. Against a far wall he can see a series of industrial ovens; almost out of view he can see wooden racks. They are making pottery. He glimpses a poorly-painted and misshapen plate; he sees half a dozen almost-matching coffee mugs; he sees a really rather elegant butter dish with an outline of the island on the lid.

He moves on, tightening his hood against the wind as he leaves the shelter of the low building.

Coming up, the new brewery, currently under construction; opposite, the recently-completed gym. He glances in: it looks like pilates. Or maybe tai chi? His strides take him away before he decides. He has not encountered anyone for a while now but suddenly he has to take evasive action as a damp but happy-looking crowd of runners turns the final corner of their lap and returns to the gym. He smiles back, empathising instantly with the expressions that are looking forward to the hot showers inside.

"Happy carnival!" someone calls as they pass, and Michael laughs out loud in agreement.

Just behind the gym is one of the periphery car-parks, largely empty. This one will need to be re-located soon. There is a handful of commercial vehicles, loading and unloading as necessary. Fragments of working banter and radio music reach Michael's ears through the rain. He watches as the forklift lowers a pallet from the side of the lorry, spins on its axis and wheedles off towards the depot.

He worries that Visco depends so heavily on the rest of the world. How can Visco really be the start of something new if it still needs other people to make the click-and-play buildings or to build the robots or to programme the tech? And what about the Trust itself, upon which the whole thing depends – doesn't that only work because there's an entire world out there for it to speculate about, an entire world of money and capital and trade and exploitation that is the very opposite of what Visco is all about?

He continues worrying: he worries about the backlash, about Tanya Golding and her associates, about the dark forces still arraigned against the fledgling Visco. He worries that he does not even know quite what he should be worrying about.

Michael checks his wristband. It is 11.30am. His meeting is at 2.

He wanders past more buildings. He sees people playing chess. He sees people playing cards. He sees people in front of their screens playing whatever it is they're playing. He wanders past the kitchen at the back of one of the refectories and, on glancing inside, he sees twenty people making cakes. He skirts the edge of one of the sports pitches, currently and, in this weather, understandably empty. As he reaches the periphery car-park at the south-eastern edge he sees a hearse: a small crowd of mourners is gathered as a coffin slides into the vehicle. He remembers Jo's dad's funeral. There is still nowhere for people to be buried or cremated on the island so funerals have to take place on the mainland. Look, there's the electric minibus. Michael stops to watch as the mourners climb in. A couple of cars are involved, too. The cortege pulls slowly away behind the hearse. Michael has removed his hood – he's not sure why, it seems to be the respectful thing to do – and he notices the rain is easing. He pulls the hood back up and feels a little cold water running down his neck.

He suddenly wonders: how many babies have been born in Visco? He sets off towards the hospital. As he walks, he tries to estimate.

"Well," he announces to the rain and the emptiness, "the population is now about 50,000, but it obviously grew over time, and it's now a year and a half since The Big Float, but most of the people here are older people and are probably not getting pregnant, although some of their carers might have, and there was the big surge of new arrivals in the summer and that was a younger crowd, so..."

He learns that there have been 122 babies born in Visco in the past year, one of them that very morning. It turns out that he knows the receptionist and he asks "Can I see the baby?" before he has really had time to think about whether this is a good or a bad idea or whether there are protocols about this kind of thing. A nurse checks with the parents who, it turns out, are entirely comfortable about his visit. Michael cautiously enters the suite where mother, father and four-hour-old baby are warmly ensconced.

"Gosh, I hope you don't mind, I just, um..." Michael suddenly feels he has made a gross error of intrusion and no longer has any idea why he is here. The parents make effusive noises of reassurance and invite him to sit near the cot where the baby is sleeping.

Michael realises and says out loud: "I don't think I've actually seen a baby this young before." The little creature is wrinkly and red and lying beneath a white knitted blanket. Michael watches as the infant stirs, appears to grimace and raises then lowers a tiny gripped fist. It opens one impossibly large eye and is gazing at something infinitely distant and mysterious. It makes a gurgling noise and opens the other eye. Michael is transfixed.

"She's a girl," the mother says.

After a few more minutes Michael makes his goodbyes and offers his gratitude and, still dazed, wanders through the hospital's corridors. At the exit he notices a large room to one side of the reception apparently full of carers and parents and elderly people in wheelchairs and sundry toddlers and babies in pushchairs. A jostling hubbub of chatter and smiles leaks from the room and Michael notices that several small wooden toys also seem to have escaped and have taken up residence on and below the seats in reception.

He floats outside. It is no longer raining. He tries to recall something about four legs and two legs and three legs and – yes, that's it, the riddle of the Sphinx! The human being: the being that crawls on all fours when young, walks on two legs as an adult and needs a stick, and thus three legs, in old age. Maybe it needs updating, he thinks: it looks like both the very young and the very old depend on wheels these days. Perhaps people in the middle, too, he ponders.

He looks back into the crèche, or whatever it's called. Young children are sitting on the laps of elderly people, reading books. Two women are craning as a child explains a ground-level game which appears to involve a complex arrangement of wooden blocks, several pieces of coloured cardboard and a fir cone. The children are animated and relaxed; the elders are shining. Carers and parents, in the corner, are trading tales over tea. The wheelchairs and buggies are still, but wheels are still turning.

Michael moves to check his wristband, pauses, then calculates that he still has a little time.

"Excuse me," he asks his friend at the reception desk, "is there a copy of the Declaration of Care here somewhere?"

"Of course!" the man replies. "There's one on the wall of the central lobby. Or there are some printed copies in the rack near the cafeteria."

Michael walks to the lobby. The document is framed and perhaps one and a half metres tall and a metre wide. He leans close for a moment: it has been made by hand. The calligraphy is beautiful. He looks even more closely and laughs – it is a jigsaw. He remembers Daniel saying something about jigsaws, the relationship between the part and the whole, the completeness and the incompleteness inextricably linked. Michael presumes that, if he were to continue a close inspection, he would find more riddles, more references, more humour, more of the adhesive bonds from which Visco is made. He takes a couple of steps back until he feels comfortable: he can see it all; and he can easily read each word.

He knows it very well, of course. He remembers the early drafts, the powerful and heated discussions, the vertiginous sense of possibility that swung into view... and then he remembers his feeling of despair as Visco seemed to succumb to the system it was supposed to overturn...

and the overwhelming mix of joy and excitement and amazement when they won the court case.

Holy shit, they won.

He stares at the Declaration. He does not so much read it as feel it. He does not see linear phrases and sentences, he experiences free-floating beliefs and aspirations as he samples its words:

- "We believe that anxiety is the most corrosive force to which a human being can be subject, and it is the duty of a good society to minimise anxiety."

- "We assert that all men, women and children are equal and are endowed with inalienable rights."

- "We assert that the society most able to support human flourishing is a society based on the primacy of giving and taking care."

- "For humans to flourish, it is insufficient to consider only their material needs – care must be given to the human need for creative expression, for playfulness, for curiosity and for joy."

- "We assert that a good society is characterised by conviviality – the condition of living in peaceful, non-exploitative and friendly exchange with others – and it is the duty of all of us to nurture conviviality in whatever way that makes sense to us."

There have been times when Michael has seen these words and been worried that they are just words, just trite statements and sentiments ill-suited to the challenge of re-building the world. There have been other times - and he thinks of Abena explaining how Visco is like a refugee camp for the world - when the Declaration seems to have been the very essence of the change he always dreamed of, a sort of fuel for his soul. That is how it seems now.

He nods to the Declaration on the wall, turns on his heel and sets off to the Council building where, a few minutes later, he finds himself surrounded by friendly faces. Jo is missing, and it is a jolt, but he understands her decision and realises that, in some ways, he might not be doing this at all if she was still in charge.

They had invited him with a simple question: "Care to save the world, Mr Smith?"

"I wanted to thank you all," he begins. "When you first asked me if I would be willing to accept this post I didn't understand why you were asking me. As some of you will remember, there have been quite a few times when none of this has made any sense to me." He pauses to allow the chuckles of understanding to rise and then fall. "But I am delighted to accept your offer. It would be an honour. I know I won't be able to do this on my own, and I shall of course need help from all of you. And I know, too, that many barriers remain. Those that tried to stop us have not yet gone away. I believe I am ready. Thank you for believing in me."

He is to be an emissary. He will leave his home in Visco and take its message to the world. He will do his best to help people and cities all over the planet to build a new future of care that truly learns the lessons of the broken, crushing past. He feels the sense of adventure in his heart like a caged beast. He has never felt so certain in all his life.

Afterword

Acknowledgements

Many thanks to all those whose perspectives, comments and support have helped me along the way, most especially James, Alex, Ellie, Robin, Ian, Teresa, Denise and Stephanie.

We'd love your feedback for research purposes. To access the short survey please scan or click here. As a thank you there is a free download of a mini eco-fiction anthology eBook

The Author

David Fell writes most regularly on his blog https://economicso fenough.blogspot.com/ where he is described as a 'recovering economist, faltering poet, grizzled navigator, occasional entrepreneur/ writer/ speaker/ activist, soul food connoisseur.

On LinkedIn he is "poet, story-teller and sometime social scientist" with skills including navigation, balance and hiding in plain sight. He tweets as @EconEnough, where he is interested in sustainability, listening as hard as I can, and improvisation.

Printed in Great Britain
by Amazon

21873719R00136